ALSO BY CAT DEVON

The Entity Within
Sleeping with the Entity

Love Your Entity

Cat Devon

St. Martin's Paperbacks

This is a work of fiction. All of the characters, organizations, and events portrayed in this novel are either products of the author's imagination or are used fictitiously.

LOVE YOUR ENTITY

Copyright © 2014 by Cathie L. Baumgardner.

All rights reserved.

For information address St. Martin's Press, 175 Fifth Avenue, New York, NY 10010.

ISBN: 978-0-312-54781-3

Printed in the United States of America

St. Martin's Paperbacks edition / January 2014

St. Martin's Paperbacks are published by St. Martin's Press, 175 Fifth Avenue, New York, NY 10010.

10 9 8 7 6 5 4 3 2 1

This book is dedicated to my big brother, Ken.
You are my rock. You don't need a "Jedi mind meld"
to know I love you from here to a galaxy far, far away.
Yes, I know that is a *Star Trek*/*Star Wars* mashup.
I did it just for you.

Acknowledgments

Special thanks go out to my Cat Devon reader street team/crew for their epic support! Thanks to Donna Carolina Ford, Maria Teresa Ayala (future Author in waiting), Alison Schooley, Pattybones 2, Sue LaShomb, Madison Fairbanks, Cheryl Smith (awesome librarian!), Misty Helm (awesome bookseller!), Jewls from Down Under, Donna Jo Atwood, Stephanie Knight, Crystal M., Miranda Sue J., Eileen Wells, Sara Sepf, Chris Mead, Nancy Wolfe, Jennifer D., Lori B., Jean S., Iris P., Sue Giroux, and the entire gang! You guys rock!

Chapter One

When Sierra Brennan opened the door to her new house in Chicago, she didn't expect to find a naked man standing inside. A very hot, sexy, well-built, and well-hung man who looked like he was hungover. He made no attempt to cover up while she made every effort to keep her eyes on his face and not his privates.

"Thank God you're here," a woman wearing a corset and little else said from right beside Sexy Naked Guy. Sexy Naked Trespassing Guy. "What took you so long?"

"What do you mean what took me so long?" Sierra said.

"Who are you talking to?" Sexy Naked Guy asked. His voice was low and rough.

"Your girlfriend," Sierra said.

"I don't have a girlfriend," he said.

"Look, I don't care what your relationship is with her, but you are both trespassing so you need to leave right now. As soon as you get dressed, I mean."

"I'm the only one here," he said.

"Clearly that's not true as I am here as well." She punched 911 into her smartphone.

He moved closer and looked deep into her eyes. He had chocolate-brown eyes and thick lashes. His chiseled cheekbones made his face as sexy as the rest of his chiseled body. "You don't want to do that."

"You really don't want to do that," the corseted woman said.

Sierra already knew what she didn't want. She didn't want to screw up her chance to inherit this house. Several others had tried and failed to fulfill the thirty-consecutive-days residency requirement. She'd only met her great-uncle Saul Brennan once yet he'd listed her in his will. Yeah, he'd listed two older cousins before her, but here she was anyway. They hadn't stayed in the house. She would. Because she had a huge advantage.

Sierra was not afraid of snakes or spiders or things that went bump in the night. Especially things that go bump in the night. That was her specialty.

Sierra saw things most people didn't. Yes, maybe it was a cliché, but she saw dead people. Ghosts. Spirits who for one reason or another didn't or couldn't move on to the other side.

Which was why she was able to write such good paranormal novels. *Write what you know.* That's what all the pros said and it was what Sierra did. Her S. J. Brennan books featured a vigilante ghost hunter and the challenges she faced in finding justice and punishment where needed.

Yep, she saw ghosts and she was seeing them now as the corseted woman moved closer and shimmered with translucency. She had short dark hair styled à la the *Great Gatsby* era, wide brown eyes, and a curvy figure. But she was definitely a ghost. Which meant Sexy Naked Guy was a ghost too, right? She put out her hand to check. Her fingertips rested on his bare chest. His *solid*, muscular bare chest.

"Why aren't you leaving?" he growled.

She yanked her hand away as if burned. "Because this is my house and you are the squatter."

"The house is mine," he said.

"In your dreams," she said. "Who do you think you are?"

"I know who I am," he said. "I'm Ronan McCoy. Who are you?"

"Sierra Brennan, the owner of this property."

"Since when?" he said.

"Since yesterday."

"Forget him. I need your help," the ghost said. "My name is Ruby, in case you were wondering."

"One thing at a time," Sierra told Ruby. "Get dressed," she told Sexy Naked Guy. Wait, his name was Ronan.

He looked deep into her eyes once more. "Get out."

Sierra shook her head. "No way."

She saw the confusion there before irritation took over. "Leave!" he bellowed.

"You leave," she bellowed back at him. She'd driven her rental U-Haul van nine hours across three states and she was beyond exhausted.

"How long has he been here?" Sierra asked Ruby.

"Who are you talking to?" he demanded.

"He's been here a few days," Ruby said. "I've been here for decades and decades."

Sierra frowned. If Ronan was a recent arrival, then he couldn't be the reason Ruby hadn't crossed over. He obviously couldn't see Ruby. She should have realized that Ruby was a ghost faster than she had, but Sierra chalked that up to the fact that she was so tired. Usually she could tell a ghost from a human, but nothing about this Saturday had been usual.

She'd done a book signing at nine this morning in Ohio. There had been a good turnout, but a majority of the audience had wanted her to pass on a message to their departed loved ones. Sierra had to tell them that she wasn't a clairvoyant, she was a writer.

Yes, her books revolved around ghosts, but that didn't mean they were real. That was her story and she always stuck to it. The rest was between her and the ghosts she helped to the other side. She wasn't about to reveal her ghost-whisperer side to the general public. She knew all too well the stigma that carried, the mocking laughter when she'd told friends as a child that she saw ghosts. She'd been labeled weird and was ostracized. Ever since then, she'd been careful not to reveal her hidden talent.

Sierra would deal with Ruby the Ghost later. First she needed to get rid of Naked Ronan. "Look, I don't know why you think you have a right to be here," Sierra said. "But I'm telling you that the previous occupants did not fulfill the requirements of the will."

Ruby raised her hand and had a sheepish look on her translucent face. "That may have been my fault."

"I had a feeling," Sierra muttered.

Ronan frowned. "You had a feeling about what? No, don't answer because I don't care."

What kind of man stood there so arrogantly while so naked? An extremely ripped one. Not in a bodybuilder-weird kind of way but in a six-pack, shoulda-been-in-the-movie-*Magic Mike* kinda way.

Sierra was finding it increasingly difficult to keep her gaze above his neck. Okay, she'd sneaked a peek down to his navel once or twice. And maybe she had mistakenly looked even lower.

Right, who was she kidding? She'd seen him in all his glory. His nudity rattled her.

Keeping her own self-preservation in mind, she had her phone in one hand while her other hand was in her purse, her fingers curled around a can of pepper spray. Because the bottom line here was that she was facing an angry naked guy and that was not a positive in the security department.

A knock at the front door startled her. She yanked it open to find a man standing there, flashing a badge of some kind at her.

"That was fast," she said. She must have pushed the 911 button without realizing it and they'd used the GPS on her phone to locate her. "Come in."

"I'm Damon Thornheart. Is there a problem?" he said.

"*He's* the problem." She turned back to Ronan to find that he'd donned a pair of jeans. That was also fast, but it didn't change the fact that he didn't belong in her house. "Get rid of him, please," Sierra said. "He's tres-passing in my house and I want him gone."

Ronan McCoy couldn't believe this was happening to him. He'd spent the past century waiting to come home and now that he had, this woman with the bad attitude and great breasts was getting in his way.

Which was why Ronan welcomed the arrival of fellow vampire Damon Thornheart. Ronan wasn't sure why he hadn't been able to compel the woman to leave. Maybe it had something to do with the fact that he'd been an indentured vampire for nearly the past hundred years.

Ronan had been turned on the battlefield during World War I, in May of 1918. The trench warfare in northern France had been brutally bloody. Hundreds of thousands had been injured, Ronan among them. But his torture hadn't ended with his death. It had only begun.

He ruthlessly shut those thoughts down. He refused to let his past dictate his future. His immortal future.

Yes, Baron Voz had sired him but, unlike most vampires, Voz had kept Ronan indentured to him for almost a century, forcing Ronan to do his bidding and his killing.

But Ronan was done with that now. When he'd left Chicago to head off to war in Europe, he'd promised his sister Adele that he'd come back. He was keeping that promise. Their mother had died in a freak boating accident on Lake Michigan in the summer of 1915. Their father, a physician, had died of a heart attack after Ronan was deployed to Europe. Ronan had received the news when he'd arrived in France. He only had his sister left, and her letters had kept him going before his death.

So here he was, home again. The returning warrior. Yeah, right.

"She won't leave," Ronan told Damon.

"Damn right, I won't," she said. "The house is mine. I have the paperwork to prove it." She dug in her purse. "No, wait, it's here. I could have sworn . . . Yes, here it is." She handed over the forms. "Those prove I am the owner of this property."

"Of the house, yes, but not the property," Damon said after looking over the paperwork.

"What do you mean?" she said.

"That you have apparent ownership of the house, but not the land it sits on or is surrounded by."

"You mean the small front yard and backyard?" she said.

Damon nodded. "That's right."

"How is that possible?" she demanded.

Damon shrugged. "You'll have to take it up with your attorney."

"He's just left on a two-week cruise to Antarctica. I can't contact him while he's away."

"Then you'll have to wait until he comes back."

"No way," she said.

"Why not?" Damon said.

"Because the clock starts ticking today."

"What clock?" Ronan demanded.

"Never mind. You still haven't said why you're here. Where is your proof that you have any right to be here?" she asked Ronan.

Her glare at his still-bare chest let him know that she wanted to add, Where is your shirt? Hmm, maybe he could read her mind and could get rid of her that way.

Ronan concentrated on Sierra, taking in everything about her, from her shoulder-length auburn hair to her green eyes to her great breasts. She had a cute nose and a stubborn chin. She grabbed her documents from Damon's hands with slim fingers.

Ronan wondered if she'd be so confrontational if she knew she was facing a pair of vampires.

Reminding himself that he was supposed to be trying to read her mind, he refocused his attention. She was angry. She was tired. She was concentrating on the papers and then looking over his shoulder. What was she looking at?

He turned but saw nothing there. He turned back to Sierra. She was wearing a black leather jacket, black pants, a lime-green top that hugged her breasts, and a pair of gold Claddagh earrings. With her coloring, the auburn hair, pale skin, green eyes, he figured her heritage was Irish. So was his. But she was a mere human while he was not.

Ronan breathed her in. All his senses were powerfully heightened to vampire strength. Her scent was tantalizing. He could hear her pulse swishing through her body. He focused on the slight quiver of her carotid artery in her neck.

As an indentured vampire, Ronan had had to kill more humans than he wanted. But that was over. He'd worked hard to develop his vampire self-control. That didn't mean he wasn't tempted, not only by her artery but also by her curvy body. His afterlife would be much simpler if she'd just obeyed his compulsion.

He didn't sense anything different about her compared to other women he'd come in contact with over the decades. Mind reading was a talent he'd developed over time but even that skill was difficult where she was concerned. It was as if he were trying to tune in to a radio station and getting very bad reception with a lot of static.

Instead of the normal clear reading he was accustomed to getting, he could only pick up a few bits of strange thoughts in her head. Deadlines, iceberg images, a woman in a corset. Whoa. Where had that last one come from? Maybe he'd mistaken Sierra's earlier appreciative looks at his body. Maybe that wasn't her thing. Maybe women in corsets were her thing.

Not that it mattered. Sierra's sexual orientation was irrelevant. She had to go and she had to go now. Ronan needed the house to himself. This was his family's home and therefore it was his if he wanted it, according to Vampire law. And he wanted it. *Badly.* The secret to saving his sister's soul was somewhere in this house.

Besides, the house was located smack-dab in the middle of Vamptown, a Chicago neighborhood inhabited mostly by vampires. This was no place for a human woman, even if she was one with courage and a surprisingly strong stubborn streak.

"She has to go," Ronan told Damon.

Nodding, Damon stepped closer to Sierra and looked into her eyes. "You need to leave."

"No way!" She narrowed her eyes, her increasing anger and frustration very evident. "I don't think you are being an impartial person in this situation. In fact, I want your badge number so I can report you to your superior."

Frowning, Damon looked at Ronan. His message was clear. Damon hadn't had any better luck compelling her than Ronan had. Which, on the one hand, made Ronan feel like he wasn't incapable after all. But on the other hand, it meant they were stuck with her for now.

"You two work it out," Damon abruptly told them before turning on his heel to walk out.

As head of security in Vamptown, Damon was no doubt going to check out every detail about Sierra Brennan. Meanwhile, Ronan had a situation to handle.

"What kind of cop are you?" Sierra shouted after Damon.

"He's the kind with fangs," Ronan drawled sarcastically. "Welcome to the neighborhood."

Chapter Two

Fangs? Sierra didn't like the sound of that. Did Ronan somehow know that she wrote paranormal books? Her books only featured ghosts, not vampires, but maybe he didn't know that.

"Hey, I was only kidding about the fang thing," Ronan said. "Can't you take a joke?"

"No," Sierra said. "And I also can't take you trespassing in my house. Even the cop said I own the house. You can stay in the backyard perhaps."

"It's February."

"Tough tinsel," she said curtly.

"Is that supposed to be a Christmas joke?"

She lifted her chin and stared him straight in the eyes. "Can't you take a joke?"

"Sure. What I can't take is camping in the cold."

"Tough tin—"

Ronan clapped a hand over her mouth. "Shh. Did you hear that?"

She shook her head.

"I heard it," Ruby said. "It's trouble."

Sierra couldn't ask what kind of trouble for two reasons. The first being that Ronan had his hand over her mouth so she couldn't say anything. Then there was the fact that she couldn't speak to the ghost while Ronan was present.

Ronan sniffed the air and then frowned. "I smell cigar smoke."

His attention was focused elsewhere yet his hand remained on her, which meant *her* attention was focused on him. Okay, also focused on herself and the feelings he aroused with his touch.

She wrapped her fingers around his wrist to yank his hand away. Or that was her intention. Instead, the feel of his pulse and the warmth of his skin distracted her.

Finally peeling his hand away, she said, "I don't smoke."

Right. She didn't smoke. But *he* was smoking hot and she'd seen him naked. Both those facts were really starting to hit her now.

"I didn't say you smelled."

She was supposed to be grateful for that?

"You don't smell cigar smoke?" he asked.

"No."

Ruby was standing a few feet away, waving her hands to get Sierra's attention. "I need you to focus on me."

"What are you looking at?" Ronan demanded.

"Not you," she assured him.

"Then what?"

"I was, umm . . . just noticing the vintage wallpaper on the walls here in the foyer."

"It's peeling. You'd be better off elsewhere," he said.

"Is that a threat?" she said.

He shrugged.

Her dwindling patience snapped. "Listen, you, I've had a long day and I don't need you making trouble."

She didn't realize she'd been jabbing him in his still bare chest until he took hold of her hand and cupped it in his. "You're different," he noted.

Uh-oh. Was he picking up on her ghost-whispering thing somehow? She sure was picking up on his sexy half-dressed-guy thing. "What do you mean?"

"Nothing." He dropped her hand. "How about a compromise? We could share the house until your lawyer gets back."

Sierra was silent for a few moments as she considered her options here. If Damon was right and she didn't own the land the house sat on, then she might be forced to leave the property, and if she did that then she'd lose it. She had to stay thirty consecutive days and nights from the moment she first set foot inside. The terms of her great-uncle's will had been very clear on that point.

Which meant that her best bet was probably to work out a temporary compromise with Ronan. "You mean like a written temporary-lease agreement?"

"I'm not sure we need anything in writing."

"I am *positive* we need it in writing. That way there won't be any misunderstandings. And if I do agree to this temporary arrangement then rule number one is no nudity."

"I don't mind if you're nude," Ronan said.

"Well, I mind if *you're* nude, so don't do it," she said tartly.

"If you insist."

"I do." She reached into her purse for one of her small notebooks. She found an empty page near the end. "The house has two floors with one bedroom and bath on the main floor and two bedrooms and a bath upstairs."

"Correct."

She moved past him to head upstairs.

"Where are you going?" Ronan demanded.

"I'm checking out the upstairs to see which floor I'd like to claim as mine during this temporary arrangement."

The stairs creaked as she climbed them. Ronan was right behind her, which made her very aware of the fact that she was a well-rounded size-fourteen woman with a butt that she considered to be curvaceous on her good days and too big on her bad ones.

Telling herself that she didn't care what Ronan thought, she quickly stepped into the bedroom to the right of the stairs.

"Did you hear that?" Ronan said.

She shook her head. All she could hear was her heart pounding in her ears. Geez, if climbing one set of stairs did that to her, she definitely needed a workout routine.

"It sounded like someone closed a door up here," Ronan said.

"Have you heard strange noises while you've been here?" she asked.

"Not until you got here."

Stung, she said, "Well, clearly I didn't close a door since I'm standing right in front of you in the middle of the room."

He looked around suspiciously.

"Maybe the place is haunted," she said.

"There's no such thing as ghosts," he scoffed.

"You sure about that?"

"Why? Do you believe in them?"

Sierra shrugged and rubbed her hands up and down her arms. There was a definite chill in this room that she hadn't detected downstairs. And there was no sign of Ruby up here. Sierra sensed another presence but saw nothing suspicious. Still, she trusted her instincts. "You can stay up here. There's no kitchen upstairs."

"Not a problem," Ronan said

"You probably eat out a lot, huh?"

"You could say that," he drawled with an enigmatic look that she found surprisingly sexy.

She opened the bathroom off the bedroom and checked that out. Nothing special there. Sink, toilet, bathtub. "Okay then. But before I print up an agreement, I will need references from you. If they turn out okay then you may temporarily stay up here and I'll stay downstairs. Hopefully our paths won't cross very often and we can get this worked out when my lawyer returns. What about your lawyer?"

"I don't need one."

She wasn't about to advise him to get legal representation, a move that might only make her own situation more complicated. While she was certain that her claim on the house and the land would stand, there were ways of dragging things out in court.

She didn't need more complications.

There was another doorway to the left of the stairs. Sierra turned the rusty doorknob. In her haste to enter, she nearly flattened her nose against the door, which stubbornly refused to open.

"Allow me," Ronan said.

Reaching around her, he managed to encircle her in his arms under the pretext of opening the door. She could feel the heat radiating from his bare chest through the back of her cotton top.

"It seems jammed," he said. He was so close that his voice resonated through her like the bass turned full throttle on a sound system in a muscle car.

She had three options. She could try to duck under his arm but that would mean rubbing against his body, probably not the best idea. She could try again to open it herself. Or she could tell him to forget it and say they'd try the room later.

That seemed the best option but she couldn't resist giving the knob one last try, which meant putting her hand over his.

The door gave way so suddenly she almost tumbled onto the floor. Ronan grabbed hold of her, preventing her from falling.

"I'm okay," she told him and herself.

Quickly moving away from Ronan, she studied her surroundings. A big window faced the front of the room and a set of French doors with a tiny balcony was at the back. The room was very large but had nothing in it aside from a large framed black-and-white photograph on one wall, of a middle-aged man smoking a cigar. He had a receding hairline, a bulbous nose, and heavy jowls. His smile was more sinister than cheerful.

The cold came creeping in. She could feel trouble

here, but she didn't know if her attraction to Ronan was to blame or if it was something else. The cold certainly didn't come from Ronan. There was definitely another presence up here. But she had other things to deal with first, including the female ghost downstairs.

Sierra told herself that she could do this. She would write up a very carefully worded agreement and have Ronan sign it today.

"If you'll give me three references, I can check them out right away," she told Ronan.

She returned downstairs and checked the rooms on that floor. A large parlor in the front led into a dining room toward the back of the house. The few pieces of furniture dated to that period. No modern Ikea pieces here.

The kitchen was dated and could use a good scrubbing.

The bedroom faced the front of the house and was on the other side of the central staircase. It was large and clean. Hardwood floors had been worn to a warm patina by generations of feet.

There was no furniture in the room. Her cousins must have taken their beds with them when they left. They were twice her age and she wasn't close to them so she didn't know any of the details of their stay. The only reason they'd given for not staying in the house was that "Life is too short."

"I'll take the ground floor. You may temporarily stay upstairs. I'll write out a *temporary* agreement," she told Ronan, deliberately repeating the word. "That doesn't mean that I in any way think you have a right to stay here or have any rights to this property. But it is February, as you said. And it is cold outside. I just want to be clear so you don't get your hopes up."

Ronan didn't deal with hope. He'd hoped that he could break free during the many decades of his long indenture, but that hadn't happened. He'd hoped that his sister had been spared the curse that his sire had cast on her soul, but that hadn't happened. So he didn't believe in hopes and dreams. He dealt with facts. And the fact was that he had to get his mission accomplished. Failure was not an option.

Sierra was plucky, he'd give her that. Nothing he'd done had thrown her for long. Granted, she'd been surprised to find him naked, but she'd bounced back and hadn't been intimidated. He didn't know why she couldn't be compelled. That was a problem. And he didn't need more problems.

He'd check in later with Damon to see what the head of security in Vamptown had dug up on her.

Ronan couldn't even flash his fangs at her because there was no way to make her forget what she saw. He certainly wasn't going to kill her. He'd seen and done enough killing over the past ninety-seven years.

He had to keep the fact that he was a vampire a secret from her.

When he'd lived here as a human, he'd no idea that he was in the midst of a vampire enclave. The talk instead had been about the increasing hostilities in Europe and the possibility that America would be drawn into the war over there.

"Why weren't you wearing any clothes earlier?" she abruptly asked him.

"I was changing." Changing from a resting vampire to an awake one.

Since arriving in Vamptown, he'd been put through a vamp inquisition by the vampire council before they'd approved of him staying. Only after that had he been given the rules.

No killing of humans.

No sharing info about Vamptown.

Not that he'd been given much info worth sharing. He had access to blood, but wasn't told where it came from. He'd been given a tattoo on the back of his neck and told he'd be able to handle sunshine in two weeks' time. He still had one day before he got there, so he spent most of his daylight hours in total darkness. Apparently he was old-school that way. He had a casket stashed in the basement.

Sierra hadn't looked down there yet.

She pointed to the door behind the stairs. "Where does that go?"

"The basement."

She headed toward it.

"Whoa." He put out his hand to stop her. "Where do you think you're going?"

"I *know* I'm going to the basement."

"Why?"

"Why not?" she countered.

"I thought you were going to write out an agreement for me to sign."

"I am," she said. "As soon as I see the basement."

"It's pretty dark down there. The lights are all out."

She flipped the switch at the top of the stairs but nothing happened.

"See?" He moved to close the door.

She moved away but only as far as her purse, where she retrieved a slim flashlight.

Shit. This woman was stubborn and persistent, neither of which he found endearing in a human.

He didn't realize he was blocking her way until she glared at him. "Is there some reason you don't want me going in the basement?" she said.

"It's not safe," he said.

"Because?"

"It's dark."

"Which is why I have a high-intensity flashlight." She turned it on and aimed it right in his face.

Ronan groaned and turned away. While it wasn't sunlight, the beam of intense light still hurt.

"Sorry," she muttered. "Are your eyes sensitive to light? I have a friend who is like that."

Ronan doubted she had any friends "like that" or like him. Even the other vampires in Vamptown had no experience with an indentured vampire. He'd seen their looks of pity. They'd let him stay because of his claim to the house . . . *this* house, his house.

"Before you go down there, I have a question for you. You referred to my girlfriend when you first arrived."

"Did I?" She fiddled with the flashlight.

"Yes. Why?"

"I just figured I may have interrupted you and some girl. I mean, you *were* naked."

"I told you, I was changing." He was changing again, into a sexually aroused vampire. He sensed her pulse quickening. He tried reading her mind again but she was blocking him.

"I'm doing the best I can," she muttered. To herself? Or to someone else? He looked around but there was no one there.

"What about the stuff in your truck?" He pointed outside. "Don't you want to unpack?"

Sighing, she returned the flashlight to her purse and reached for her set of keys.

She opened the door to find Damon and another man standing there with her desk. "Where do you want this?" Damon demanded.

"Come in. I, uh, wasn't expecting—"

Damon interrupted her. "Where do you want this?"

"In my bedroom. Follow me."

"She likes giving orders," Ronan told his fellow vampires. The newcomer was Nick St. George, the head of the local business association.

"How did you get into my U-Haul van?" she asked them.

"You left it unlocked," Damon said.

Ronan stood there and watched as Nick introduced himself to Sierra. It didn't take them long, even traveling at human rather than vamp superspeed, to unload the pieces of furniture. Bed, bookcases, a dresser.

Ronan took the boxes of books that Nick handed him at the front door. He noticed that one was full of the same book by one person. S. J. Brennan. Suddenly that confusing thing about deadlines, one of the few bits he'd picked up from her thoughts earlier, made sense.

"You must really like this author's books," he noted as he set the box in Sierra's bedroom.

Sierra nodded. "She's one of my favorite authors."

"Not surprising since *you* are S. J. Brennan," Ronan said.

Chapter Three

Sierra eyed him suspiciously. "How do you know that? And what's with the detective helping me to move in?" Damon and the other guy had moved so fast, Sierra hadn't had time to protest. She was becoming increasingly brain-dead. She just wanted to crawl into her bed, but couldn't. Not yet.

"Damon is just being friendly," Ronan said.

"As in he's *your* friend, not mine. He's not really a cop at all, is he? You both set me up." Sierra rubbed her fingers over her forehead. A massage therapist had once told her it was a good way to release stress.

"Hi, welcome to the neighborhood," a woman said from the bedroom doorway. "My name is Daniella Delaney, the owner of Heavenly Cupcakes. I can't believe I'm talking to S. J. Brennan! I really enjoy reading your books."

"Thanks, but I think it would be best if you all left now. Especially you." She glared at Ronan.

"What did you do?" Daniella said, joining Sierra in

glaring at Ronan. "Do you know how lucky we are to have her move into the neighborhood?"

"My uncle left his house to me but Ronan refuses to leave. Then Damon came and lied by saying that I might own the house but not the property around it," Sierra said.

Daniella frowned. "That doesn't make sense."

"Right." Sierra felt like hugging her. "My point exactly."

"What does your lawyer say about all this?" Daniella asked.

"I can't reach him at the moment," Sierra said.

"I'm staying upstairs until her lawyer gets back and we settle this. Sierra is drawing up a temporary agreement for me to sign," Ronan said.

"Don't sign it!" The order came from a newcomer, a tanned blonde wearing stiletto boots, a spandex micromini skirt, and a tight T-shirt. She'd just removed her faux-fur coat.

Sierra was starting to feel like she was in the midst of some bizarre flash mob scene taking place in her own bedroom. "Who are you?" Sierra demanded.

"My name is Tanya and I'm your biggest fan. I'll move in with you instead."

A crash from the kitchen drew everyone's attention. Sierra headed there, and everyone else followed. Or so she thought, but the truth was that somehow the three men entered the kitchen first, as if intent on protecting their womenfolk. Sierra was surprisingly touched by the chivalrous gesture.

"What does a ghost have to do around here to get a little attention?" Ruby demanded. "Oh wait, I guess I have to smash something." She pointed to the kitchen wall clock now broken on the floor.

"Is that oak?" Daniella asked in a tense voice.

Sierra looked down. "It's plastic."

"It was plastic. Now it's broken," Ruby said. "This is so frustrating! I've been waiting so long for someone to finally see me and now that you do, you don't pay any attention to me."

"I'm a little busy here," Sierra said.

"Right. Everybody out," Tanya ordered. "The muse is calling her and Sierra has to write now."

Ruby fluffed her hair. "So I'm a muse now? Can she see me?" Ruby floated over and waved her hand in front of Tanya's face. "No." Her luminescent face reflected her disappointment before she returned her attention to Sierra. "Are you afraid of me?"

"I'm not afraid," Sierra said.

"You should be," Ronan said. "Look what happened to that guy in the Stephen King novel when his biggest fan got hold of him."

"I would never do anything to upset my favorite author," Tanya assured her. "I've read your books about a thousand times."

"I didn't know you liked reading," Daniella said.

"Usually I don't, but I loved these books," Tanya said. "Especially the latest one. The sex was really hot."

"The sex?" Ronan raised an eyebrow.

Tanya made it sound like Sierra had written the latest *Fifty Shades of Grey* book. Sierra could tell by the look on Ronan's face that he was thinking the same thing.

Tanya clapped her hands. "Everybody out."

"I'm not going anywhere," Ronan said.

"Maybe you should all step out for a bit while Sierra and I have a cup of tea and some cupcakes," Daniella said.

Sierra couldn't deny that the cupcakes looked delicious and her stomach was growling. The last food she'd had was . . . she couldn't remember. Had it been a burrito from the Quik-Mart place near the Indiana border where she'd filled the car with gas?

"I'll stay," Tanya said.

"No you won't," Nick said.

One look from Nick stopped Tanya's protest.

Damon, Nick, and Tanya left but Ronan stayed. Daniella gave him a look, as did Sierra.

"I'll be in the basement checking the lighting," Ronan finally said.

"You should go with your friends," Sierra said.

"I'm not leaving," he said.

"If you go down there, you'll need a flashlight," she reminded him.

"I have excellent night vision," he said.

"It's your funeral." It was a trademark line from her books.

He shrugged. "I'm not into funerals."

From the kitchen doorway leading to the hall she could see him open the basement door and descend the stairs.

"Okay, then." Daniella flipped open the cardboard box she still held in her arms. "Do you prefer chocolate, red velvet, or cookies and cream?"

"Chocolate."

"Ah, a girl after my own heart."

"I see you've got them decorated for Valentine's Day."

"It's only a few days away and it's one of our busiest times of the year."

Sierra looked at the cupcake Daniella handed her.

Picking up on Sierra's uncertainty, Daniella said, "What's the matter?"

"I'm never sure how to eat one of these in front of someone. I mean, it's okay if I get frosting on my nose, but not in public. And what about the paper lining? Do I take it off completely or just partially?"

"There is no wrong way to eat a cupcake," Daniella said.

"I'm sure there must be and I probably do it," Sierra said.

"Don't be so hard on yourself. Just take a big bite. Go on." Daniella's grin urged Sierra on. Sure enough, she got icing on her nose. Instead of feeling self-conscious, she grinned back.

"Good, huh?" Daniella said.

Since she had a mouthful of cupcake, Sierra made no reply other than an *mmmm*. Then it hit her—here she was standing in the kitchen chowing down without offering her guest a drink or a seat.

Wiping the icing off, Sierra swallowed. "I don't have any tea, but I do have my Keurig. How about some coffee?"

A few minutes later, Sierra and Daniella were seated at the hefty dining room table. It looked like it weighed a ton, which was probably why it was still in the house. It would take an army to move it out. So it, the sideboard, the living room couch, and the other furniture had stayed.

Staying wasn't in Sierra's history. Her thoughts were interrupted by Daniella.

"I'm sure this must all be hard for you," the cupcake maker said. "Moving to a new place is always a challenge."

"It's a bigger challenge when you open the door to find a naked guy standing there," Sierra said.

Daniella's jaw dropped. "Did Ronan kick him out?"

"Ronan *was* the naked guy."

"Wow, I don't know what to say."

"I didn't either for a split second. Then I told him to leave." Sierra didn't bring up the part about talking to Ruby and thinking the ghost was Ronan's girlfriend.

"I don't know what I would have done in your place," Daniella said. "I probably would have turned around and left."

"I don't give up easily." Which was how she'd survived a challenging childhood. Sierra's father was an alcoholic abuser who'd beaten Sierra's mom. When Sierra was five, her mom took Sierra with her and left him.

Her mother hadn't trusted the judicial system to protect her so she hadn't filed a restraining order. Instead she'd taken off with Sierra in the middle of the night and never looked back. Or to be more accurate, her mother had always looked back over her shoulder to stay one step ahead of her father. Sierra remembered enough of her father's fury and violence that she never doubted his promise that he'd make them pay. So they'd kept moving.

That had gone on for nearly a decade before they got the word that he'd died of a massive heart attack.

They'd returned home to the Chicago area and re-connected with the few relatives on her mom's side that remained. Great-uncle Saul had been just about the only one left. But Chicago hadn't really seemed like home. No place did.

Maybe that was the result of a transient lifestyle. Sierra had spent almost all her life moving every six months or so. The longest they'd ever stayed in one place was a year.

Perhaps that's why Sierra's mom had never worried about Sierra's "invisible friends." Even when she real-ized that Sierra was talking to ghosts, she hadn't wor-ried. "It's your Irish heritage," she'd proudly tell Sierra. "My grandmother had the sight as well. She saw the future. You see ghosts. You come by it honestly."

Sierra saw her first ghost at her seventh birthday party. Only Sierra and her mom were present until a little girl in pigtails showed up. She was in the shadows at first but came forward when Sierra held her hand out.

Her name was Bonita and she wanted Sierra to tell her mom, who lived in the apartment across the hall, that it wasn't her fault that Bonita had drowned in the apartment-complex pool.

When they were alone, Sierra had tried telling Bo-nita that she didn't think an adult would appreciate the message. But Bonita was persistent. So two days later, Sierra had screwed up her courage and knocked on the neighbor's door.

"Bonita wants me to tell you not to feel bad. It wasn't your fault," Sierra said in a rush.

The woman reached out as if she were going to slap Sierra.

Bonita quickly said, "Tell her it wasn't our dog Ti-to's fault either."

Sierra repeated Bonita's words in a rush.

"It was an accident," Bonita said. "I love you, Momma, and Tito too."

Once again, Sierra said the words.

Bonita's mother started to cry. Sierra could still re-member feeling guilty that she'd made the woman so unhappy. She turned to Bonita, who was looking at a bright light at the end of the apartment hallway. "Tell her I hid her ring in the purple vase." Bonita waved and then disappeared into the light.

Sierra had repeated the message about the ring be-fore she ran back to her own apartment and hid under the covers. The white light hadn't frightened her. She sensed it represented something good, not bad. But Bonita's mother had scared her.

A few minutes later, Sierra's mom knocked on the door. "The strangest thing just happened. The woman across the hallway wanted me to thank you. She wouldn't say why."

Bonita's mom moved shortly after that.

Later, Sierra had asked her mom if she'd ever seen ghosts. Her mom had replied that she was too busy for such things. Sierra suspected it was more likely that her mother already felt haunted by the memories of the terror and pain Sierra's father had inflicted on her. She hadn't wanted anything or anyone else haunting her.

Sierra lost track of how many ghosts she'd seen since then. There weren't hundreds but there had been a number. Sometimes their message was simple, some-times it was more complicated, sometimes there was no message and they were just confused. But they always moved on once Sierra dealt with them. But their memory remained with Sierra, which wasn't always a good thing.

At least Sierra's mom was in a better place now. A few years ago her mom had met Paul James, who treasured her. The two of them were living in New Zealand at the moment, where Paul was on a yearlong teaching sabbatical.

Her mom had been hesitant to leave her but Sierra had convinced her to go. Paul was an incredibly giving soul and Sierra could see the goodness in him. Trusting someone didn't happen often for Sierra, and it hadn't happened overnight but over the course of several years with Paul. He was one of the few good guys.

Normally Sierra's mom would frequently Skype with her from New Zealand, but for the month of February they were in an area with few Wi-Fi or cell phone connections.

Her mom had been nervous about Sierra moving into the house in Chicago by herself but Sierra had convinced her that she'd be fine. It was hardly her first move, even though her mom had helped with the others.

The bottom line was that Sierra had this moving thing down pat. It was the "staying" part that she wanted to work on now.

Given Sierra's background and the fact that she saw dead people, her romantic relationships tended to be few and short-lived. The longest had been her most recent. She and Steve had been together almost seven months when she'd decided they were better off as friends than as lovers. Steve had agreed. So the move to

Chicago had come at a good time for Sierra, allowing her to move on.

"You're braver than I am," Daniella said.

Sierra carefully folded the cupcake liner and dropped it in her now empty coffee mug. "I don't know about that."

Sierra certainly wasn't as brave as Nicki Champion, the heroine in her books. Although, the more time she spent writing about Nicki, the more Sierra took up the gauntlet of courage and control. Which was why she hadn't turned tail and run when she'd seen Naked Ronan.

Those days of being afraid of her own shadow were over. It was time to put down roots for a bit and she might as well start here, with her great-uncle's house. It would take her seven months to finish the book she'd just started writing. Since it revolved around a bootlegging Chicago Mob plot dating back to 1920s, this was the perfect place to find inspiration.

So, yeah, she didn't give up easily. To her way of thinking that just made her persistent, not brave. Because if she really were brave, she wouldn't still want to run sometimes.

Another crash came from the kitchen. "That better not be my Keurig," Sierra growled.

Ronan sat on the closed casket on the basement floor. Nick sat beside him. Nick had come in from the tunnels leading beneath the house that dated back to the bootlegging days during Prohibition. That all had happened after Ronan had been turned. When he'd grown up in this house he'd been afraid to come down here. Now nothing scared him.

Not true. The possibility that he couldn't save his sister's soul scared him.

"You like the dark," Nick noted.

"I live in the dark," Ronan said.

"You won't have to after tomorrow," Nick said.

Part of Ronan would always remain in the dark. There hadn't been any lights guiding him home. Only desperation.

He'd arrived here in the dark. Being able to survive sunlight meant he'd have more opportunity to find the key to breaking Voz's hold on Adele's soul. It didn't mean that his afterlife would be all light and cheery.

Ronan pointed upstairs. "Can't you get rid of her?"

"I assume you are referring to Sierra?"

Ronan nodded. "You're in charge here—"

"No," Nick corrected him. "The council is in charge. I'm not even the most senior member of the council. Pat Heller is. He's been here in Vamptown the longest."

"Were there vampires here when I lived here as a human?"

"Probably. You'd have to ask Pat. You could have asked him when he gave you the tattoo. Why didn't you?" Nick said.

Ronan just shrugged and absently rubbed the back of his neck and the inked fleur-de-lis there. Instead of answering, he changed the subject. "Did Damon tell you that Sierra can't be compelled?"

Even though it was pitch-dark, Ronan could see Nick nod.

"She's not the only one. Daniella can't be compelled either."

"So human women can't be compelled here in Vamptown?" Ronan was incredulous. "How does that work?"

"It wouldn't work. Daniella is a hybrid," Nick reminded him. "She's part druid."

"Then that's what Sierra must be."

"She's not. We already checked her."

"How?"

"You already know we have surveillance cameras all over Vamptown and in the buildings as well."

"Right."

"For some reason, we can't get them to work well in this particular house. But we used the image we got of her entering the house and put it through our computers' specialized heat sensor test," Nick said. "If she had any druid or vampire blood, it would have shown up in those results. She's human."

"She's not a normal human. I'm sure of it. Maybe she's a witch or something. Do your computers show that?"

"No. But your neighbors are witches and they would know if she's a witch. Damon checked with them the moment he discovered Sierra couldn't be compelled. And she's not a witch. But now that I think about it . . ."

"Yes. Now that you think about it?"

"Perhaps she can be slightly compelled. It's not completely logical that she'd agree to let you stay here until her lawyer can be reached. I mean, what did you say your claim was to owning the house?"

Ronan tried to think back. Having a good memory was critical to a vampire but the fact that he'd been around for nearly a hundred years meant there was a lot of stuff in his head. Just as a vampire's senses of hearing, smell, and touch were heightened, so too was his ability to remember. Which was more a curse than a blessing at times.

"No, I didn't tell her why. I could hardly say that my family owned this house before World War One. Damon told her that the paperwork she has only applies to the house not the land but I didn't go into details about my claim to the place."

"So why did she agree to let you stay even if only temporarily? I doubt it was because of your charm."

"It would be easier if she'd just leave."

"We're still trying to figure this out. She's only been here a few hours. We'll get to the bottom of it soon. Until then, just try to get along."

"Getting along is not a vampire thing."

"I am well aware of that," Nick said. "I'm also aware that you haven't told us everything about your vampire past."

"And I never will," Ronan said.

"Then tell me the parts that might affect us here in Vamptown."

"There is nothing. I already told you that when you approved of my staying. You checked me out."

"I know that you were an indentured vampire turned by Baron Voz. Vamptown has already survived a rival vampire attack followed by a demon infestation. We don't need a Master Vampire coming down on us."

"I put in my time," Ronan said. "I'm no longer indentured. Check it out with Voz if you don't believe me."

"I did."

"And?" Ronan said.

"And he confirmed your story."

"It's not a story. It's the truth."

"Not all of it."

Ronan clenched his fists. "It's all you need to know."

"If you bring trouble here, you will pay," Nick said.

"Understood." Nothing Nick could threaten him with could compare to what Voz had already threatened. Ronan had bargained with the devil. The devil known as Voz. He'd done so to save his sister. But if he didn't find the key Voz wanted then Ronan would be indentured to Voz for eternity.

"I thought you'd *never* get rid of her," Ruby said after Daniella left.

"Step away from my Keurig," Sierra ordered the ghost.

"The what?"

"The coffeemaker. And anything else you can break. I only own four mugs."

"Now you own three." Ruby pointed to the shards still on the floor.

Sierra angrily picked them up and tossed them into the garbage. Luckily the mug had broken into three pieces instead of many. "Stop breaking stuff! I don't need this. I've had a long day."

"Long?" Ruby put her hands on her ample hips. "You want to talk long? How about waiting ninety years or more for someone to hear you, or see you? Do you have any idea how it feels to be invisible?" Ruby said.

"Actually I sort of do."

"Were you a ghost?"

"No," Sierra said. "But growing up, we moved around a lot. I was always the new kid who never fit in. I coped by blending in to the background and becoming invisible so I wouldn't stand out."

Ruby played a tiny violin. "Tough tinsel."

"Hey, that's my line," Sierra said. "I'm a writer. We're sensitive to other people stealing our lines."

"Like I said, tough tinsel. Let's get down to the bottom line here, shall we? You owe me. It's thanks to me that you inherited this house and not the other two that came here before you. I helped scare them off," Ruby said.

"Then scare Ronan off as well."

"I can't do that."

"Why not?" Sierra demanded.

"Because Ronan must stay," Ruby said. "Or we will all perish."

Chapter Four

"What? What are you talking about? What do you mean Ronan has to stay? Why?" Sierra demanded.

"To save you from the man upstairs," Ruby whispered.

"Do you mean God?" Sierra whispered back.

"I mean Hal," Ruby said.

Sierra frowned. "I don't understand. Who is Hal?"

"He's the ghost upstairs."

"Why do we need saving from him?"

"Because he's evil."

Before Sierra could ask more questions, Ronan interrupted her.

"Who are you talking to?" he said.

She whirled to face him. "Don't do that!"

"Do what?"

"Sneak up on me that way."

"You're tired." He looked at her with those chocolate-brown eyes of his. "You should go to bed."

"Yes, I should but not because you said so. And

don't think I've forgotten about needing those three references."

He pointed to the empty cupcake box on the counter. "Daniella will vouch for me."

"She's not here anymore."

"You can call her. The number is on the box."

Ruby was waving her hands behind him.

"Fine," Sierra said. "I'm going to bed now. Just for a couple minutes' rest."

She stomped into her bedroom and slammed the door. Or she would have if the box of her books hadn't stood in the way. She shoved the box with her foot and closed the door.

Ruby floated right through and sank onto the bed.

"You don't have much stuff," she noted.

"I have more than I used to. When I was growing up, I couldn't have more stuff than would fit in two black garbage bags."

"Don't make me play that pity violin again," Ruby said. "Can we finally talk about me now?"

Sierra nodded, reached for a pillow from a nearby box, and sat on the other end of the bed.

"Okay, like I said, my name is Ruby. I was murdered in this house and I need your help punishing my murderer."

Sierra wasn't surprised to hear Ruby had been murdered. Spirits who couldn't move to the other side often had ties to this world caused by a violent death or some other intense unresolved situation.

"Who murdered you?" Sierra asked.

"Hal."

"The evil ghost upstairs?"

Ruby nodded.

"Shit," Sierra said.

"I know."

"Start at the beginning. Did you live in this house? Did he?"

"I worked here," Ruby said.

"Worked here? As what?"

Ruby pointed to her scarce attire. "What do you think?"

"I didn't want to make any assumptions."

"I was a prostitute. I'm not real proud of it, although I was very good at it. I don't like to brag but I was the most popular girl in Al's prostitution ring."

"Al?"

Ruby nodded. "Al Capone."

"You knew him?"

"In the biblical sense?"

"In any sense."

"Yes, I knew him. So did Hal. Hal was in charge of the prostitution division of the business."

Great. So the ghost upstairs was a former gangster. That didn't bode well.

"And no, I never knew Al in the biblical sense," Ruby added. "Al never lived here. He had a house on South Prairie Avenue on the South Side of the city."

"What was he like?"

"Forget about Al. This is about me, remember?"

"Okay, well then . . . when did you die?"

"I didn't just die. I was murdered. On Valentine's Day in 1929."

"That's the date of the Valentine's Day massacre when Al Capone's gang allegedly gunned down a rival gang." Sierra leaned forward. "Did you know about that? Is that why you were killed?"

"I was never involved in those kinds of dealings. I was killed because I wanted to leave the business. I was dressed for work at the time, which is why I am stuck in these clothes instead of some mysterious white dress like girl ghosts are supposed to wear."

"Spirits often appear wearing the clothes they wore when they died."

"Yeah, well, after wearing these garters for ninety years I am sick of it," Ruby said. "At first I thought this was a version of hell, that I was sent here because I was a prostitute. I thought being stuck here forever was my punishment."

"Why is Hal here?"

"Maybe that's his punishment. He spends most of his time upstairs. Didn't you see him up there?"

"No. You're the only ghost I've seen so far."

"His portrait is up there on the wall. The large framed photograph on the wall. He's smoking a cigar."

"Ronan said he smelled a cigar."

"I wonder why you can see me and not him."

"I don't know."

"How much experience do you have with ghosts?" Ruby asked.

"Most of the spirits I've dealt with don't go back as far as you do," Sierra admitted.

"What does that mean?" Ruby demanded. "That I've been here so long there's no chance of me moving on?"

"Did you see white light when you died?"

"Was I supposed to?"

"Did you see anything?"

"I saw red. A lot of red. I was stabbed like twenty times. Blood gushed everywhere."

Feeling faint, Sierra rolled onto her side and tried to catch her breath. It was one thing to write about stabbings and battles, but it was another to actually be speaking to a ghost who had died that way. She quickly sat up again, reprimanding herself for the momentary show of weakness. She was a writer. She should be viewing this as research. And neither the sight of blood nor the discussion of it had ever bothered her before.

Ruby was eyeing her suspiciously "What's the point of you being able to see me if you don't have the answers?"

"I never claimed to have the answers to everything."

"Okay, how about this one question. What are we supposed to do now?"

Sierra countered with a question of her own. "Why did you say that Ronan had to stay or we would all perish?"

"Because he can protect us from Hal."

"How?"

"I'm not sure. I just sense that he can."

Sierra had never dealt with a ghost's intuition before so she wasn't sure how reliable it was. But she did know that the presence she'd sensed upstairs had been a very powerful one.

"Was Hal murdered too?" Sierra asked.

"I don't know."

"Did he die in this house?"

"I'm not sure."

"Did he die when you did?"

"No, I don't think so. Can't you find that stuff out? Can't you sense stuff?"

"Not really," Sierra said. "It doesn't work that way."

"Then how does it work?"

"I work with the spirit to help them come to terms with whatever is keeping them here instead of moving on."

"Do all the ghosts you see move on toward the white light?"

"So far, yes."

"Why did you say it that way? You think I'm different?"

"You *are* different," Sierra said.

"Because I'm a prostitute?"

"Because you're a prostitute who died in 1929 and who had ties to Al Capone." Sierra rubbed her hands with excitement as her inner writer came to the fore. "This has the makings of a great story!"

Ruby smiled and did a brief flapper dance of joy. "That means I get a happy ending."

Sierra didn't have the heart to burst Ruby's bubble by admitting that happy endings were a lot easier to achieve in fiction than in real life.

Feeling frustrated, Ronan went outside to examine the exterior foundation of the house. Was the key buried somewhere in the concrete that bound the bricks together? Was the key even really a key or something symbolic of a key?

Ronan only had until the middle of the month to figure it all out. Not only to figure it out, but also to retrieve the key and hand it over to Voz.

All of which was hard enough to do without having a human getting in his way. Whenever humans had gotten in his way before, he'd either killed them or compelled them, thereby quickly getting them *out* of his way.

He wondered if Voz was behind Sierra's sudden appearance in the house. He wouldn't put it past the Master Vampire to pull something like that. But he hadn't sensed any vampire ties with Sierra. Not that he could always tell. But surely Damon would have checked her out.

Sierra's inability to be compelled irritated Ronan. Damon had assured Ronan that Sierra wasn't the first woman to come to Vamptown with that ability. There were two others—Zoe Adams, who lived next door, and Daniella Delaney, who ran the local cupcake shop.

Somehow that information didn't do much to decrease Ronan's frustration with the situation. He was still adjusting to nearly a hundred years of being an indentured vampire, sleeping in a coffin during the day and doing whatever his Master Sire wanted during the night.

Now that he was free he should be able to move on and enjoy the rest of his immortal life. But Ronan couldn't do that. Because he had to save his sister's soul.

He kicked a shrub along the foundation wall. His vamp strength yanked it out of the ground and sent it flying fifty yards across the street, over the top of a house and into the alley behind it.

"Chicago is known as the Windy City but we don't usually have flying bushes," Damon said from beside him. "Or burning bushes either."

"Vamps and fire do not get along," Ronan said.

"Right."

"Sorry," Ronan said abruptly.

"Is your anger going to be an issue? I've heard that indentured vamps can have a hard time making the transition."

"From human to vamp?"

"From indentured to free."

"Are we ever really free?" Ronan's voice was as dark as the night.

"Depends on your definition of freedom," Damon said.

Ronan didn't know what his definition of freedom was anymore but it sure as hell didn't include a female named Sierra.

"So you're saying that you are willing to give Ronan a good character reference?" Sierra asked Daniella over the phone.

"Sure."

"How long have you known him?"

"Long enough to know he seems like a reliable kind of . . . um . . . person."

"That seems rather vague."

"Damon and Nick would not have befriended Ronan if they had any doubts about his character. They are both real particular about that sort of thing."

"Where does Ronan work?"

"I believe he's between jobs at the moment. But he's not broke if that's what you're worried about."

"How do you know that he's not broke?" Sierra said.

"Nick told me."

"He's not exactly an objective person."

"Sure he is," Daniella said. "I'd trust Nick with my life."

Yeah, but would Sierra trust Ronan with *her* life? Holding her smartphone, she walked from the kitchen to her bedroom to make sure there was a lock on the door. There was. In fact, it was a surprisingly strong double lock that looked as if it had been installed recently.

That made her feel better. After completing her call with Daniella, she checked her phone for a nearby Chinese takeout place that delivered.

While waiting for her dinner to be delivered, she printed up an agreement for Ronan to sign.

"You're responsible for your own food," she told him half an hour later.

"Not a problem. I'm not into Chinese takeout."

"High salt content, I know," she said. "But I am such a sucker for Shanghai noodles, moo shu pork, and pot stickers."

She set her food on the dining table, took a seat, then opened the white container and used the chopsticks to eat some of the noodles.

"They look like worms," Ronan said.

"Cutting the noodles would be bad luck since they represent a long life."

Ronan snickered.

"So you don't believe in bad luck?" she said.

His expression darkened but he made no comment.

She ate a pot sticker before speaking again. "You never did say what your claim was to this house."

"You didn't ask."

"I'm asking now."

Ronan sat across from her. "I have a prior claim."

"What kind of prior claim?"

See, this was why Ronan preferred compelling humans to do his bidding. Because explanations got messy and complicated. He could hardly say that the place had been his family's home in 1900.

"My family has a claim prior to your family's." Ronan made sure to maintain direct eye contact with Sierra as she sat across from him in the hopes that some amount of compelling would work on her.

He wasn't sure how well it worked because all she said was, "We'll see about that."

He'd been telling the truth for once. His family had moved into the house when it was brand-new. He remembered that summer. It had been very hot. He'd just turned ten and his sister Adele was five. Their birthdays were only a week apart in July, which had aggravated them as kids.

Sierra reached for another container of food. "My great-uncle owned this property for ages."

Ronan almost smiled. He doubted "ages" had the same meaning for her that it did for him. When you were immortal, your perspective about time—and everything else—changed. As for those long noodles of hers representing a long life, again the concept of a long life changed when you had forever.

Realizing she was waiting for him to reply to her last comment, he repeated her words back to her. "We'll see about that."

"I printed out the temporary living arrangement for you to sign. I talked to Daniella. She said you were trustworthy. She said Damon and Nick would vouch for you as would a number of others in the neighborhood."

He made no comment as she slid the agreement and a pen across the table for him to sign. He did so, scrawling his name across the bottom of the page.

"It must be nice to have friends who will vouch for you like that," she said.

"You say it as if you aren't familiar with the concept."

"We moved around a lot when I was a kid. I kept doing that as I got older. So I don't have many close friends."

"Is that the only reason?"

"What other reason could there be?"

Ronan noted that she avoided all eye contact. She was hiding something. Shit. He didn't need more mysteries.

Sierra's dream started out innocently enough. She was in a large room filled with people all dressed in vintage clothing. Everyone seemed happy.

Then she was in a house with no lights. It was pitch-dark. Suddenly little beady red eyes appeared all around and above her. One of them came closer until she could see it was the burning tip of a cigar held in a stocky man's hand. He smiled at her before striking her face and trying to burn her eyes out with his cigar.

She screamed and sat bolt upright in bed.

Chapter Five

Sierra wasn't alone. There was someone else in the darkened room. Fear ripped through her. Was it the ghost with the cigar?

No, it was Ronan.

He reached for her hand. "I've got you."

She wrapped her fingers around his and instantly felt safe. "I thought I locked the door."

"You must have forgotten to do that because it wasn't locked."

"I could have sworn . . . I guess I was so tired that I meant to do it but didn't."

"That must be it," Ronan said. "I heard you scream. Bad dream?"

"That's putting it mildly. It was a nightmare about that guy in the photograph upstairs."

"The one with the cigar?"

"Yeah. Is he a relative of yours?"

"What?"

"You did say that your family had a prior claim to my family's," she reminded him

"No, he's not a relative," Ronan said.

"You're sure?"

"Yeah."

"Do you know who he is?"

"No. Do you?" he countered.

She didn't know how to answer that. She hadn't had time to do any research on Hal. Ruby hadn't even told her his surname. Sierra would have to ask her tomorrow. Glancing at her watch, she corrected herself. Today. It was three-thirty in the morning and she was still holding on to Ronan's hand. She needed to let go and she would in a second.

There. She missed his touch immediately but she refused to give in to the temptation to grab his hand.

Instead she asked, "What do you know about the history of this house?"

"It was built in 1900," he said.

"And?" she prompted when he fell silent.

"And what?"

"And what else do you know? About the house, I mean."

"Do you really want to talk about this in the middle of the night?" Ronan said.

She reached out to turn on the bedside lamp. "You're right. Sorry. Did I wake you when I screamed?"

"No. I was awake."

"So you're a night owl, huh?"

"Something like that. I don't need much sleep," he said.

There were nights when Sierra didn't get much sleep

because she sensed the spirits around her. That had been especially true during her teenage years. She'd done some research around that time and discovered that teenage girls are often the most frequent recipients of earthbound spirit visitations.

Yet Sierra's interactions with ghosts had started much earlier than that. She'd never found the answers she was looking for like "Why me?" Instead she learned to accept her talent but to keep her mouth shut about it. In middle school she'd once made the mistake of talking about seeing the ghost of a girl in their class who had died in a car crash.

She'd gotten written up and sent to the principal's office. Her mom had had to take time off from her waitressing job to come to the school. Sierra never talked with outsiders about seeing ghosts again. But she still saw them. Sometimes they were clear like Bonita or Ruby while other times they were filmy projections of mere orbs of light.

But none had been murdered like Ruby and none had had their murderer also haunting the same place.

"I'm okay now," Sierra said as much for her own benefit as Ronan's.

She read for an hour before dozing off again. This time her dreams featured a naked Ronan holding her close and telling her, "I've got you."

Sierra didn't see any ghosts as she made her morning coffee. She loved her Keurig. Sipping her favorite brew from one of her few remaining mugs, she ran a mental review of her to-do list for today. Number one was returning the rental U-Haul.

It looked cold outside, so Sierra was wearing a warm yellow cashmere sweater and jeans. She checked her smartphone to make sure there were no e-mails from her editor or agent. Nothing. Good. That meant all was well and she could focus on the errands that needed doing before she had to hunker down and focus on her writing.

Grabbing her navy wool winter coat, she headed outside.

She was still on the front porch when she looked to her right and saw a woman on the porch of the house next door.

"Hi, my name is Zoe Adams," the dark-haired young woman said with a wave and a big smile. "Welcome to the neighborhood."

"Thanks. You're the second person to welcome me." Sierra wasn't including Ronan or Ruby.

"Let me guess," Zoe said. "Was the first one Daniella?"

"Yes."

"She was one of the first to welcome me too. I bet she brought cupcakes, right?"

"Yes, she did and they were delicious." Sierra looked over her shoulder nervously. She was uncertain about leaving Ronan in the house. She'd heard him moving around upstairs just as she was leaving. What if he changed the locks and she couldn't get back in? Sure, he'd signed that agreement but would he stick to it?

"Is something wrong?" Zoe asked.

"I'm just a little jumpy about leaving the house."

"Why?"

"Do you know Ronan?" Sierra asked.

Zoe moved closer so she was standing on the sidewalk near Sierra. Zoe was wearing a red down jacket with a black scarf artfully wrapped around her neck. "I've met him," she said.

"He thinks he has a claim to my house."

"Damon told me."

"So you know Damon too?"

Zoe grinned. "I know him very well. We live together."

So that's why Damon had showed up so fast yesterday. He lived right next door.

"I heard you and Ronan signed an agreement to share the house," Zoe said.

"A *temporary* agreement," Sierra said.

"Well then, you don't have anything to worry about. Where are you off to?"

"I have to return the U-Haul van this morning," Sierra said.

"Do you need a ride back?" Zoe asked.

"I can take a taxi."

"Save your money. Unless you're independently wealthy?" Zoe teased her.

Sierra laughed. "No, I'm not."

"Then I'll give you a ride back. My car is already out front." She pointed to a red Mini Cooper.

"I've been thinking of getting one of those," Sierra admitted. "I sold my used Ford Fiesta back in Cleveland. It was on its last legs anyway."

"At least we've got sunny weather," Zoe said. "February in Chicago means temperatures can go either way. Fifty degrees like it was yesterday or barely thirty like it is today."

"So you've been in Chicago a long time?"

"Almost a year," Zoe said. "We moved from Boston."

"You and Damon?"

"No. My grandmother and me. She's out with a friend this morning. Let me grab my keys and we can be off. I'll follow you."

"At least let me treat you to breakfast as a thank-you," Sierra said an hour later as they returned to the neighborhood.

"Deal." Zoe pulled in front of Heavenly Cupcakes a few minutes later. "They have great coffee here too."

"Daniella makes great cupcakes *and* great coffee?"

"Yes, she does. She's also a really nice person."

"She gave me a good reference for Ronan."

"Hi, Zoe. How are you doing? Who's your friend?" the young woman behind the counter said as they entered the shop. Her dark blond hair had attention-grabbing streaks of purple that matched the neon-purple earrings she wore. The tag on her navy blue Heavenly Cupcakes T-shirt said her name was Xandra.

Zoe made the introductions, then she and Sierra placed their orders. Sierra went for a latte and a mocha cupcake while Zoe went for an espresso and a devil's food cupcake.

Then they sat at one of the bistro-style tables next to the front window.

"This is a nice place," Sierra said. "I love the Art Deco architectural details, the decorative moldings, and the framed angel prints. The black frames really pop against the pale pink walls."

"Daniella has done a great job with it." Zoe took a sip of her espresso before saying, "I hear you're an author."

"That's right."

"I looked you up on Amazon. You've gotten some wonderful reviews, including in *Booklist* and *Library Journal*."

"You sound very knowledgeable," Sierra said.

"I sound like what I am," Zoe said. "A former librarian."

"You're not a librarian now?"

Zoe shook her head. "I'm a soap maker. I have my own line of botanical soaps and creams. I sell them online. Bella Luna is the name of my business."

"I'll have to check it out," Sierra said.

"And I'll have to check out your books. It sounds like your vigilante ghost hunter Nicki Champion is quite the woman. She always gets her ghost."

"Not always," Sierra said.

"Oh, now I am intrigued."

"No one is always successful," Sierra said.

"Not even ghost hunters?"

"Especially them."

"A number of the reviews on Amazon said how realistic you made the ghost world sound. As if you had experience yourself."

"Yeah, I hear that a lot," Sierra said.

"And?"

"And it's a nice compliment."

"That's all it is? You know your house is rumored to be haunted," Zoe said.

"I love those kinds of rumors. I've got research books on haunted bridges, mines, and hotels. What about your house? Is it supposed to be haunted too?"

"It's not my house. I'm renting. Nick owns the property. I think you met him last night," Zoe said.

"He and Damon started unloading my U-Haul without even asking me if I needed their help."

Zoe frowned. "Didn't you need their help?"

"Yes, but—"

"They're not the type to wait for permission to do something."

"Yeah, I got that impression."

"I suspect Ronan is the same way," Zoe said.

"I agree."

"Let's get back to you. Can you tell me what you're working on now?" Zoe asked.

Sierra took a sip of her latte before replying, "I'm writing another Nicki Champion book. This one involves Chicago history during Prohibition."

"In that case, you should speak to Pat Heller. He owns Pat's Tats a few doors down. Oh look, there he is now." She tapped the front window and waved at a man with a gray ponytail wearing a gray sweatshirt that said GOT BRAINS?

The man came inside.

"Pull up a chair," Zoe invited.

As he did so, Sierra noticed that he had tattooed symbols on the back of his fingers.

"This is Sierra Brennan. She's a published author and she just told me that her work in progress involves Chicago history during Prohibition. I said you were the guy to talk to about that."

"Are you interested in that time period?" Sierra asked.

"I'm interested in all periods of history," Pat said.

"She's moved into the house next door to me," Zoe said. "I told her it's rumored to be haunted."

"Do you know its history?" Sierra asked Pat.

"I believe the story is that a member of Al Capone's gang lived there," he said.

"I heard a rumor that the upstairs may have been used for prostitution," Sierra said.

"A house of ill repute?" Pat paused. "Well, Capone was certainly into prostitution as a means of income, along with bootlegging illegal liquor among other things."

"Do you happen to know the name of the alleged Capone gang member?"

"Hal something or other. Hal . . . Bergerstock."

Great. At least she now had a surname. Sierra made a mental note.

"Al Capone may be famous but he isn't the only historical figure in Chicago. I'm not a big fan of his but I am a fan of Bertha Palmer," Pat said. "She lived around the turn of the century. The turn of the twentieth century not the twenty-first. Her husband built the Palmer House Hotel for her. It burned down two weeks later in the Chicago Fire."

"I did consider having a ghost from that time period," Sierra said. "I still might for another book."

"Much of the city was burned to the ground. But it's one of the reasons Chicago is now famous for its architecture. Those buildings had to be rebuilt, and they used new technology to do so. New to that time period anyway. Steel and concrete. The Palmer Hotel was rebuilt and promoted as the first fireproof hotel. The gala balls put on there were really something."

"You make it seem like you were there at the time. That's a real talent. I'm guessing your family has lived in this area for a long time?"

"A *very* long time," Pat said.

"That must be nice," Sierra said somewhat wistfully. "We never stayed in one place very long. It meant I got to see a lot of the country but I've always tried to imagine what it must be like to have deep roots to one place."

"One of the ghosts in your first book has very deep roots to one place," Zoe said. "A funeral home, wasn't it?"

Sierra noticed a flash of suspicion cross Pat's face before it was gone. Instead he sounded calm as he asked, "What made you choose that location?"

Sierra shrugged. "I heard him say that's where he was. I write a character-driven book. They're real to me. I've often said if I could teach them how to type I'd be in great shape."

"Your characters are real?" Pat said.

"Obviously they aren't *really* real," Sierra said. "I write fiction."

"Why ghosts?" Pat asked.

"Why not?" Sierra said. She'd heard this question before.

"How do you do your research?" he asked.

Another common question, but something about the way he asked it was new.

"The same way other writers do. Research books and the Internet," Sierra replied.

"Do you have any paranormal skills yourself?" he added.

Again, not a new question.

For some reason she didn't give her standard reply of no. Instead she said, "Maybe."

"Really? Do tell," Pat said.

Sierra vehemently shook her head. "I was just kidding." What was wrong with her? Why had she said that? Granted, she hadn't confessed she spoke to dead people but she'd left the door open.

It's good PR, she told herself. Let readers think there is a chance you know things about the other side without going into specifics.

The silent pep talk had her pulling on her author mantle and becoming S. J. Brennan instead of Sierra. Reaching into her purse, she pulled out a bookmark with her current and future books listed as well as her author website, Facebook, and Twitter pages. "Would you like one?"

Zoe nodded eagerly. Pat paused before nodding.

"Do you want me to sign it for you?" Sierra asked.

"That would be great," Zoe said before confessing, "I didn't just look you up on Amazon. I actually downloaded your first book onto my iPad yesterday evening and was up most of the night reading it. I didn't say anything before because I didn't want you to think I was a crazy fan girl or something."

"I'm her number one fan," Tanya shouted from outside the window before running inside and repeating the words. "Not you. *Me!*"

"I'll sign a bookmark for you too," Sierra said. "Spell your name for me."

Tanya did. "Write 'To my number one fan,'" she added.

Tanya leaned over Sierra's shoulder as she wrote.

"Why are you bothering Sierra?" Tanya asked Zoe and Pat. "Don't you know that she has a book to write?"

"They weren't bothering me. In fact, Pat was telling me a little bit about the local history."

Tanya looked at Pat in surprise. "Really?"

Pat gave Tanya a look Sierra couldn't decipher.

"He told me the name of the man who owned my house during Prohibition," Sierra said.

"That was before my time," Tanya said.

"Mine too," Zoe said.

Sierra noticed Pat didn't say the same thing. Instead he stood and took Tanya by the arm. "Time for us to leave."

The other woman went with him, clutching her autographed bookmark and leaving Sierra wondering what else she'd learn about her new surroundings.

Ronan sat across from Damon at a table in the All Nighter Bar and Grill. He'd spent the past fifteen minutes complaining about Sierra while Damon remained quiet.

"You could always kill her," Damon told Ronan.

"I thought killing humans was frowned upon here."

"It is."

"Then why suggest it? Was it some kind of weird test?" Ronan demanded. "Because I was indentured?"

"No. If I thought you were dangerous I wouldn't have approved your staying."

"Then why did you say that about killing Sierra if you weren't trying to trip me up?"

Damon shrugged. "It's what I do."

"You mean you aggravate the hell out of people?" Ronan said.

"People and vampires."

"And witches," Ronan added. "So I've heard."

Damon leaned forward. "What did you hear? What did Zoe tell you?"

"Nothing."

"So it was her grandmother."

"No, it was her cat," Ronan said.

"Bella is a blabbermouth."

"She had a nightmare last night," Ronan said abruptly.

"Bella?"

"Sierra. She was terrified. I should have used that fear to make her leave but instead I comforted her."

"Afraid you're going soft?" Damon mocked.

"I've killed before," Ronan said.

"So have I," Damon said.

"You're a Demon Hunter. You kill demons. It's not the same."

"We're all bound by the reality of our circumstances," Damon said.

"Some of us are bound by more than that." Ronan's voice was flat.

"Yeah, some of us are," Damon agreed.

Looking down, Ronan realized he was clenching his fists. He took a deep breath and relaxed his fingers.

"What have you told Sierra about your claim to the house?" Damon asked.

"That my family has a prior claim to the property,"

Ronan replied. "But I could hardly tell her that it went back over a hundred years."

"I could have Neville forge some paperwork for you that would back up your claim. We'd have to come up with another story to update yours."

"Who is Neville?"

"He's our resident computer geek," Damon said.

"Computer genius," Neville corrected him as he joined them.

Ronan instantly picked up on the fact that Neville was a vampire. The glasses held together with duct tape did give him a nerdy appearance.

"I'm also a financial guru," Neville said.

"What's got you so full of yourself?" Damon demanded.

"This." Neville waved a piece of paper at them. "It indicates they didn't do a thorough title search when the property in question was sold."

"Is it real?" Damon asked.

"Of course not," Neville said. "But it looks real enough to gain us some time. Note that I did this before you suggested I come up with another story regarding ownership of the house."

"Once Sierra's lawyer comes back won't he be able to tell this is a fake?" Damon said.

"It was my understanding that he won't return for two weeks," Neville said.

Which was all the time Ronan needed. Actually it was longer than he needed. He was on a deadline here with Voz. He only had a limited amount of time to save his sister's soul. As in mere days.

Damon studied the forged paper. "This will do."

"Are you a lawyer?" Ronan asked.

"I went to law school. Then I went to war. The American Civil War."

"That's before my time," Ronan said.

"Same here," Neville said. "I was turned in the eighties when I accused my stockbroker boss of being a greedy bloodsucker. My bad. He was a vampire and he turned me."

Ronan didn't talk about when or how he was turned. It wasn't a topic of conversation he enjoyed, even with other vampires. In fact, he hated the memories.

As was often the case when his thoughts turned to that period, he felt a darkness entomb his soul and the need to move on. Thanking Neville, he grabbed the forged paperwork and made a hasty retreat.

It was so hasty that he almost knocked Sierra down on the sidewalk outside the bar.

Putting his hands out, he steadied her. "Sorry," he said.

"No, it was as much my fault as yours," she said. "I was thinking about a scene in my book instead of paying attention to where I was going."

"Does that happen often?"

"Sometimes."

"Are you heading back to the house?" he asked.

She nodded.

"Me too. We might as well walk together."

"Okay." Sierra was acutely aware of the man at her side. He had a naturally fluid swagger that was very sexy. He was wearing a black leather jacket and black T-shirt and jeans. He looked as good in clothes as he did out of them. Chiseled cheekbones. Chiseled body.

All of those things increased her attraction to him. Then there was the rumbly sound of his voice that got to her as well. And there was something else, something she couldn't identify yet. She'd never had a man get under her skin so quickly.

She could count on one hand the number of men she'd been intimate with, including Steve. One had told her she was woefully inexperienced because she hadn't been open to a threesome. She'd dumped him immediately.

Okay, so maybe she lacked the slutty gene. That didn't mean there was anything wrong with her. Being this close to Ronan proved that. Every feminine cell in her body was humming and celebrating.

Her brain reminded her that hooking up with him would not be a good move. Her body indicated that any move with Ronan would be good, good, good!

She couldn't remember what she said during the short trip back to their house. No, not *their* house. *Her* house.

Sierra unlocked the front door but Ronan opened it for her and ushered her inside. The courtly gesture took her by surprise. But even more surprising was finding Ruby in the foyer, clearly frightened and shaking in her corset and silk underwear. "I didn't do it!" Ruby said.

Chapter Six

Sierra couldn't reply to Ruby because Ronan was at her side. Instead she mouthed "What?"

Ruby pointed toward Sierra's bedroom.

Sierra rushed forward. The place was up for grabs. Books, papers, and clothes were all tossed around.

"Not a neatnick, huh?" Ronan said by her side. "You must have been in a hurry to get up and out this morning. Because the room didn't look like this in the middle of the night."

"What was he doing here in the middle of the night?" Ruby said.

Sierra ignored her. "I had to return the rental van this morning," she told Ronan.

"So you threw your books all over the place?" He bent over to pick a few up.

"Nice butt," Ruby noted.

Sierra had to agree although she didn't say so.

"That's okay. I'll tidy up," she told Ronan, hurrying

him out of the room so she could speak to Ruby in private.

Pressing her back against the closed door, she asked Ruby, "What happened? Who did this?"

"It was Hal. He doesn't want you here."

Sierra frowned. "I thought he stayed upstairs."

"I thought so too. This is the first time he's come down."

"Did he hurt you?" Sierra asked.

"I'm a ghost," Ruby said. "I'm already dead. Besides, I can do a disappearing act. Now I'm here. Now I'm not." Sure enough, there was no sign of her. Then she suddenly reappeared. "And now I'm back."

"Where is Hal now?" Sierra demanded.

"He's not down here."

Sierra reached for the doorknob.

"Where are you going?" Ruby said.

"To talk to Hal upstairs."

"He won't like that," Ruby said.

"Well, I don't like him messing with my things," Sierra said. "I don't have that many things."

"You can't go upstairs."

"Why not?"

"Because Ronan lives upstairs. That's his territory. His and Hal's."

Sierra paused. "You're right." She looked around and then started tidying up. "I need to think of a plan first. Then I'll go upstairs."

"Hal is a very powerful ghost," Ruby said.

"So you're saying I should *not* go upstairs? Hal invaded my space. Why shouldn't I invade his?"

"Because he could go all poltergeist on you. Do you have experience dealing with something like that?"

"I've read about it," Sierra said.

"Great. So that's it? You've only read about it?"

"No, that's not all. I've also written about it."

"Bully for you."

"I found Hal's last name."

"It's Bergerstock. I could have told you that," Ruby said.

"Yes, but you didn't." Sierra opened her tablet. She was glad that the Wi-Fi was working. One of her distant cousins ahead of her on the inheritance ladder had gotten the house wired for the Internet and then only stayed a day after that. She hadn't considered that when she'd checked her e-mail first thing that morning on her smartphone. She'd used her phone carrier rather than Wi-Fi to access the Internet in the house.

"What are you doing?" Ruby said.

"A search on the Internet," Sierra said.

"Who is Mr. Google?"

"Google is a search engine."

Ruby looked at the thin tablet. "There's an engine in there?"

"No. It's done via the computer. That's what this is." Sierra pointed to her tablet. "So is that." She pointed to her laptop.

"And that?" Ruby pointed to Sierra's smartphone.

"It's a phone and a camera and a computer. Actually the tablet has a camera too. None of that is important. Stay focused here."

"Usually that's my line," Ruby said.

"I'm not finding anything," Sierra said.

"That's not surprising. Capone and his gang liked keeping things quiet. They were good at keeping secrets. And paying off officials."

Sierra already knew that from the preliminary research she'd done of that period in Chicago. "What about the bootleg tunnels? Have you gone in them?"

"Sure."

"Since you died?"

"I don't like it down there and I can only go in the part of the tunnel that is attached to this house."

"How do you get into the tunnel?"

Ruby shook her head and looked around fearfully. "I can't tell you that."

"Why not?"

"Because it's forbidden."

"By whom?"

"By Hal."

"He's not the boss of me," Sierra said.

"He will be if we don't get rid of him," Ruby prophesied.

"Then help me. Give me more information. How many girls worked upstairs? What were their names? I can't remember if you told me this already but did Hal live down here when he was alive? Did he have his family here?"

"He did not have his family here. The main floor was more of a lounge and an office area. Plus the kitchen. Oh and it was also a place for security. We had armed bodyguards around the clock. They used to play billiards in the basement."

"There are only two bedrooms upstairs," Sierra said.

"Four of us were assigned here. This was the upper tier. Only the very best—best clients and best prostitutes. One was known as 'Belle of the Balls' because she specialized in that part of a man's anatomy."

Sierra laughed so hard, she snorted, which made her laugh even more. Wiping the tears from her eyes, she said, "Sorry. Go on."

"We worked in shifts. Twelve hours on, twelve hours off."

"Where did you go when you were off duty?"

"I had a little apartment a few miles away. One of Hal's drivers took me back and forth."

Something about the way Ruby said that made Sierra look up at her. "What was the name of Hal's driver?"

"I don't remember," the ghost said hurriedly.

Ruby was lying. Sierra wasn't sure how she knew that, but she did. She was certain of it.

Sierra was lying. Ronan suspected that she hadn't told the truth about creating the mess in her bedroom. Her bedroom wasn't just messy, it looked like it had been trashed by someone searching for something.

His silent questions came fast and furious. If she hadn't done it, who had? What were they looking for? The key? Who sent them? Did the local vampires know about it? Did Damon?

Sure, Damon had been with Ronan, but in the short time it took Ronan to walk with Sierra from the bar to the house, Damon could have moved with vamp speed ahead of them and searched Sierra's room.

Was there a connection between Sierra and the key? Was that why only her belongings had been messed up?

Who could he trust? The answer was no one.

Ronan went upstairs to check his stuff. He didn't have much, a few changes of clothing, that was it. The casket in the basement was on loan from the funeral home courtesy of Damon.

Damon had said the surveillance cameras didn't work in this house but what if that was a lie? What if they were watching his every move?

"Paranoid much?" Baron Voz said from beside him.

Ronan refused to show how much the Master Vampire's surprise appearance caught him off guard. Instead, Ronan stoically stood his ground and put up a shield against his thoughts. He hadn't felt the need to do so sooner because only a Master Vampire could read another vampire's thoughts and even then only the thoughts of one they'd turned and indentured.

As always, Voz was impeccably dressed in an Armani suit with a hand-tailored, crisp white shirt and a fine burgundy silk tie held in place with a gold tie clasp with his family's coat of arms on it. A matching ring with the same coat of arms was on his right hand.

Ronan knew that ring well. He had been branded with it on more than one occasion. He could still remember the searing pain, the stench of his flesh burning. As a Master Vampire, Voz had the power to brand his indentured vampires like cattle.

"What are you doing here?" Ronan demanded.

"I thought I'd see how things are progressing."

"No one can see you," Ronan said.

"Of course they can."

"I mean, you mustn't be seen here by anyone," Ronan said.

"By *anyone* I presume you mean the sexy redhead downstairs? No problem. Just compel her to forget. Why is she here anyway? She's not one of us. She's human."

"She inherited the house."

"Get rid of her."

"I will."

"Now," Voz said.

"No," Ronan growled. "I'm no longer indentured to you. I don't have to obey your orders."

"You do if you want to save your sister's soul."

"No. Our agreement was that I find the key and turn it over to you by midnight on February fourteenth. There is no requirement on my part to obey your orders until then."

"Time is running out," Voz said. "Ticktock, ticktock."

"Then leave me alone so I can get back to my search."

"Or get back to your redhead. Don't let her distract you," Voz warned.

"I don't intend to."

Since Ruby clammed up and disappeared after Sierra questioned her about the driver, Sierra spent the rest of the day restoring order to her room and working on her book.

At least that was her plan. But when she heard voices coming from upstairs, she couldn't help herself. She had to go look.

The door was open into Ronan's room, but he was alone. "Who were you talking to?" she asked.

"Nobody," he said curtly.

"I heard voices."

"I was talking to myself."

"Oh."

Apparently he could tell she wasn't buying that answer one hundred percent, because he got an irritated look on his face. "I don't go nosing around when I hear you talking to yourself."

"I wasn't nosing around."

"The upstairs is mine. We signed an agreement."

"A *temporary* agreement," she reminded him.

He waved her words away and glared at her. "Don't come up here uninvited again."

Could he have been talking to Hal? Had Ronan been lying when he said he didn't believe in ghosts? "Has something weird been going on up here?" she demanded.

"What part of 'mind your own business' do you not understand?" he said curtly.

"All of it. If you're involved in something dangerous up here—"

"It's none of your business," he interrupted her.

"Yes it is. Because it could endanger me."

"I wouldn't let that happen."

"You might not be able to stop it." Especially if Hal the gangster went all poltergeist on them.

"You underestimate me," he said.

"Promise me you'll tell me if you experience something strange," she said.

"Are you worried about me?"

"Just promise me."

"Define 'something strange.'"

"Lights flickering on and off or doors slamming or windows opening."

"Because it could be a ghost?" he mocked.

"Because this is an old house and it could have electrical issues."

"Electrical issues wouldn't make the doors slam or windows open."

"The house might not be plumb. If there's a slight angle to the floors then strange things can happen."

"Have you noticed any particular floor at an angle?"

She looked around. "This one."

"How can you tell?"

She pulled a marble from the pocket of her jeans and set it down. Sure enough, it rolled away from the door and toward the sleeping bag Ronan had thrown on the floor to distract her in case she came snooping. He definitely didn't want her looking in the basement and finding that casket. She was sure to wonder where he slept if he hadn't created some semblance of human normalcy.

Why the hell did she have to be so . . . *everything*? Stubborn, sexy, strong-willed, and smart.

The jeans curved over her butt as she bent down to retrieve her marble. He'd noticed the way she'd checked him out when he'd bent down to pick up a book in her bedroom earlier. He could tell she'd liked what she'd seen. So did he.

And that was a problem.

"I know what you're thinking," she said.

He seriously doubted that. Because he was thinking of kissing those lush lips of hers. She really did have a very kissable mouth, curvy and full.

"You're wondering what I'm doing with a marble in my pocket," she said.

Wrong.

"It's kind of a good-luck thing. I've had this marble since I was a little kid." She rolled the glass ball between her fingers.

He wished she'd roll his balls between her fingers. He was instantly hard.

When he stayed silent, she finally said, "Well, I guess I'll head back downstairs and get something to eat."

"You do that." His voice sounded like he'd gargled with gravel.

He slammed the door after her, then opened it again to call after her, "*I* did that. Not some damn ghost!"

She turned on the stairs and gave him the finger.

Ronan slammed the door again then started pacing the room. He needed to forget Sierra and focus on his mission. He'd been here two weeks and had yet to even figure out what key Voz wanted, let alone where to find it.

Voz had told him next to nothing when he'd entered into this agreement with him. That alone should have been a red flag. But this was his only chance to save his sister Adele's soul.

She was an innocent in all this.

Ronan shoved his hand through his hair. He had to focus. But his hatred for Voz momentarily blinded him. How dare he show up here. Ronan already knew that Voz didn't want him to succeed, but he'd never considered the possibility that the Master Vampire would show up uninvited here in Vamptown.

Was he uninvited? Or had Damon or Nick approved his visit? He couldn't come out and ask them directly or they'd know Voz had been here, and if they hadn't approved the visit then they might toss Ronan out. If the Vamptown Council didn't approve you then you weren't part of their clan and you were not welcome here.

During his nearly hundred years of indenture to Voz, the Master Vampire had told Ronan that his sister Adele had lived a long life, found love, had had a family, and peacefully died at the age of eighty-eight.

But the moment his years of slavery were done, Voz told him the truth. That Adele had died from the Spanish influenza of 1918 that had killed millions and that Voz had been holding her soul in limbo until now.

Ronan had nearly torn Voz's throat open, not caring that doing so would kill him and all the others that Voz had turned, not caring that he probably had no chance of killing him because the Master's powers were so strong. Indeed, upon hearing Ronan's feral growl, Voz had waved his hand and sent Ronan crashing into the stone wall of his castle in Romania.

"You can't hurt me," Voz had said, "but even if you could, doing so would insure your sister's soul will never be saved. I'm the only one who can save her. And I will if you just do one little favor for me."

Ronan had wiped away the blood trickling from his temple. "What do you want?"

"A key."

"What kind of key? To what?"

"It's in that family house of yours. That's all you need to know. Oh, and the fact that you have until midnight on Valentine's Day to find it. If you do, then I will free your sister's soul."

"And if not?"

"Then you will return to being an indentured vampire."

"For another hundred years?"

Voz had laughed. "No, for all eternity."

"How do I know you will keep your end of the bargain?"

Voz put his hand on the family coat of arms carved into the stone wall of his castle, the crest right above Ronan's head. "I swear it on my family's honor."

Voz might be devious and evil at times, but he did value his family's honor. He'd been turned during the Crusades and valued loyalty. He didn't care whether it was given willingly or not.

"Remember, I let you end your indenture early because of good behavior," Voz had said.

"Big deal. You freed me three years early."

"It *is* a big deal," Voz said. "Do you accept my offer?"

Ronan had no choice but to agree. Their conversation had taken place a few weeks ago, yet the emotions still roiled deeply within his gut. Hatred, betrayal, guilt.

At that time he'd been so sure of his ability to save his sister's soul. Now desperation was setting in. Which was precisely what Voz wanted.

He supposed he should be grateful that Voz hadn't tortured him about Adele's soul earlier in his indenture. But Ronan suspected that was because Voz wanted Ronan to remain loyal. Had Ronan known the truth, he would have been harder to control.

As it was, Ronan had to fight the rage that threatened to unbalance him.

Returning to the present, Ronan stared at the hardwood floor. Could the key be hidden beneath one of the floorboards?

He knocked on the floor, using his vamp superhearing to try and detect any differences that would indicate a storage space. If the key was only a few inches long then this was a useless test. Perhaps he should get a metal detector.

"Stop that pounding," Sierra shouted from downstairs. "Do not make me come up there!"

Since he'd just ripped up several floorboards, he didn't want her returning, so he left things as they were and went down to confront her. He could hear her banging around in the kitchen.

This arrangement was not going to work as long as Sierra kept hassling him. He had enough issues to deal with at the moment. He didn't need some paranormal author who apparently wrote hot sex scenes getting in his way.

Voz was right. Ronan couldn't afford to allow Sierra to distract him. He needed to try and compel her again.

As Ronan entered the kitchen from the hallway entrance, three dinner plates came flying through the air. They were headed straight for his head.

Chapter Seven

Ronan instantly caught all three plates. His hands moved faster than a mortal could see.

Sierra stared at him in amazement. "How did you do that?"

"I'm good with my hands."

"You moved so fast. It's like the plates were in the air one second and in your hands the next. Are you a juggler or something?"

"Or something. The question is, why were you throwing plates at me?"

"I wasn't. They um . . . slipped out of my hand when I was getting them out of the cabinet," she said.

Another lie. She really did not have a poker face. "Really?" Ronan said. "They slipped out of your hand?"

"I didn't throw them at you if that's what you're thinking."

Okay, now she was telling the truth.

Sierra knew she was no good at lying. At least she wasn't good at it with Ronan.

Maybe in the beginning she'd been better at lying by omission, as in not telling him she saw ghosts, but the more time she spent with him, the harder it was becoming to keep her secrets. She needed to turn the spotlight off herself and back onto him. "You never talk about your life before you came here. Why is that?"

"I'm not real talkative."

"That's putting it mildly."

"You don't talk about your life before you came here."

"You already know I'm a writer," she said.

"I *guessed* that," he reminded her. "You didn't volunteer the information."

"Because I'd just met you."

"And I wasn't wearing any clothing. Is that why you don't trust me?"

"I didn't say I don't trust you. If I didn't trust you, I wouldn't allow you to stay in the same house with me," she said.

"You lock your bedroom door at night."

"Apparently I didn't do that last night."

"Do you frequently have nightmares?" he said.

"Sometimes. How about you?"

Darkness seemed to descend upon his face. He didn't say a word. He didn't have to. She could feel the emotions vibrating from him.

"You also never told me much about your supposed claim to this property," she said.

"My family has ties to it."

"You used to live here?"

Instead of answering, he said, "Your great-uncle never lived here."

"No, he didn't. He bought it as an investment property and then rented it out. But he had a hard time keeping renters for very long."

"My bad," Ruby said, raising her hand. She was sitting on the kitchen counter, swinging her feet. "At first I liked the company, but then I got frustrated when they couldn't see me so I scared them off."

"What are you looking at?" Ronan demanded.

"Nothing," Sierra said.

"You seem to look at *nothing* a lot," he said. "I can't help wondering why that is."

"And I can't help wondering why you still haven't told me anything about your life."

"What do you want to know?" he countered.

"How about where you lived before this?"

"Here and there," he said.

"That's real specific. If you don't want to answer the question, just say so."

"I don't want to answer the question," he readily admitted.

"Fine. Be that way."

"I don't want to answer it, but I will. I spent a lot of time in Europe."

"Doing what?" she said.

"Traveling."

"Were you a travel guide or something?"

"Or something," he said.

Sierra was losing what little patience she had left. "When I asked how you were able to catch those plates so fast, you said you were something like a juggler and now you just said you were something like a travel guide. Which is it?"

"It's complicated. I've done a lot of things in my life."

Pissed off at his attitude, she said, "How about male stripper? Have you done that?"

"Are you asking me to give you a demonstration?"

"I'm asking you for the truth, but apparently that's too much for you to handle."

"Right back at you." His voice was curt. "You didn't mess up your room yourself. Who did it?" Stepping closer, he looked deep into her eyes. "Tell me who did it."

She had to clap a hand over her mouth to prevent herself from speaking.

"Who did it?" Ronan repeated, his voice darkly hypnotic.

"It was me," Ruby piped up to say. Jumping down from the counter she floated close to Sierra, breaking the spell Ronan seemed to have on her.

"It was me," Sierra repeated.

"Like hell it was." With that, Ronan stormed out of the house.

"She's asking questions," Ronan said as he joined Damon at the All Nighter Bar and Grill.

"I hate when that happens," Damon replied.

"Yeah, me too."

"So what kind of questions was Sierra asking?"

"Stupid ones," Ronan said, drinking half a bottle of blood before wiping his mouth with the back of his hand. He'd had enough of being polite.

"Well, she *is* human. Naturally her questions will be stupid."

"*She's* not stupid."

Damon sighed. "Why don't you just tell me what she said."

"She wanted to know where I lived before I came here."

"And you told her what?"

"That I was in Europe."

"Doing what?"

"Yes, that's what she asked next."

"And you said?"

"Not much." Ronan's voice reflected his impatience.

"Wise move," Damon congratulated him. "Then what's the problem?"

"She wants to know more."

"They always do."

"You speak like someone who has experienced this yourself."

"Zoe knew I was a vampire the first time I met her," Damon said. "And I knew she was a witch. I knew and wasn't happy about it."

"Just as I'm not happy about Sierra's presence. Have you figured out yet why Sierra can't be compelled like other humans?" Ronan asked.

"We're still working on it."

"How long is it going to take?"

"She's hasn't even been here two full days yet."

"I'm on a deadline." The words slipped out and Ronan instantly regretted saying them.

"What kind of deadline?" Damon's voice turned hard.

"She gave me two weeks to stay in the house until her lawyer comes back. I have to get rid of her before then."

"That's it?" Damon asked suspiciously. "There's no other deadline?"

Ronan shook his head. He was lying but it had to be done. He couldn't reveal the bargain he'd made with Voz. Instead he focused on his cover story. "The longer Sierra stays, the bigger the risk that she'll discover what I really am."

"And what you are really?"

"A vampire."

"And?" Damon demanded.

"And what?" Ronan said.

"You tell me. There's something else going on here."

"I've already assured Nick that no one in Vamptown has anything to fear from me."

"What about those outside of Vamptown?"

"Is it so hard for you to consider the fact that I just want to return to my home?" Ronan said.

"Yeah, it is hard for me."

Ronan tried turning the conversation to Damon. "Where was your home when you were human? Was it here in Chicago?"

"No."

"See, you don't like talking about your past either."

"Good point."

"Are the surveillance cameras in the house working yet?" Ronan asked.

"No." Damon's voice hardened again. "And I'm not happy about that. Neville says it's a software problem and he's working on it. What makes you ask?"

"I just thought it might provide some answers as to why Sierra can't be compelled."

"We will find out soon, I can promise you that," Damon said.

Ronan managed to sidestep any further questioning but he didn't relax until he'd left the bar. He was always on guard. Not that other vampires were the type to spill their guts. But being indentured made you different from your own kind. He knew it and Damon knew it.

Thanks to the still malfunctioning surveillance cameras, Damon didn't know that Voz had paid Ronan a little visit and Ronan planned on keeping it that way.

"Have you come up with a plan yet?" Ruby asked Sierra.

"No."

"What are you doing?"

"Research," Sierra said.

"About what?"

"Hal." Sierra shivered after saying his name. "Is he here?"

"He's everywhere."

"He can leave the house?"

"No. At least I don't think so. He never has in the past."

"Has he ever come downstairs in the past?"

"Not often."

"What about the tunnels under the house? Can he go there?"

"I already told you that I can't talk about that."

"The tunnel under this house was an escape route, wasn't it? In case there was a raid. It wasn't just used to bring liquor in, it was used to smuggle people out."

Ruby remained quiet.

"What happened to that driver you had a crush on?"

"I don't know," Ruby whispered.

"Tell me his name, and I'll find out what happened for you."

"I'm not sure I want to know."

But Sierra could tell Ruby was tempted. "Come on, tell me."

"His name was Johnny. Johnny Olivetti."

Sierra did a Google search. Nothing. Then she tried other subject headings, like Capone's drivers.

"He never drove Al," Ruby said. "When Al came to the house, he used his own driver. Johnny was only used for the girls' transportation. And liquor deliveries."

"What about money drops? Is that why Al came to the house?"

"No, he came every once in a while to talk to Hal. Not very often. Maybe twice a year."

"Where did Hal take the money?"

"Various bank accounts. Hal kept two sets of books. One for himself and one for the—"

"The Chicago mob. Was Hal skimming money off the top? That could be why he was killed," Sierra said.

Sierra kept searching. Finally she found Hal's obituary. "Died for undisclosed reasons. Wait, here's another one that is tied to a police report. Died from a gunshot wound to the back of the head."

"Who shot him? It wasn't me. I was dead by then," Ruby said.

"They didn't find the shooter."

"Maybe it was Johnny. If he knew that Hal killed me, Johnny would have done something about it."

"We could always ask Hal."

"Are you crazy?" Ruby turned even whiter than usual. "He'd go ballistic."

"He's already trashed my room. What else can he do?"

"Plenty."

"Can he throw dishes at Ronan like you did?" Sierra asked.

"I didn't like the way he's been talking to you. And yes, Hal can do much worse."

"How do you know? Has he done something to others in this house?"

"Your cousins, you mean? No, I was able to get rid of them on my own," Ruby said.

"Then why . . . ?"

"Shortly after his death, when he first was here in this house as a ghost, Hal shoved someone down the stairs."

Fear shot through Sierra. "That's not good."

The temperature in her bedroom suddenly dropped and Sierra felt a thick stillness that did not bode well. She sensed an evil presence growing and she could tell from Ruby's frightened face that she was aware of it as well.

The sound of the front door slamming made them both jump.

The next sound was Ronan swearing. The feeling of an evil presence disappeared and was replaced with the continued curses of Sierra's clearly unhappy temporary housemate.

Yanking open her bedroom door to confront him, she said, "What is your problem?"

It belatedly occurred to her that it might have been smarter on her part to stay out of his way instead of confronting him.

"You," he said. "You're my problem."

"Hey, I already told you that I did not throw those plates at you."

"Right. They just happened to fly halfway across the kitchen on their own."

"Stranger things have happened," she muttered.

"Like what?" he immediately demanded.

"Like you smelling cigar smoke," she said, silently congratulating herself for coming up with something that was in his bailiwick.

"That wasn't strange."

"You thought it was at the time."

"I changed my mind." He paused for a moment. "I don't suppose you have the original blueprints for the house?"

"No."

"*Any* blueprints for the house?"

"No."

She thought she heard him mutter "Good" under his breath but she couldn't be sure. What was he hiding? She knew what she was hiding—a pair of ghosts, one good and one bad. But Ronan had some sort of secret of his own.

"Where are you going?" Ronan demanded.

"I thought this would be a good time to check out the basement."

"You thought wrong."

"What do you have stashed down there?"

"There's a lot of old stuff down there."

"So?"

"So . . ." He looked deep into her eyes. "You don't want to go into the basement."

"I am not falling for that," she said impatiently.

"For what?"

"For that I'm-so-sexy-look-at-me look. It doesn't work on me."

"Yeah, I noticed," he muttered.

"Doesn't seem to stop you trying though."

"No, it doesn't."

She put her hand on the doorknob.

He put his hand over hers.

She felt a strange kind of zing. His touch was responsible for making her heart go faster and her hormones to race out of control. He'd touched her last night when she'd had that terrible nightmare and she'd felt safe. Now she felt something else. Not danger exactly. Desire.

Yep, this was definitely desire. She hadn't felt it for a while, not since . . . well, actually never. Not this strong. Not just from a man's hand covering hers. Which made her wonder what it would feel like to have his mouth covering hers, or his naked body covering hers.

She already knew his naked body was damn fine. The chemistry between them was undeniable. Was this lust at first glance? She'd never wanted a man so badly so quickly. What was going on here?

She was still wondering about that when the basement door suddenly flew open, knocking her backward off her feet and into Ronan's arms.

Chapter Eight

Ronan caught her in his arms, preventing her from falling. She felt the air humming, but maybe that was because her entire body was humming. Especially the parts that were pressed against his body, like her breasts.

Putting her hands on his broad shoulders didn't help matters any. Instead, it seemed to make it eaier for him to lower his head until his lips covered hers. She should have minded him taking possession of her mouth so totally but she didn't because it felt so damn good. The touch of his tongue was darkly seductive.

He tilted his head to increase the angle and therefore the intimacy of their kiss . . . their slow, erotic, irresistible kiss.

But she should resist. She couldn't remember why exactly because her mind was filled with the waves of pleasure and the excitement of the moment. This was far and away the best kiss she'd ever had. She should be thinking of ways to extend it not end it.

Every breath brought her closer to wanting more of him. She wanted his mouth on her naked body, his lips pressed against her breast, his tongue seducing her nipple.

No, wait, this wasn't right. Ronan was kissing her to distract her from going into the basement and she was letting him. She surprised him by breaking off their embrace and sliding under his arm to hurry down the stairs.

Ronan rushed after her. "I can explain," he began.

She kept racing down the stairs. Only when she was at the bottom did she turn and say, "Explain what?"

Frowning, he glanced around.

"What are you looking for?" she asked suspiciously.

"Nothing."

"Did you kiss me to try and prevent me from coming down here?" she demanded. "If so, it didn't work," she added proudly.

"Yeah, I noticed."

"So you're not even bothering to deny it?"

"There was nothing in our agreement about kissing you," he pointed out.

"About *not* kissing me."

"Nothing about that either."

"Because I never thought it would be a problem," she said.

"It wasn't a problem. I liked it," he said.

"Liked it?" Talk about damning with faint praise. Here she thought the earth moved and he says he "liked" it?

"Didn't you?" he said.

"No," she said. A huge lie. So sue her.

"It certainly seemed as if you were really into that kiss," he said.

"You're mistaken."

"Am I?" he said.

"Yes, you are. Definitely mistaken. As in terribly wrong. Big-time."

"Prove it." He snared her in his arms and kissed her again.

This time she was a little more prepared. Not much but a little. Her response remained anything but little, however.

Parting her lips, she allowed his tongue in to tangle with hers in a sexy thrust and withdrawal that once again made her want more. He had a talented tongue. Extremely talented. A touch to the roof of her mouth was followed by a teasing swipe across her teeth.

Kissing him was better than any sex scene she'd ever written. And that was saying something. Because she'd written some pretty damn good sex scenes. And this was just a kiss.

Just a kiss? Right. Who was she kidding? Not him for sure as he kept devouring her and she kept letting him. No, not merely *letting* him but returning the favor.

She had to stop this. He was trying to distract her again. And dammit, he was succeeding.

She freed herself and pointed a finger at him. "Stay there! Do not come any closer."

"Or what?" he mocked her.

"Or I will tear up our temporary agreement and kick you to the curb."

He tilted his head and eyed her the way a tiger eyed fresh meat. "You're cute when you're—"

"Don't you dare tell me I'm cute when I'm mad," she said fiercely. She marched over to the far wall, examining it carefully for any sign of something that might be a trigger to the secret entrance to the tunnel.

"What are you looking for?" he asked.

"None of your business. Now go away."

"And leave you all alone down here in this dark basement?"

"I've got a flashlight."

"Who knows what's down here?" Ronan said. "Snakes? Spiders? Rats?"

"You're the rat," she muttered under her breath.

"Seriously. You do not want to be down here."

"Seriously. The more you tell me that, the more determined I am to be down here. Your lease only covers the second floor, not the basement. So leave."

"I've got stuff stored down here."

"Where?" She aimed the flashlight around. "I don't see anything." A second later, she truly couldn't see anything as the flashlight went dead. She sensed a dark presence. Or maybe she was just sensing the enveloping darkness, period.

There was enough light coming down from the still open door at the top of the stairs to light the way back out. Sierra wanted to accuse Ronan of sabotaging her flashlight, but chances were that a ghost was responsible.

She really couldn't waste more time on this. Giving up for now didn't mean giving in. She'd come back later, when Ronan was out of the house and wouldn't bother her.

An hour later, Sierra was sitting in front of her laptop, trying to write. She was behind on her daily quota of pages required to meet her deadline. She had to create five pages today, or what was left of today, to get back on track.

She'd never considered the possibility that moving into this house would be a distraction. Instead she'd thought it would be a great inspiration. The house was old enough to have been here during the Prohibition period that the ghost in her story lived through. The fact that two *real* ghosts, as opposed to fictional ones, were sharing the house with her was a distraction. The fact that one of them had trashed her room was definitely a problem.

But the main issue was Naked Ronan. Okay, she really needed to stop thinking of him that way, of visualizing him that way. That shouldn't be as difficult as it was. She for sure should not be sitting in front of her laptop thinking about him instead of her characters.

She'd put on her headphones as a tool to increase her concentration. She created a playlist for each book, sometimes for individual scenes. She was about to write a sex scene between her heroine Nicki Champion and the Chicago detective who was giving her a hard time. She was listening to Imagine Dragons' latest, which usually inspired her to get her thoughts in order and her fingers flying over the keyboard.

Instead all she could think about was her reaction to falling into Ronan's arms and their resulting kiss. The song "Radioactive" by Imagine Dragons should have been a warning that Ronan was radioactive to her. The man was a rival trying to steal her inheritance from her. Instead he'd stolen her breath and her common sense.

There was no way she was justified in returning his kiss. Of course, there was no way that he was justified in kissing her in the first place. Still, it was her job to remain the calm one. Instead she'd turned into a hot mess complete with weak knees and a racing heart.

At least she could brag that she'd come to her senses and pushed him away to end the kiss. She was glad she'd been the one to walk away.

Damn. There she went again, thinking about Ronan instead of Nicki.

No way Nicki, the heroine of her book, would be sitting here mooning over a guy. Instead she was rolling in black satin sheets with a hot cop. A naked hot cop. Right. There was the naked thing again, which led Sierra's thoughts right back to Ronan.

She clicked on her playlist so it moved on from Imagine Dragons to the next song up. "Lessons in Love" by Neon Trees. Not a lot of help there. No way she was falling in love with Ronan. Not after one kiss. That was ridiculous.

Lessons in lust, maybe. Okay, she could deal with that. She'd pour her feelings onto the page . . . er, the screen.

Wait, she had to check her e-mail to see if her attorney had answered her. He'd said that he wouldn't have much e-mail access, that it would be spotty at best, but there was a chance . . . No, no response.

But there was an e-mail from a reader saying she'd loved reading Sierra's first book and asking for a signed bookmark. Sierra didn't have an assistant, so she took care of the promo things herself. Someday soon she hoped to have help, but right now her funds were limited.

Focus. Her readers were waiting for the next Ghost Games book and Nicki's next adventure.

Back to those black satin sheets. She'd never needed wine to write a sex scene before but maybe she should try it now. Too bad she didn't have any alcohol in the house. Besides, her readers wouldn't be tipsy on chardonnay while reading her book so she probably shouldn't be tipsy either.

Maybe she should forget the satin sheets and try making that indelible image of Naked Ronan work for her. And so it was that the Chicago cop got brown eyes and dark hair just like Ronan. And bingo, suddenly Sierra was inspired and Nicki and the as-yet-unnamed Chicago cop got naked, got busy, and got orgasmic.

Nicki didn't care that she didn't know his first name. She knew his kiss. Recognized it. Wanted it to distract her from the devastating mess she'd seen. Bernie had come to her as a ghost, asking for her help in capturing his murderer. Instead, she'd been unable to prevent his wife from nearly being killed by having acid thrown on her.

So yeah, Nicki needed sex. To avoid the guilt. She needed molten hot, epic sex and she knew this man could give it to her. She'd known it from the first moment she'd seen him. And she was right.

She wasn't wearing much when he'd come to her door to talk about the case. Now she was wearing nothing but the scent of desire.

He backed her against the wall as she fumbled with the fastening of his jeans. He had her roll the condom on his penis before he plunged into her, banging her against the wall. Wrapping her legs around his hips, she welcomed the wild reck-lessness of his possession.

"Faster!" Nicki told him. "Faster. Deeper!"

"You like giving orders," he muttered against her mouth before grabbing hold of her butt to yank her into his thrusts.

"Yes!" Nicki shouted as she came, her orgasm gaining momentum.

"Satisfied?"

The question startled Sierra out of her writing zone. She looked up from the screen to see Ruby standing near the door.

Sierra looked back at her screen and the page count. Yep, five pages done. "Yes, I'm satisfied. So are Nicki and her cop."

"Who?"

"My characters," Sierra said.

"I don't care about them. I'm talking about me."

"You asked me if I was satisfied. I thought you meant was I satisfied about getting some writing done."

Ruby made a scoffing face. At least that's how Sierra translated it. "Why should I care about your writing? I was referring to Hal. Are you satisfied that you have a good plan to deal with him?"

"Not exactly."

"Which means no." Ruby floated closer and peered

at the screen. "I charge double to do that. I didn't know you were writing about a prostitute."

"I'm not!"

Ruby would have read on but Sierra slammed her laptop shut.

"Why did you do that?" Ruby said.

"Because I don't like people reading my work while I'm writing."

"I can see why, if you're writing pornography like that."

"It's not . . . never mind," Sierra said. "I can't work under these conditions. I'm going upstairs."

Sierra let her anger carry her as she climbed the creaky steps and headed to the portrait of Hal. She made it halfway across the room when he materialized. He looked just like his photograph. The same receding hairline and sinister smile. As he stood before her she could observe his short and bulky build in his 1920s tailored suit, which was not apparent in his framed head shot. He looked like the mobster he was. Sierra didn't have much time to focus on any of that because the most important thing about his appearance was that it had a dense darkness that was very unsettling.

"I want you gone," Hal told her.

"I want you gone too," Sierra shot back.

"Who are you talking to?" Ronan asked from behind her.

She whirled to face him. "What are you doing here?"

"I live here, remember?"

"You said you were going out."

"I came back," he said.

"And took a shower." Which was why he was wearing a towel around his waist, a sexy smile, and a few droplets of water meandering down his bare muscular chest.

"Yeah, I took a shower. Is there some law against that? I didn't see anything against that in the agreement."

She could *see* too much of his body, and that towel was way too little to properly cover him. Not that he was flaunting his package at her or anything. Although after writing that hot love scene, she wouldn't have minded seeing Ronan naked again.

"Who were you talking to?" he repeated.

"You."

"You didn't even know I was here, yet you were saying I want you gone?"

At a loss for words, she merely nodded.

"You do know that doesn't make any sense, right?" he said.

She just shrugged and tried to move past him to the hallway and an escape. He took hold of her hand. That might not have been enough to stop her in her tracks but he used his other hand to trail his fingers up her arm. "Is this about our kiss?"

She nodded. What else could she do? Say she'd come to kick a gangster ghost to the curb?

"You want more," he murmured.

She shook her head. "No, I don't," she added for good measure.

"It's okay. You don't have to be embarrassed."

"No, it's not okay."

Ronan had one hand holding hers and his other hand

caressing her arm. Which is why he wasn't able to do anything when his towel suddenly fell to the floor.

Sierra was about to yell at Ronan for breaking the terms of their agreement when the startled look on his face held her back.

The sound of cruel laughter made her turn to find Hal puffing on his cigar and grinning. "If ya got it, flaunt it, boyo."

Ronan released her and grabbed for the towel. "I smell cigar smoke."

"That stinks. Not you," she hurriedly assured Ronan. "I meant the cigar smell."

"You smell it too?"

"Yeah, I do."

"I don't like it."

"I'm no fan either," Sierra assured Ronan.

"Your friend looks a little green," Hal noted with a huge puff.

She turned to face Ronan. "Are you okay?"

He didn't answer her at first.

"Ronan?" She waved her hand in front of his face. "Are you okay?"

He pulled away from her and left without a word, slamming his bedroom door. A moment later, he strode out dressed in jeans and a black T-shirt with his black leather jacket in his hand.

"Where are you going?"

"Out."

"There's something going on at the house," Ronan announced as he joined Damon at the bar.

"Let me guess. Sierra is asking questions again."

"No. I smelled cigar smoke."

"Sierra is smoking cigars?"

"No. You told me that there was something weird about the house that didn't allow you to put your customary surveillance cameras in there."

"We put them in. They just don't work."

"Why is that?"

"Don't know," Damon said. "Like I told you a few hours ago, we're working on it. Neville thinks it's a software problem. You do realize this is the third time you've come into the bar today, right?"

Ronan ignored his comment. "Have the cameras ever worked?"

"Sometimes."

"When was the last time?"

"I think for the human before Sierra."

"Did you see anything suspicious?"

"Like what? Like a ghost maybe?" Damon paused to hand Ronan a bottle of blood. "You look like you could use this."

Ronan had fed a few hours ago when he'd come to speak to Damon, but felt the need for sustenance so he drank the entire thing.

"I've heard the same stories you have about that house being haunted," Damon said. "After all, I do live next door."

"And?"

"I haven't seen any ghosts."

"But some humans have?"

"They didn't stick around long enough to say one way or another."

"Nothing showed up on the surveillance tapes?" Ronan said.

"No ghosts."

"But something else?"

"No entities. Just strange human behavior."

Ronan wasn't freaked about the possibility of ghosts. In fact, he'd welcome that news. Because the other option was much worse. Voz smoked cigars. And if Ronan could still smell that scent, it meant Voz hadn't gone far. Which meant Ronan had to keep his thoughts tightly locked up. If Voz discovered that Ronan didn't know what he was looking for or that he was sexually attracted to Sierra, the Master Vampire would use those things against Ronan.

During the two weeks he'd had the house to himself, Ronan had checked the usual places to hide things. The cubbyholes he knew about from living there as a teenager. The loose brick above the fireplace provided space to hide something. But it was empty. The fake bottom beneath the built-in bookshelf. Again nothing but cobwebs and spiders. The attic was full of junk but no key. Maybe full was an exaggeration but that's how it had felt to him. Most of it was old furniture. He'd even checked the tunnels used by the vampire residents of Vamptown. Nothing.

When he returned to the house a short while later, he was happy to find that Sierra was gone. She'd left a note on the dining table saying she was getting groceries and that Zoe next door was giving her a ride.

While she was gone, he made fast work of ripping up the floorboards in the bedrooms upstairs, and when he found nothing, swearing incessantly as he hammered them all back into place at vamp speed.

Nothing. Yet again he had reached a dead end in his hunt. Striding across the hallway, he went right up to the large framed photograph Sierra had been standing near. "If you're a freaking ghost, I need to know about it now! Show yourself," Ronan demanded.

Nothing. If this guy lived in the house, he might have some idea about what hidden treasures were inside. Ronan didn't care if the guy was dead. He was good at dealing with the undead. Not that he'd ever dealt with ghosts before. Hell, for all he knew they didn't even exist.

But on the odd chance that they did, he needed to make contact. "Show yourself!" he said, louder this time.

Again nothing.

So no ghost. Just the lingering scent of cigar smoke reminding him of Vox. Moving at vamp superspeed, Ronan knocked on the walls and the floor. He tore up more floorboards and had to put it all back. He hated this. Not the work, but the frustration.

Voz had granted Ronan his freedom and then reeled him right back in by holding his sister's soul hostage. Ronan didn't even realize he'd punched a hole in the wall until after the fact. He'd used such force that his bones cracked and broke.

He didn't care. As a vampire, he healed quickly. He welcomed the intervening pain.

What if this was a mission for which there was no chance of success?

Was this his punishment then? Were the fates conspiring against him for becoming a vampire, a monster? Not that he'd been given a choice. He later learned that vampires are supposed to ask for permission before turning a human. And even then, a large percentage of the fledgling vamps didn't survive the transformation.

But Master Vampires were immune to those rules. At least they were in Europe and Russia where vampire history went back to the beginning of time. There they could enslave a human, turning them into an indentured vampire at will to fight and to kill at their master's bidding. That was how they got their jollies, but most importantly it was how they maintained their power among rival vampire clans.

There was no bargain involved, no requirement for the human to agree to the transaction. This was no volunteer vampire army. Voz drafted those he wanted, those he felt would be strong enough to fight his battles. Dressed as a medic there on the battlefield in northern France, Voz forced Ronan to drink blood, blood from Voz's own vein where he'd sliced open his wrist. Then he'd moved Ronan to Romania and his remote castle there. Or to be more specific, he'd moved him in a flash to the cold and brutal dungeon beneath the castle.

The transition had been horrific. Only the strong survived. Ronan heard the tortured howls from those who didn't make the grade. It was a relief when their voices and their afterlives were stopped.

The smell of blood had been all around him in that dark dungeon just as it had been in the trenches in France. But there had been a big difference. Now he was hungry for that blood.

When he'd been released from that hellhole, he'd

gone on a feeding frenzy promoted by Voz. Only then, when he'd drunk his full, was he told he'd be indentured for a hundred years. Voz likened it to the gladiators in ancient Rome, battling it out. Voz didn't like the hundred-year rule; he wanted it to be for an eternity, but that century limit, which had been decreed by the Ancients, had been in place forever.

Vamps could get time off for exceptional valor, shortening their hundred years by a few years. After that point additional bargains could be made. A handful in Voz's army had signed agreements in blood to extend their term beyond the first century. They'd become addicted to the killing and now they were there for an eternity or until a strong, smarter, faster vamp destroyed them.

There was a limit to how many humans could be transformed into an indentured vampire in any given year, or so Voz had told him. But then he'd told him that Adele was well and had lived a long life.

Ronan had believed that his sister had done well. It was the only thing that kept him sane during the nearly hundred years of bloodshed at Voz's bidding. He'd had no choice or voice in who was killed. The guilt of that would stay with him forever. There were moments when he'd wanted to die, when he'd wanted to end it all.

But that hadn't happened. Instead he'd fought on. Been covered in blood from numerous vampire uprisings of various rival clans. So many that Ronan had lost count.

But each time it happened, Ronan was reminded of the blood of the battlefield at Cantigny in northern

France. He had no idea why his human memories remained after he'd been turned. But they did.

Ronan wondered if he'd lost his humanity there and then, back in France with the injured screaming as their guts oozed out of them or their limbs lay beside them. Maybe he'd no longer had a soul when Voz had turned him. Maybe that's why Voz had chosen him in the first place.

Sierra set the bag of groceries on the kitchen counter a second before Ruby appeared.

"I thought you were going to work on your plan of getting rid of Hal," she said impatiently. "Why are you shopping?"

"Because there's no food in the house." She opened the refrigerator and put a dozen eggs in along with some Parmesan cheese and crusty bakery bread. She added fresh zucchini, broccoli, and a bag of russet potatoes to the fridge's vegetable bin. The potatoes didn't have to be refrigerated but she didn't want them lying around in case Ruby decided to throw them like she had those plates.

Ghosts couldn't get into refrigerators. Although sometimes they could make them, and other appliances, go on the fritz. Toasters seemed to be a popular target for some reason.

"What did you do about Hal?" Ruby demanded.

"I went upstairs before I went out."

"And?"

"And I confronted him."

Ruby looked doubtful. "Really?"

"Okay, he confronted me first, but only because he talked first."

"He always does."

"Good to know. I'll remember that for next time." Sierra folded the paper bags and set them beneath the sink.

"What happened when he confronted you? Did you turn around and run?" Ruby said.

"Of course not," Sierra said. "He told me he wanted me gone and I told him I wanted *him* gone."

"And then what happened?"

"Ronan showed up right out of the shower, wearing a towel and nothing else."

"So you were distracted by a naked Ronan again?" Ruby looked incensed.

"I was not distracted, despite the fact that Hal practiced his usual tricks and yanked the towel off Ronan."

"I've never heard of Hal doing something like that before."

"There's always a first time," Sierra said as she gathered up the ingredients for a mushroom omelet. Cooking made her feel more in control, more everyday normal.

Ruby grew bored and disappeared when Sierra took her plate into the dining room. Her omelet might not be fluffy and perfect—in fact, it was rather brown on the bottom—but it tasted good.

She liked eating alone. It gave her time to think about her book and upcoming scenes. She kept a notepad nearby. She'd nearly spilled food on her iPad so she didn't use that during meals. Instead she went old school—back to pen and paper.

Thinking about the transition from World War I to

the roaring twenties reminded her that she'd seen a book on that subject in the massive floor-to-ceiling bookcase in the living room.

Leaving her empty plate on the table, she stood and walked over to the built-in bookcase. She reached for the book on the second shelf from the top. She heard a strange noise and a second later the entire bookcase came away from the wall and crashed toward her so fast that she couldn't move.

Chapter Nine

Ronan was there, pulling her to safety. It happened so fast it was a blur. And not blurred because she was traumatized but because he had moved faster than any human could. And no human could have pushed away the heavy bookcase with such ease, not even the strongest man on the planet. It had to weigh a ton. Okay, not literally a ton but it had weighed a lot. Granted it wasn't completely full of books but it was still a huge piece of furniture.

"What the hell just happened?" Sierra's voice shook. Books encircled her on the floor but miraculously none had actually hit her.

"A bookcase almost crushed you," Ronan said.

"I know that."

"There's no way that should have come loose from the wall like that. It's almost like someone pushed or pulled it over," he said.

"They did," she said.

"Who? There's no one here."

"Hal is here," she whispered.

"Who the hell is Hal?" Ronan demanded.

"The ghost upstairs. He used to be upstairs. Clearly now he's gaining strength." She waved her trembling hands. "I want to know about *you*."

"I'm fine."

"How did you move so fast and how did you push that bookcase away from me? It was too heavy for one person to move that way and you did it with ease."

"What makes you think it was a ghost?"

"Because I see ghosts. I have all my life. But I've never seen what you just did." She poked his arm as if to test his density. "Are you real?"

"I'm real. How long has Hal lived here?"

"Before he died or after?" she said.

"I need your help," he said.

He didn't seem the least bit fazed that she saw dead people. "Not until you tell me who you are."

"I'm Ronan McCoy and I just saved your life. You could say you owe me."

"Or I could say you're not human. Would I be right?" Her mind was racing a mile a second. Was he some kind of ghost she'd never heard of before?

"You're in shock," he said.

A crash behind him had him turning superfast. He was poised as if ready to attack. But it was the gleam of his fangs that totally freaked her out.

She wasn't alone. Ruby freaked too. "He's a vampire!" Ruby shrieked.

Sierra didn't bother shrieking. She focused her energy on getting the hell out of the house. She ran as fast as she could, praying the vampire wasn't right on her heels, the few steps to Zoe's house.

The moment Zoe opened the door, Sierra started talking. "Oh my God! Ronan is a vampire!"

Zoe gently put an arm around her shoulders. "You better come in."

"A bookcase fell over and almost crushed me. I would have been killed if Ronan hadn't rushed in and pushed it away from me. And by rush I mean go so fast I couldn't even see him move."

"Are you saying he pulled the bookcase down?"

"No, that was a poltergeist gangster ghost named Hal." Sierra gulped back a sob. "I should probably tell you that I can see ghosts. I have most of my life."

"So the house next door is haunted?" Zoe asked.

"Yes."

"I knew it," Zoe said.

"Do you see ghosts too?"

Zoe shook her head. "Not exactly."

"Is . . ." Sierra's voice shook. "Is Ronan some kind of—"

"He's a vampire. So am I," Damon said as he joined them in the foyer.

"You didn't have to spring it on her like that," Zoe reprimanded him. "Can't you see she's upset?"

"She's not the only one," Damon said. "Here's yet another human trying to blow our cover."

Sierra's heart stopped and her ears started ringing. She couldn't be hearing correctly. This couldn't be real. "You're . . . you're all vampires?"

"Absolutely not," Zoe said.

"Zoe isn't a vampire," Damon said. "She's a witch."

Zoe glared at him. "I'm not allowed to share that information with a human."

"You didn't. I did," Damon said.

"You can't compel her to forget. You already know that doesn't work." Zoe tapped her foot impatiently. "So what's your plan, Damon?"

This was all too weird for Sierra. Backing up until she was against the door, she felt for the doorknob behind her. She needed to get out of there.

She needed to hop in a car and leave—wait, she didn't have a car yet. What if Damon could move as fast as Ronan had? What if they both ganged up on her? She wouldn't have a chance.

The door behind her was pushed open and Ronan stood on the threshold.

"You might as well come in," Zoe told him.

"Sierra can see ghosts," he said.

"We know," Damon and Zoe said.

For a surreal moment, Sierra wondered what her heroine Nicki would do. She'd probably kick ghost butt, but vampires and witches had never been involved in Sierra's plotlines. She'd considered it, given the popularity of vampires. But she wrote what she knew. Ghosts.

Besides, she wasn't Nicki. Sierra was scared. She was shaking so hard her teeth were chattering.

A sudden thought hit her. Did her distant cousins who had inherited the house before her really leave the house or had these . . . these vampire people drained them of blood and killed them?

Was she going to suffer the same fate?

Not without a fight.

Right. How was she supposed to fight two vampires and a witch? Maybe she'd fallen asleep and this was all a bad dream. She pinched herself hard. Shit. That hurt. Which meant she wasn't asleep.

"We're not going to hurt you," Zoe reassured her.

"Damn right you're not." She reached for the wide sterling silver bangle she wore and held it up. "Stay back!" Wait, did silver work on vampires or just were-wolves? She wrote paranormal novels, she should know this stuff.

And what about witches? What worked on them? Hell if she knew.

"I realize this is a lot to take in, but you shouldn't panic," Ronan said.

"Sure. You're right. The fact that you're a vampire and my neighbor says she's a witch is no big deal."

Damon raised his hand.

"Right," Sierra said. "You're a vampire too. I'll take your word for that."

"I can show you—" Damon said.

"I don't want to see," Sierra said. She tried to think logically here. She'd seen stories on the Internet of people who'd had their teeth changed to become fangs. But were those retractable fangs? Because Ronan sure as hell hadn't had fangs when she'd kissed him a few hours ago.

"Would you like to sit down and talk about this?" Zoe offered. "We could have some of Daniella's cup-cakes."

"I need to leave." After she spoke, Sierra realized it might not have been smart stating her intention to exit this craziness. "Do not try to stop me."

Zoe put her hand on Ronan's arm. "Let her go."

Sierra wasted no time in getting out. Once in the cold February air, she tried to figure out a plan. She sure as hell wasn't leaving without her laptop. Her book was on there. Yes, she'd backed up part of it to the cloud but that was several days ago.

She'd rush into her house and grab a few things and get out. She'd go to the cupcake shop and call a cab on her cell from there.

Ruby greeted her the moment she walked in.

"How could you not know he's a vampire?" Sierra demanded. "You were here with him before I came."

"I never saw his fangs until today. Besides, he couldn't see me, so what difference does it make?" Ruby said.

"It makes a lot of difference to me."

"Well, it doesn't to me."

Sierra's anger flared. "And that's all that matters, right? *You*."

"No," Ruby said. "You matter too."

"Only because I'm useful to you."

"Not yet, but I have hopes."

"You are incredibly self-centered, do you know that?"

"Talk to me after you've been stabbed two dozen times and had to parade around in your underwear for decade after decade. I've been waiting forever." Ruby paused as Sierra reached for a bag and quickly tossed a few fave books and a handful of clothes in it. "What are you doing?"

"Leaving."

"But you can't. You'll lose the house."

"I could lose my life if I stay," Sierra said bluntly. She grabbed her laptop, purse, and the bag. Her furniture could stay. As for the box of her books, she'd ask her publisher to send more. She could just imagine the conversation with her editor, Lily Janeway.

"You know that box of books you sent me? I had to leave it behind for fear of being attacked by vampires and a witch plus a poltergeist ghost and Ruby the garter girl." Yeah, right. Like that talk was ever going to take place.

She turned but only got as far as the foyer before Ronan appeared in front of her. He didn't appear out of nothing the way ghosts did, although it was pretty damn close.

"You have to stay," he said.

"No I don't. I am totally out of here."

"My sister's soul depends on you."

The anguish in his voice should not have gotten to her but it did. Still, she tried to hide that fact by using sarcasm. "Is she a vampire too?"

"No."

"So you want to steal my soul and give it to her?"

"No, nothing like that. Where do you come up with this stuff?"

"I'm a writer," she muttered.

"Which means you have a vivid imagination," he said.

"Not so vivid that I ever imagined I'd inherit a house full of vampires," she shot back.

"And ghosts. Don't forget the ghosts."

"The ghosts were no surprise. You are the surprise."

"Just so you know, the house is not full of vampires. My family lived here before I was turned. The house is mine by Vampire law."

"Yeah, well, it's mine by every other law," she said. "Like the state of Illinois law."

"Vampire law trumps all others."

"Says you."

"Check it out with your lawyer."

"Right. I'll do that," she said sarcastically. "I'm sure he's up-to-date on all the intricacies of Vampire law."

"If you leave then you will lose the house," he said.

"And if I stay I will lose my life."

"No you won't. Where did you get such an idea?"

"From you. You're a vampire."

"I'm not going to kill you."

"So you just want to turn me into a vampire?" she said.

"No."

"Then what do you want?"

"I'm trying to tell you, but you won't give me a chance."

"I'm too scared to think straight," she muttered, before pointing to the mirror in the foyer. "Wait, I can see your reflection."

He nodded. So did his reflection. "That's right."

"Are you trying to punk me or something? Is this some kind of reality show gone bad?"

"I have no idea what you are talking about."

"The fact that you aren't really a vampire."

"How do you figure that?"

"If you were, then I wouldn't be able to see your reflection," she said.

"That's an urban myth, dating back to the days when mirrors were backed with thin sheets of silver. At that time, most vampires were not able to see their own re-flection. No one else could see their reflection either."

"Right." She looked around. Vampires seeing their reflection? She didn't think so. She'd seen a few epi-sodes of the first season of the BBC version of *Being Human*. The vampire on that show couldn't see his re-flection, although he was dark and sexy. Maybe Ronan was an actor like that one, only American not British. "So where are the hidden cameras?"

"They don't work in this house. I'm assuming it's because of the ghosts haunting the place."

Bingo. He'd just confirmed there were cameras. Wow, she'd almost fallen for that vampire stuff. Maybe this could be tied into some publicity for her book. As far as she knew there was no mention of television cov-erage in her promo plan or her publisher's. Unless they hadn't told her because they'd wanted to surprise her?

What about the bookcase? Maybe they'd replaced it with a fake one like on TV. And the freaky-fast speed? A hologram or special effects or something. She didn't know the details. "So this is a reality-show hoax."

"No, the cameras to which I was referring would be part of the area's surveillance system."

"The city of Chicago is watching you all?"

"No."

"So you are watching the city instead?"

"No, just our small corner of it."

"How do I know this is real?" she demanded. "I mean that *you're* real."

He held his arms out. "You can touch me, feel me."

"No way."

He looked hurt. Like she should care? If she was talking to a real vampire, she needed to get the hell out.

Then he got angry and, as he did, his eyes did something strange and his fangs appeared. "I swear on my sister's soul, I'm a vampire," Ronan grated. "Get over it!"

Looking at him now, she finally accepted his word. She took one step back, then another. "Look, it was one thing inheriting a house with a ghost or two. But moving into a nest of vampires is quite another. You say this was your house at one time and that it should be yours again. Fine. You can have it. Life is too short for this crap. Not *your* life of course since you are immortal. Or is that an urban myth as well?"

"No, that's true."

"Well then, I hope you and your house are very happy together." Sierra rushed to the front door.

"Noooo!" Ruby plastered herself against the door. "You can't leave!"

Chapter Ten

"Step away from the door," Sierra told Ruby.

"No!" Ruby shouted. "You can't desert me in my hour of need."

"Yes I can. Watch me."

She would have stepped forward but a sudden force sent her flying backward to land on her butt on the floor. Sierra was stunned. That energy had come from Ruby, not Hal.

"I'm not letting you leave," Ruby said.

"You are not locking me in this house with a vampire, Ruby," Sierra told her.

"You can leave as soon as you help me go into the light."

"Are you talking to the ghost? Ask her about my sister," Ronan said.

"Thanks for asking how I am," Sierra said with mocking bitterness. She ignored the hand that Ronan belatedly put out to help her up. "Too little, too late."

Sierra scrambled to her feet before facing Ruby.

"After everything I've done for you, this is how you repay me?"

"What have you done for me?" Ruby countered.

"I talked to you. I listened to you. I said I'd help you."

"And then you walk away before you help me."

"He's a vampire."

"He said he wasn't going to hurt you," Ruby pointed out.

"He drinks blood for a living."

"Tell him I know something about his sister."

Sierra shook her head. "No, I am not doing that."

"Fine. Then I'll tell him."

Ruby moved to the mirror, and breathed onto it, creating a mist she wrote in. *Addie*.

Sierra could hear Ronan's indrawn breath before he said, "That's my sister's nickname."

"Like that was hard to figure out," Sierra scoffed. "Ruby heard you talking about your sister Adele and she made a lucky guess. Fake clairvoyants do that all the time."

"Tell me about Ruby," Ronan ordered her.

"She's the ghost who just pushed me onto my butt. She was a prostitute in Al Capone's establishment until she was murdered here in this house."

"That's why I need your help," Ronan said.

"Clearly Ruby can communicate with you without my assistance. She can mirror-write. Good thing you can look in mirrors now, huh? You two have a good time. I'm outta here."

"No," Ronan said. "I just saved your life and this is how you repay me?"

"He thinks you are ungrateful too," Ruby said. "Tell him I agree with him."

"Tell him yourself," Sierra shot back. "Write it in the mirror, why don't you." She turned her attention to Ronan. "As for you, how do I know that you didn't yank that bookcase down yourself as a ploy to con me into thinking you saved my life?"

"Because *I* yanked the bookcase onto you," Hal stated from the top of the staircase. "I told you to get out. You didn't listen. Just like Ruby didn't listen. I told her she couldn't leave. Instead of backing away, she just stood there looking at me as if I ain't worth shittin' on. She still looks at me that way."

"Because you murdered her, Hal," Sierra said.

"Who are you talking to now?" Ronan demanded.

"Hal. The upstairs ghost who smokes a cigar and was a member of Al Capone's gang."

"Shit. You need a scorecard to keep track. How many ghosts are there in this house?" Ronan said impatiently.

"I've only seen two," Sierra said.

"You haven't seen my sister, have you?" Ronan reached into his back pocket and pulled an old photograph out. The young woman had a Gibson girl hairstyle piled on top of her head. She wore a white gown that covered her from her neck to her feet per the fashion of the early 1900s. She had Ronan's smile.

"No, I haven't seen her."

"I don't know if that's good or bad," he muttered.

"Can we get back to me?" Ruby said with an impatient tap of her foot. "Get rid of Hal. Have the vampire do it."

"Ruby wants you to get rid of Hal," Sierra told Ronan.

"How the hell am I supposed to do that?"

"I have no idea. You're a vampire. Think of something."

"He's got no powers over me," Hal bragged, before pointing to the grandfather clock, which flew toward Sierra. "Time's running out."

Ronan instantly stepped in front of her, preventing it from hitting her. It hit him instead and shattered.

"I never liked that clock anyway," Ruby said.

"That belonged to my family," Ronan growled.

Sierra's fear grew. "Look, I want no part of a turf war between vampires and ghosts. You entities can figure it out among yourselves. A word of warning," Sierra added. "Ruby smashed the plastic clock in the kitchen the first day I was here. These two may have a thing against clocks. I'm just saying . . ." Her hands were shaking but her voice was strong. She'd pushed the 911 button on her phone in her pocket and the speakerphone. The police would be here soon. "The house at 661 Nikolas Street has trouble. They've tried to kill me. Help needed urgently." She disconnected before the dispatch operator could say anything. She also turned it off in case they tried to call her back. She didn't want a callback. She wanted an entire SWAT team.

It took ten minutes, but officers banged on the front door. "Chicago police. Open up!"

"If I don't do what they say, they'll knock down the door," Sierra said.

Ronan opened the door.

"We got a report of a disturbance here," a sexy dark-haired officer said.

"That came from me." Sierra hurried to his side, praying he wasn't a fake cop from a strippergram. He sure looked good enough for that job. "They are keeping me here against my will. Get me out of here, please."

"What's going on, Ronan?" the sexy cop said.

"I can explain, Alex," Ronan said.

Sierra stepped away. "You're another fake cop! Just like Damon."

Alex said, "I assure you, I am a real cop."

"She can't be compelled," Ronan told Alex.

"What about you?" Sierra asked the other cop. "Are you a real cop?"

"Yes."

"Are you human?"

"My wife doesn't always think so."

"A simple yes or no would do," Sierra said shortly.

"What drugs did you take?" the unsexy cop asked.

"I did not take any drugs. I'm telling you, I am being held against my will."

"Are you afraid for your safety?"

"Hell, yes."

"I'll escort her out," the unsexy cop said. "You talk to the guy."

"He's not a guy. He's a vampire," she said as she scurried past Ruby. Or tried to. Ruby was not budging. Sierra couldn't get past her. It was as if the ghost had put up a force field of some kind of kinetic energy to stop Sierra.

"Come on," the unsexy cop said impatiently. "You said you wanted to leave."

"They won't let me," Sierra said.

"Who?"

"The ghosts," Ronan said cheerfully. "She sees ghosts."

"Push up your sleeves and show me your arms," the unsexy cop said.

"He's looking for needle marks," Ronan told her.

Sierra was infuriated. She was the victim here but they were treating her like she was the problem. "I am not a drug addict!"

"You just have fun with drugs on a recreational basis, right?"

"No, that's not right! I'm telling you, he's a vampire." Sierra pointed to Ronan. "Didn't you hear him say that he can't compel me?"

"I heard."

"So why aren't you arresting him?"

"Because it's not illegal to be a vampire," Alex said.

Sierra looked at Ronan and pointed accusingly at Alex. "Is he another cop with fangs?"

"That would be an affirmative," Alex said.

"I suppose you'll compel your partner now to forget you just said that."

"I don't have to," Alex said. "He's a vamp too."

Sierra couldn't believe what she was hearing. "What is it with this town? Is everyone a vampire?"

"Chicago is a city not a town," Ronan said. "And no, not everyone is a vampire. You aren't."

"I'm not," Ruby piped in. "I'm a ghost."

Sierra's head was spinning and her anger growing. "I can't believe this is happening. You cops are vampires yet you think *I'm* on drugs because I see ghosts? How messed up is that?"

"Most of the people we come in contact with who see hallucinations are drug addicts," Alex said.

"I'm not most people," she shot back.

"Yeah, I get that," Alex said.

Ronan stepped in front of her. "She's mine."

"Listen, I am not a piece of property. You already claim you own this house. Fine, you can keep it. But no way does anyone own *me*." She leaned closer to look him right in the eye. "You got that?"

The fact that he was a vampire who could rip her throat open was momentarily blocked out by the knee-jerk reaction to something her biological father had said the night she and her mother had left. "You are both mine and if I can't have you, no one can." That kind of maniacal control was a trigger for her, one that instilled terror and anger at the same time.

"It's okay." Ronan gently took her hand in his. "You're safe now."

"She's a feisty one," Alex said.

"Hello, enough about you," Ruby said. "Back to getting rid of Hal. There are three vampires in front of us. You're telling me that three vampires are powerless to get rid of one ghost named Hal?" Ruby demanded.

"They're vampires not ghost busters," Sierra said.

"You got that right. What happened to the clock?" Alex asked, noticing the fragments of wood for the first time.

"The ghost did it," Sierra said.

"Right. Well then, we'll leave you to it, Ronan.

We've got another call to take." Alex nodded Sierra's way. "Good luck."

"Thanks for nothing," she said.

"Definitely feisty," Alex said.

"And fiercely loyal," Ronan said.

After the two vamp cops left, Sierra belatedly realized she was still holding Ronan's hand. Or he was holding hers. "What makes you say that?"

"That you're loyal?"

She nodded, unable to take her eyes off their entwined fingers. Why did that look so right? She was holding hands with a vampire. How weird was that? Totally weird. Or it should be.

"Because you've helped spirits in the past." He slid a strand of her hair behind her ear and then caressed her cheek. "I saved your life twice tonight. Here's your chance to help me."

"You're not a spirit," she whispered.

"No, I'm not."

"You're something dark and scary."

"Yeah, I am," he said gruffly.

"I'd be stupid to trust you."

"You aren't stupid. But you can trust me." He squeezed her hand.

"Prove it."

"How?" he said.

"Let me leave."

Ronan sighed and took a step back, releasing her from his hold. "I can't do that."

"Sure you can."

"I'm not the one keeping you here," Ronan said. "Your ghosts are doing that."

"Hal wants me gone," Sierra said.

"Damn right," Hal said.

"Ruby is the only one who wants me to stay."

"No she's not. *I* want you to stay."

His voice was intense and demanding but the look on his face was what grabbed hold of her heart. There was a yearning there that was unspoken but fierce. Those brown eyes of his displayed the briefest flash of vulnerability and that was her downfall.

Why was Ronan able to get to her? She was so conflicted about all this. Was it really his expression and his eyes or was it a vampire thing? He'd claimed he couldn't compel her but what if that was a lie?

If he could compel you, you wouldn't still want to leave. You'd blindly do his bidding, her logical self pointed out.

Okay, that made sense. But her feelings for him didn't make sense. Why was he able to make her feel safe when she knew she should run a million miles away?

Given her past, she was jumpier about trusting a man than others might be. Always being on the run, fearing that an abusive father would catch them, created a sense of never being able to relax.

Yet things were different with Ronan.

Yeah, because he was a vampire.

She should have left when she'd first walked in and found him naked. No house was worth risking her life. Not that she'd had a clue at that time that he was anything other than what he'd stated—a guy with a claim to the house.

"So that line you gave me about the house not having a clear title was a lie?" she said.

Ronan didn't answer.

He didn't have to. She knew it was a lie. "How am I supposed to believe anything you say to me?" Sierra said.

"You can't," Hal said. "Another reason you should leave. As if this vampire shit isn't enough. You are one seriously messed-up broad."

Without warning, the large foyer mirror flew off the wall and toward Sierra. Ronan stepped in front of her. The mirror broke into large pieces, one of which embedded in his arm.

"At this rate, we won't have much furniture left," he noted dryly, yanking the glass out.

As blood gushed down his arm, Sierra was glad that she was the only writer in her writer's group who hadn't passed out during the tour of the medical examiner's office and the talk about blood splatter at crime scenes.

"Let me help," she automatically said. She didn't realize she'd been cut as well until a drop of her blood ran along her arm and fell onto his open wound.

"Shit!" He reared away from her as if burned by acid.

There was glass all around them. "Careful."

"It's too late," Ronan said.

Chapter Eleven

Sierra blinked in confusion. "What's too late? What happened?"

"Your blood mingled with mine," he said.

She froze. "Does that mean I'm going to turn into a vampire?"

"No. It means there is now a vampire bond between you and me."

"What's a vampire bond?"

"We're linked together."

"Define *linked*."

"It doesn't happen that often. Usually when a vampire is exposed to human blood we want more."

"More?"

"More blood. Depending on when we last fed."

"When did you last feed?" she asked nervously.

"Earlier this evening."

"Okay, so that's a good thing, right?"

"Your blood blended with mine."

"How can you be sure of that?" she said.

"I could feel it."

"Well, I couldn't."

"You will."

"When?"

"Now." Ronan leaned forward to kiss her.

His mouth was hot and wet. So was her body. She sucked his lower lip. The taste of him was driving her wild. She was on fire for him. Every cell in her body ached with the need to have his bare skin against hers.

Her hips undulated against his. She could feel his erection pressed against her. She wanted him buried deep within her doing all kinds of wicked things to her.

Reaching down, she tried to unzip his pants.

"No." Ronan's voice was rough and unsteady as he put his hand over hers. "This isn't you. It's the vamp bond making you act this way."

Sierra couldn't believe this was happening to her. Ghosts, vampires, and witches weren't enough to cope with? Now she turned into a nymphomaniac each time Ronan touched her?

Sure, there had been times in her past when she'd wished she was a little more confident where sex was concerned. Times when she wished she could make the first move and respond without any inhibitions. But those thoughts had all been geared toward having sex with a human male, not a vampire.

Looking for any possible silver lining here, she wondered if this might make her write superhot sex scenes. Ronan had already inspired her to write that last scene against the wall.

No, she couldn't think that way. She had to find an exit strategy.

"How do you break a vamp bond?" she demanded.

"By having sex," he said bluntly.

"That's convenient," she muttered.

"I'm not having sex with you. The bond keeps you tied to me. You won't want to leave."

Damn, Sierra silently swore. He was right. Sort of. Part of her—the tiny sliver of logic left—still wanted to leave. But that tiny inner voice was drowned out by the blare of wanton desire telling her to stay. Ordering her, *demanding* that she stay.

So she had to stay. Did that mean she had to like it? Absolutely not. "You trapped me! I'll bet you deliberately broke that mirror so you'd be injured and I'd try to help you."

"A vampire bond can't be staged. It has to be a natural rare occurrence."

"Says you."

"I don't make these rules up," he said.

"How do I know that?"

"You saw your reaction when I kissed you."

"It could have been a freak—" The rest of her sentence was cut off by his mouth covering hers. An instant later she was in his arms again, and reaching for the zipper on his jeans before he set her aside.

"Okay, so it wasn't a freak occurrence," she muttered.

This was so humiliating. It was bad enough wanting to have sex with him when he was just Naked Ronan, but now that they shared a bond it was downright mind-blowing. As in, her mind couldn't comprehend it while her body welcomed it.

"We need to talk," he said.

"You think?" She didn't care if she sounded snarky.

"Not here. Outside."

As he reached for her coat from a hook by the door, she realized his wound was already healing. Looking down at hers, she saw that it was no longer dripping blood but certainly hadn't healed the way his had. She rolled down the sleeves of her shirt before putting on her coat.

They took a few steps away from the front porch before he spoke. "I'm trusting you with something very personal. You can't tell anyone."

"I know already. You're a vampire."

"That's not what I meant."

"So now you're saying you're not a vampire?"

"I am a vampire."

"But you have a pulse and your skin isn't cold. Well, maybe it is now since we're standing out here in the cold."

"Outdoor temperatures don't bother me."

"What about sunlight?"

"No longer a problem, but that isn't important. This is. The reason I'm here at my former home is because of my sister."

"Yeah, you said that earlier but I don't get the connection unless she's a ghost?"

"No, I don't think she is."

"You're not really making much sense."

Ronan realized that. There was so much at stake here that he needed to get it right. The memories of what he was about to reveal came flooding back. Not just what had happened after he'd been turned—but before. When he'd slid in the blood in the trenches and fallen facedown in it. The metallic taste in his mouth, abhorrent to him as a human, was necessary to him now that he was a vampire. He tried to keep his explanation brief. "I was turned on the battlefield in France during World War One by a Master Vampire named Baron Voz. As a result, I was indentured for nearly a hundred years. I only recently gained my freedom."

"How recently?"

There she was, quick with the questions. "Two weeks ago."

"What does *indentured* mean? Not the dictionary definition of the word, but in regard to you. I'm still trying to come to terms with this entire vampire thing," she said.

"It meant that I had to do whatever Voz wanted." He had no intention of going into detail about what that entailed.

"How do I know that you aren't still following this Voz's orders? If he controls you then—"

"He doesn't. Damon or Nick would both confirm that. They wouldn't allow me to stay here in Vamptown otherwise."

Instead of asking for more proof, she surprised him by asking, "How old were you? When you were turned, I mean."

"Twenty-eight."

Ronan tried reading her mind. He'd had some minimal success before. Now that they were bonded, he should be able to access more of her thoughts, but they were so jumbled and coming so fast that it was hard to keep track.

Five pages. I have to write five pages tomorrow.

How am I supposed to do that when I'm tied to a vampire? I have an interview. Wear black. What must it be like to have been human once and been turned? I don't want to find out. I don't want to be a vampire. I can manage seeing blood but drinking it is something else. Ronan's sister has his smile.

He almost commented on her last thought about his sister but doing so would let her know that he could access her thoughts and he knew her well enough to know that would not go over at all. His redhead had a temper.

Shit. He couldn't think that way. She wasn't *his*. Yes, they shared a bond but he couldn't act on it. Doing so would risk everything. He couldn't have sex with her.

Yet he wanted to. Look at her standing there so close, with her great breasts and bad attitude. Those were the first things he'd noticed about her. Her breasts and her attitude.

But now he knew so much more, like the way she nibbled her bottom lip when she was thinking hard or the way her green eyes flashed when she was angry yet went soft when she was wrapped up in the stories in her head. Then there was the delicate shape of her fingers yet the strength in her grip. When he'd held her hand and twined his fingers through hers it was as if they were meant to fit together. When she'd given him that incredible vamp bond kiss, it had taken every iota of his control to stop her and not tear her clothes off and have her right there and then.

He cut those thoughts cold. He couldn't have sex with her. The dangers were too great and the stakes too high.

Sierra's voice jogged him back to the matter at hand.

"I don't understand. What does all this have to do with your sister?" Sierra said.

"I only recently discovered that she died during the Spanish flu epidemic in 1919."

"I'm sorry to hear that."

"It gets worse. When he released me, Voz told me he's been holding her soul hostage. In order to free her, I have to retrieve a key for him that is hidden in my house."

Maybe it was her experience with spirits trying to head toward the other side that made her more accepting of his story.

"What kind of key?" she said.

"I don't know. Voz didn't say. I don't even know if it's literally a key or not. But I only have until midnight on Valentine's Day." He realized that sounded lame, but she didn't ask him how the hell he was supposed to find something when he had so little to go on.

Instead she asked, "So what's the plan? Do you intend to stay in this house forever looking for this mysterious key? You might have forever, but I sure don't. I have a book deadline."

"I have a deadline as well. Valentine's Day, remember? I just told you that."

"What happens if you can't find this mysterious key?"

"If I fail, then I remain indentured to Voz," Ronan said.

"For another hundred years?"

"Forever."

He saw her gulp. "How am I supposed to help you?" she said.

"By communicating with the ghosts. Ask them what they know about the key and about my sister."

"What if it's the key to something bad like the key to hell?"

"Then I'm in deep shit."

"I'm serious. Would you hand over the key to hell to save your sister's soul?"

"No."

"Even if it means that you'd be indentured to Voz for eternity?"

"Even then." He couldn't justify letting more evil into the world. He'd done enough evil things. Maybe that was meant to be his punishment. But it wasn't Adele's punishment. She hadn't done anything wrong. She wouldn't want him causing more malevolence, even if it was done to save her.

Sierra looked at him uncertainly. "How can I be sure?"

"I'm willing to swear on my sister's soul."

"If you even have a sister," she muttered.

He could have pointed out that Sierra had already noticed that Adele had his smile, but didn't. He knew she was grasping at straws, trying to find a way out. He couldn't fault her for that. "I showed you her photograph."

"That could have been anyone."

Then it hit him. There was more to a vampire bond. During his years of being indentured to Voz, Ronan had tried to research various elements of vampirism, looking for an out from his original indenture, and in doing so he'd learned about other elements. Like a vampire bond. "You can tell when I'm lying." He paused before saying, "I don't want to touch you."

His words said one thing but his message said the opposite. His desire for her was radiating toward her with intrinsic heat. She looked at him a moment. "You're lying." Her voice was husky.

"How can you be sure?"

She put her hand to her chest. "I could feel it."

"Exactly. Everything I've told you out here is the truth."

"Except for you not wanting to touch me."

He nodded. "Except for that." His voice was low and deep.

At that moment she felt exactly the way her heroine Nicki had when she wanted mindless sex. Not just with anyone. With Ronan. Sierra had wanted it before. She wanted it even more now.

She straightened her shoulders and tried to shake off the intimacy they'd just shared. "So you are a vampire turned on the battlefield in France during the First World War and you were then indentured to a Master Vampire for almost a hundred years. You do have a sister named Adele. You need my help to talk to the ghosts to get information about the key to save your sister."

"Right. But you can't share this information with anyone else. Anyone at all."

"What are you two doing out here?" Zoe asked, a look of concern on her face as she joined them in front of their house.

"We're talking." The look Ronan gave Sierra was a reminder that he was trusting her with his secret.

"You can't do that inside?" Zoe said.

"I didn't want the ghosts to eavesdrop," Ronan said.

Damon joined them a moment later. Ignoring Sierra and Ronan, he took Zoe in his arms and kissed her deeply. She wrapped her arms around his neck and ran her fingers through his hair. Their love and passion was obvious. Their embrace seemed to go on forever.

When it was over, Zoe had a huge grin on her face, as did Damon. But Damon's faded as he looked at Ronan, indicating with a tilt of his head that he wanted to speak to Ronan privately. The two of them moved to the side of the house, leaving Sierra alone with Zoe who was still starry eyed.

"Wow," Sierra said.

"I know." Zoe sighed and touched her fingers to her lips. "I just can't get enough of Damon. I love him so much."

"He obviously feels the same way about you."

"We're lucky that way. But enough about me. What about you? How are you holding up?" Zoe asked.

"What do you know about a vampire bond?" Sierra said.

"A sire bond?"

"No, not a sire bond. A sex bond."

Zoe's eyes widened. "I don't know anything."

"But you and Damon are a couple. He said he's a vampire. You said you're a witch."

"I'm a good witch. I don't worship the devil or anything."

"Maybe a vampire bond doesn't apply to you because you're a witch. I can't believe I'm even talking to you like this," Sierra muttered.

"Is it really so strange? You already have paranormal abilities. You see ghosts."

"I don't just see them, I communicate with them."

"How?"

"They talk to me. Whether I want them to or not."

"Given that, are you surprised that witches and vampires exist?" Zoe said.

"Hell, yes!" Sierra answered emphatically.

"Okay then. Just breathe. There's no need to panic."

"Of course there's a need to panic. I just bonded with Ronan and now I can't leave him."

"You two had sex?"

"No. Having sex would break the bond between us."

"I have no idea what you're talking about," Zoe said. "Maybe you should ask Damon about this."

"No way. I am not going to talk about sex with him."

"Okay, then I will."

"No."

"Maybe there's nothing to it."

"Oh, there's something to it all right. One of the ghosts went all poltergeist and made the large mirror in the foyer fall off the wall and fly toward me. Well, it would have if Ronan hadn't stepped in front of me. The glass shattered and cut his arm. I didn't realize I was cut as well, although not as badly as Ronan, until a drop of my blood blended with his. That's what did it. Now I am totally hot for Ronan. He kisses me and I want to strip him bare and . . . well, you know."

"You want to do what your heroine Nicki did to the hero in your last book?"

"Yeah, that and more."

Zoe shared a knowing look with her before reaching into her back pocket for her phone.

"Who are you calling?" Sierra demanded.

"Pat. If anyone would have info on vampire bonds, it would be him."

"Because he has an interest in history?"

"Because he's a vampire who has an interest in history."

Pat showed up a second later with another man, more heavyset, by his side.

"I'm Bruce," the man said. "It's so exciting to meet you. I've been saying we need more artists and writers here in Vamptown."

"Vamptown?"

Bruce looked at Zoe. "I thought you said she knew about vampires."

"Why are we all talking outside? It's freezing," Pat said.

"Sierra doesn't want the ghosts eavesdropping on our conversation," Zoe said.

"So the house is haunted." Bruce just about jumped for joy. "I told you so," he said to Pat.

"Have you heard of something called a vampire bond?" Zoe asked Pat.

"You see ghosts?" Pat asked Sierra.

She nodded. "And hear them and talk to them too."

"Then you are a powerful entity empath," Pat said. "If so much as a drop of your blood merges with a vampire's—"

"With Ronan's in this case," Sierra said.

"Then you are bonded with him. You must stay near him. It's like you are compelled to do so."

"What else am I compelled to do?" Sierra demanded. "Whatever he wants?"

"No. You won't want to leave him and you will feel a powerful attraction to him."

Sierra had already been attracted to him before this blood stuff had come up. She knew from the two kisses they'd exchanged since then that things were now basically on fire.

She couldn't believe she was standing here talking to vampires and a witch about all this, but she had to get answers.

"What about lies? Can I tell when Ronan is lying to me?" Sierra asked.

Pat nodded. "While you are bonded with him, yes."

"How can the bond be broken?" she asked Pat.

"Once you have sex with Ronan, the bond is broken," Pat said.

"There's no other way?"

Pat shook his head.

"How can you be sure?"

"I've been a vampire for over four hundred years," Pat said dryly. "I've learned a few things along the way."

"Wait a second. When I met you and we talked at the cupcake shop, you talked about Chicago history. Were you here for that? The Chicago Fire? The Roaring Twenties? Prohibition?"

"Yes."

"Did you know Hal Bergerstock when he ran this place?"

"I knew of him."

"He's haunting the place now."

"He doesn't seem very nice," Zoe noted. "He just broke a mirror inside the house."

"Uh-oh," Bruce said. "Seven years' bad luck."

"That's just a superstition," Zoe stated before asking Sierra, "What about your cut? Are you okay?"

"What's going on out here?" Tanya demanded as she came rushing down the sidewalk to join them. "I happened to be in the Vamptown security center watching surveillance screens and saw everybody gathered around Sierra. Is something wrong?"

"I'm okay," Sierra said.

"Then why are you bothering her? I told you, she needs to be writing. Everyone step away from the world-famous author," Tanya ordered.

"I'm not that famous," Sierra said.

"And modest too. The sign of a true talent," Tanya said. "Back up, people. Get a move on."

"How did you know we were out here?" Zoe said.

"I told you. The surveillance cameras. But there is no audio out here. Why are you all out here anyway?" Tanya tugged her faux-fur coat tighter. "Zoe, were you having hot flashes again? Menopause is a bitch, huh?"

"I am not menopausal," Zoe growled.

"Trouble?" Damon inquired as he strolled over.

"Yes," Tanya said. "These . . . people are bothering Sierra when she needs to be working on her next book."

"Sierra knows we're vampires," Damon said.

"Wait a second," Sierra said. "Don't vampires have to be invited in before they can enter a place?"

"Yes," Damon said. "You invited me and Nick in when you moved in. And Ronan was already there. It's his house according to Vampire law."

"I didn't invite Tanya in," Sierra said.

"The previous resident did," Tanya said. "I only need to be invited into a location once within the past six months. What, you don't believe that I was here and invited before? Check the surveillance tape."

"The cameras don't work in the house," Damon said.

"No, but they work on the front porch," Tanya said.

Damon checked his smartphone. "Okay. Your story was confirmed."

"I should hope so," Tanya said. "Now please leave Sierra alone so she can get back to work on her story. The one she's writing about her kick-ass ghost-busting heroine Nicki's adventures here in Chicago. All of you, go away!"

"Not gonna happen," Ronan said.

Tanya sighed. "Okay, you can stay, but everyone else—"

"Is coming inside." Ronan's voice was steely, the look in his eyes daring anyone to contradict him.

Chapter Twelve

Sierra entered her house followed by a bunch of vampires. Yet another surreal moment to add to the growing number of them indelibly imprinted on her mind since arriving here in Chicago . . . or more specifically here in this house in a neighborhood she'd just learned was known as Vamptown. At least the local vampire residents referred to it as such. She doubted it showed up that way on Google Maps.

"I just want to confirm something," she said. "I'm guessing that unless you have fangs, you don't know anything about Vamptown."

"*You* don't have fangs, and you know about it," Ronan said.

"I don't have fangs and neither does my grandmother," Zoe said. "We both know about it."

"I know about it too," Daniella said as she joined them for the first time. Nick was by her side. "And I don't have fangs," she added.

Sierra was confused. "So tons of people know? I

would have thought that its very existence would be top secret and unknown to humans."

"That was the plan," Nick said.

"Is it safe?" Zoe asked, looking around nervously. Pointing to the broken shards of glass from the mirror still on the floor, she asked, "Do you want me to clean that up for you?"

"That would be nice but I can do it," Sierra said.

"Not as fast as I can," Zoe said with a wave of her hand. Presto, the glass was gone.

Sierra was speechless.

Tanya wasn't. "Show-off," she muttered.

"You're sure that Hal won't try to bombard us with something else?" Zoe said.

Sierra shook her head.

"You're not sure?" Zoe said.

"I meant he can't do that. He doesn't have unlimited power," Sierra said. "He'll have to shut down to recharge, so to speak."

"Like the electric car I almost bought," Zoe said.

"You need to invite Pat and Bruce in," Ronan told Sierra.

"I'm so sorry," Sierra said. "Come in, both of you."

Wait, why had she let all these vampires into her house? She might be able to tell when Ronan was lying to her, but that didn't mean she could trust these others.

If there was trouble, Ronan would protect her because he needed her. Yeah, but that made it Ronan versus four . . . no, make that five vampires counting Tanya. Not good odds.

Okay, so Tanya probably wouldn't hurt her because she needed Sierra to keep writing the next book.

Maybe Sierra could put vampires in the next book. Everything was grist for the mill in a writer's life. Write what you know. She already knew ghosts. Now she knew vampires too. Let's not forget Zoe the witch who could clear messes with a single wave of her hand.

"No wand?" Sierra didn't realize she'd said the words out loud until she saw Zoe roll her eyes and heard Tanya say, "That's what I asked her."

"And as I told you at the time, I'm a witch not freaking Tinkerbell," Zoe said impatiently.

"No need to get crabby about it," Tanya said. "No one likes a crabby witch."

Yeah, inviting them all in had definitely been a mistake, Sierra silently decided. Now the issue was how to get rid of them.

"Can you see a ghost now?" Bruce asked Sierra.

She looked around and saw Ruby in the far corner of the living room, shaking her head and putting her finger to her lips in the universal *shhh* sign.

"Uh, no, I don't see any ghosts right now," Sierra lied.

Bruce looked around. "So this place used to be a brothel, huh?"

"No, it was a bordello," Ruby said, and Sierra repeated without thinking.

"What's the difference?" Bruce said.

"Damned if I know," Sierra muttered.

"Then why did you say that? Did the spirit speak through you?" Bruce asked eagerly.

"I'm not a medium," Sierra said.

"No, you're a large," Tanya said. "A size fourteen if I'm not mistaken."

"A medium is someone who can communicate with spirits via telepathy. I'm clairvoyant and clairaudient in that I can both see and hear ghosts. Just not right now," Sierra hurriedly added as Ruby put her fingers together and made a zip motion across her mouth.

"One of the hard things about being a vampire is having your friends and family pass on," Bruce said. "I was hoping maybe you would be able to contact some-one for me."

"I don't know . . ." Sierra said.

"I'd pay you," Bruce assured her.

"Who do you want to contact?" Pat asked him.

It was only as Bruce put his arm around Pat and kissed his cheek that Sierra realized that the two were a couple.

"There's no need for you to get jealous," Bruce told Pat. "I don't want to get in touch with any old lovers. But I would like to contact Mother."

"I thought she was the reason you ran away and joined the circus," Pat said.

"I was a professional clown," Bruce told Sierra. "Be-fore I was turned into a vampire, I mean. And yes, my Bible-thumping adopted momma was the reason I ran away when I was fifteen. She'd thump me upside the head but good with that Bible of hers."

"Then why do you want to contact her?" Pat asked.

"Mother is a nickname for the bearded lady in the circus who took me under her wing. She choked on some kernels of popcorn and died in her trailer all alone. I just wanted her to know how much I appreciated her kindness."

"I'm sorry but I've never done séances," Sierra said.

"And the other ghosts might object to having a new spirit in the house," Zoe said.

"Ya think?" Ruby said. "Damn right I'd object! Not that I have anything against bearded ladies. I saw one once in the circus when it came to town."

Sierra was prevented from further discussion about séances or circuses by a phone call. "I have to take this," she told all the supernaturals in her living room.

The call was from a reporter, Bob Nolan, from the *Chicago Tribune*. "I just wanted to confirm our interview for tomorrow," Bob said.

When Katie Katz, Sierra's publicist at her publishing company, heard Sierra was moving to a historic house in Chicago that might have ties to Al Capone's gang, she'd set up an interview with Bob.

But that was before Sierra knew about Vamptown.

"Uhm, maybe we could meet somewhere else instead of my house."

"Is something wrong?" the reporter asked.

How to answer that question? Yes, a million things were wrong. A handful of them were standing in her living room arguing about bearded ladies.

"I'd prefer if we could meet at another location," Sierra said.

"I already assured you that I would not be revealing your address in the article and that the photos would be taken inside your new home not outside."

"I haven't really had time to settle in and unpack—"

"I'm on a deadline. If you're not interested, then I'll have to move on to another story," Bob said.

"No, don't do that." Sierra hoped she didn't sound as desperate as she felt.

"Okay then. So are we on for tomorrow around four in the afternoon?"

"Yes."

After disconnecting, Sierra turned to face everyone. "Listen, people . . . er, vamp . . . er . . . everyone. I have a reporter coming here tomorrow and I don't want anyone doing anything weird."

"Define *weird*," Ronan said.

"She means Zoe flying on a broomstick," Tanya said. Zoe rightfully looked affronted.

"No, that's not what I mean," Sierra said hurriedly.

"She means no blood-sucking," Zoe said.

Now Nick, Damon, Pat, and Bruce all looked affronted. Ronan merely looked amused.

"Actually, I meant to just let the guy come and interview me without any trouble," Sierra said.

"Hear that?" Tanya said. "No trouble."

"Is he bringing a photographer?" Ruby asked.

"I have no idea," Sierra said, before recalling that she shouldn't be answering a ghost's question in front of others. "I mean, I have no idea what to wear for the interview tomorrow."

"Basic black is always a classic," Zoe said.

"Because you're a witch," Tanya said.

Zoe pointed to Nick, Damon, and Ronan, all of whom wore black. "Vampires like black too."

"Sierra, as a redhead, you would look great in black," Bruce agreed. "I watch *Project Runway* so I do know a little about women's fashion."

"Very little," Tanya said.

"You definitely don't want to look like her." Bruce pointed to Tanya.

"What's wrong with my outfit?" Tanya demanded.

Bruce shook his head. "Where to begin?"

"With the spandex neon lime ultramini skirt," Zoe suggested.

"I don't know about you, but I definitely have better things to do than stand around and talk about fashion," Nick said. "I'm heading back to work."

Damon tilted his head toward Ronan. "We need to talk again. Now."

Ronan sat on the closed coffin in the basement while Damon paced the cement floor. Luckily Sierra's flashlight had gone out before she spotted it earlier.

"I'm not happy about any of this," Damon said.

"I need to warn you that the ghosts may be able to hear you," Ronan said.

"I took care of that," Damon said.

"How?" Ronan asked.

"I'm a vampire Demon Hunter. I have ways of establishing secure sites."

"That's all you're going to say?"

"Damn right." Damon was pissed and making no attempt to hide that fact. "You're the one who needs to do the talking."

"About what?" There was so much to be pissed off about that Ronan couldn't decide which took top place.

"About the fact that you told Sierra you're a vampire."

"I didn't tell her. Not at first. I had to save her. Hal had just yanked a huge bookcase onto her. Or that was his intention. She would have been killed. You told me not to kill humans."

"Yeah, well, I'm having second thoughts about that," Damon said.

Ronan clenched his fists. He didn't want to have to fight with his fellow vampires to protect Sierra, but he would do so in a heartbeat.

Damon rolled his eyes. "Relax. I'm not going to hurt Sierra. That doesn't mean the ghost won't, though."

"I'll protect her." Ronan was surprised at how intense the need to save her from harm had become. Was this a result of his vampire bond with her? He wasn't sure. He only knew that he would do anything to ensure that bastard ghost Hal didn't hurt her.

You haven't done a very good job of being her protector so far, an inner voice mocked. Ronan was very familiar with that voice. He'd heard it in his head often enough while indentured to Voz. At the slightest hint of a conscience, that inner voice came out to verbally thrash him. Vampires weren't meant to have a conscience.

He had plenty of inner demons. He refused to give them all a voice. But some remained stronger than others.

"My first priority is the security of Vamptown," Damon said.

"Understood."

"What is your first priority?"

"To stop others from treating me like a subservient in my own home." Ronan's voice reflected his anger.

Damon eyed him for a moment before nodding. "Understood. I just want to point out that we don't like outsiders invading our turf. And by *outsiders* I am referring to humans in this case."

Ronan said, "Sierra isn't here because of me."

"No, but a reporter is coming here because of her. You have a vampire bond with her. Can't you talk her out of it?"

"She still can't be compelled," Ronan said. "She just is willing to stay with me."

"Willing? Or required to stay?" Damon asked.

Ronan remained silent.

"So if you leave the house when she's supposed to have her interview, she would have to follow you?" Damon continued.

"And the reporter would follow her."

"That's okay. Go to Daniella's cupcake shop."

"Do you really want more publicity for her cupcakes? I heard that she's already pretty well-known for them."

"Good point," Damon allowed. "Get off the coffin. I'm returning it to the funeral home."

Ronan hopped down. "I'm sure the reporter won't be staying long. He'll do his interview and leave. I'll be here to make sure that happens. I'll compel him to leave if things get out of hand."

"Things always seem to get out of hand around here," Damon said.

Ronan had the feeling that things were going to get much worse before they got better . . . *if* they got better.

Chapter Thirteen

Serena didn't get much sleep that night. She told herself it was because she was nervous about her big interview the next day, but that wasn't the only reason. How could she not be nervous when ghosts, vampires, and witches surrounded her? Come on. Really?

It was amazing that she wasn't a babbling, sobbing mess.

What was also amazing was that she'd written twelve pages before going to bed. That was two days' worth of work.

Maybe being bonded to Ronan made her supercreative? Superproductive? Definitely superhorny.

She'd have to ask Ronan. Not about the horny stuff but the creative, productive stuff. He'd been her last thought falling asleep and now he was practically her first thought waking up.

Which wouldn't be such a problem if he weren't a vampire. A vampire she wanted to have sex with. No, not just *wanted*. When he kissed her, she immediately

felt like she *had* to have sex with him. The way she had
to have air to breathe.

Sierra was getting hot just thinking about it, thinking about *him*. Every hour, every minute increased her
feelings for him as she replayed every touch, every
kiss, every embrace he'd given her. She grew moist
between her legs as she remembered the feel of his
arousal rubbing against her there.

She ran her hand down her body and pressed against
her mound, all the while imagining it was his hand on
her. She was stunned by how quickly she came, the
spasms rolling within her. That had never happened to
her before, not that way, not that fast, not that intensely.
Wow.

Jumping into the shower and washing her hair helped
calm her down somewhat. She had most of the day before the reporter showed up. Which meant she could
focus on her writing not on orgasms.

She was considering various nonorgasmic scenar-
ios for the next chapter as she padded on bare feet into
the kitchen and her beloved Keurig. Her editor Lily had
e-mailed her yesterday, asking if she was going to make
her deadline because the book was already scheduled.
The fourth book in her S. J. Brennan series was coming
out in three months' time and the cover flats were supposed to be arriving in an e-mail today.

Cover art and blurbs were important marketing elements. As a reader herself, she knew that she'd picked
up a book because of the cover. Then she'd read the
back cover copy and then the opening page. If she liked
what she read, she bought the book.

But e-books had turned things upside down in some

ways. Yet even with the high-tech changes, reader word of mouth was still an incredibly important element in helping sales. Given that fact, Sierra was considering adding a street team of readers to spread their enthusiasm over her books among their friends.

She remained totally engrossed in her thoughts about the business of publishing as she brewed her coffee. The first three books in her series had done well, each one slightly increasing in sales. She needed to continue that trend, which wasn't easy to do given the fact that she was competing with free downloadable books on the Internet.

So she worked hard to keep up her presence in social media platforms like Facebook and Twitter as well as doing blog tours and online chats when a book was released. Sierra had a cult following of very enthusiastic fans but that hadn't yet translated into major financial success. Her editor remained hopeful that things would continue to improve and her readership would grow. Sierra had one more book coming out this year and then the manuscript she was currently writing before her contract ran out and was up for renewal.

She needed to be sure to e-mail her publicist Katie after the interview today and let her know how it went. She should also check with her to see if any new reviews had come in. Sierra had met Katie last summer during a trip to New York. She'd immediately bonded with her. Katie was brimming with energetic enthusiasm and was a consummate professional. She also had a thing for cupcakes. Sierra made a mental note to send her some of Daniella's cupcakes.

She was just about to take her first sip of coffee

when she felt a hand on her shoulder. Startled, she dropped the mug, which shattered on the floor. As it did so, she realized that Ronan was the one touching her. If she hadn't been so distracted, she would have recognized that fact immediately because her body had such a powerful reaction to him. But the way he was able to show up out of nowhere was disconcerting.

She was accustomed to ghosts suddenly appearing, so she should be able to deal with a hot, sexy vampire doing the same thing. But Ronan was special in so many ways.

He looked so hot in his jeans and black T-shirt, standing so close, smelling so good. She was a writer. She should be able to come up with more creative ways to describe the way he made her feel. But she couldn't.

None of the previous men in her life had ever ignited this passion in her. But Ronan wasn't a man. He was a vampire. She was still grappling with it all.

"Watch out," Ronan said as he tightened his hold on her while she gazed down at the mess on the kitchen floor.

She tried to ignore her intense connection and the physical need to be with him. Instead she focused on the mundane. Two mugs down, only two to go. Clearly she should get Styrofoam cups or something from now on.

Luckily she hadn't burned herself from the spilled hot coffee. That may have been her last French Roast flavor though. She'd have to go out and buy more.

"Careful," Ronan said before sliding his arms around her and picking her up.

Now her thoughts were a thousand percent focused on him. "What are you doing?"

"Preventing you from cutting yourself on the broken china."

She'd never had a man carry her before, let alone a vampire. Putting her arm around his neck, she held on tight as he cradled her against his body. Her face was close to his, which meant her neck was close to his mouth. She hoped he wasn't tempted to take a bite. She was tempted to kiss him but she didn't.

"Where are we going?" she asked breathlessly. She wasn't breathless on purpose. She wasn't trying to sound like Marilyn Monroe. The words just came out that way.

"Where would you like to go?" he said.

To bed with you were the first words that came to mind, but luckily she didn't say them aloud. She hoped he wasn't reading her thoughts. Could she post "Vampires Out" on her mind? She definitely wanted "Vampires In" regarding the rest of her body. The more she tried to stop thinking about him in bed with her, the more she did it, imagined it, fantasized . . .

"I'm waiting," he said.

"My shoes are in my bedroom." So was her bed.

As he walked toward her room, she responded to the way his arms felt around her. Heat surged throughout her body. The side of her breast was pressed against his chest. She was wearing a NYT BESTSELLER WANNABE T-shirt and had forgotten to put on a bra underneath it. Or maybe she'd deliberately omitted putting on that lingerie item. She was glad she had. She didn't want any additional layers of clothing between them.

The truth was that she wanted to rip his T-shirt off and lick her way across his chest. She didn't normally have a photographic memory but the image of Ronan standing naked when she'd walked into the house that first day seemed to be clearer than ever.

Her breathing became faster and faster. At this rate, she'd be hyperventilating soon.

When he crossed the threshold into her bedroom, she noticed how thick his eyelashes were. His dark hair tumbled over his forehead, lending him a rakish air that she found irresistible. Which is why she lifted her hand to run her hand through his hair.

He tightened his hold on her.

She licked her lips. The feel of the silky strands between her fingers was incredibly arousing. Was that because of the vampire bond? Or just because he was Ronan?

He stood there with her, a few feet from the bed, his mouth mere inches from hers. She wanted to taste his lips. So she did. Or tried to. But he abruptly dumped her on the bed.

She landed on her back and bounced on her soft mattress. Her breasts bounced. He watched them with heated eyes. For a moment, she was certain he was going to join her, stripping off her clothes and his before thrusting into her. But he didn't.

She told herself she shouldn't be so deeply disappointed that he walked away. Her mind might be buying the argument that he'd done the right thing, but her body was still on heightened hormone alert.

She grabbed her laptop and wrote a scorching sex

scene for Nicki while silently admitting the irony of the fact that her fictional character was getting more erotic satisfaction than Sierra was.

Time flew by as Sierra entered the world she'd created. Her cell phone chimed, reminding her that it was time to get dressed for the interview.

She chose a black V-neck sweater and tailored black pants. The gray color of the labradorite beads on her necklace shimmered with shades of blue as the light hit it. Her hair fell onto her shoulders, behaving for once instead of sticking out in all directions. She'd carefully applied her makeup, ending with her extravagant purchase of red Chanel lipstick. She only used it on special occasions.

She turned from the bathroom mirror to find Ruby watching her.

"Remember. Behave," Sierra told the ghost. "No funny stuff."

"I promise. Cross my heart and hope to . . . um . . . fly?"

"No flying."

"Why not?" Ruby said. "You're the only one who can see me."

"Because you'll distract me. I can't be looking over the reporter's shoulder or in the other direction while he's interviewing me. Just go wherever you go when you disappear."

Sierra was going to ask where that was but the knock on the front door had her rushing out of the bedroom into the hallway.

"That's him. How do I look?" Sierra asked Ruby.

But it was Ronan who answered. "You look great."
He reached out and rubbed a few strands of hair between his fingers. "I love this color."

"It's my natural color," she said.

"I know."

She wanted to ask how he knew but kept her mouth
shut. He lowered his hand to his side. "You better answer the door," he said.

Turning the doorknob, she pasted a smile on her
face and greeted the reporter, who was in his thirties as
was the woman standing beside him. They were both
blond, and had athletic builds and overly generous
smiles. He wore horn-rimmed glasses while she had
her long hair tied back in a ponytail.

"This is my photographer," Bob said. "She's also my
wife, but that's not why she got the job."

"I was a photographer for the paper before we got
married," she said. Putting out her hand, she added,
"I'm a freelancer now. My name is Mary, by the way."

Sierra noted the other woman's strong grip and her
interest in the house as they stepped inside.

"This house dates back to the early nineteen hundreds, right?" Mary asked.

"That's right."

Mary turned to look in the living room.

"Much of the furniture came with the house," Sierra
explained as she ushered them into the room.

"This is beautiful." Mary's attention was focused
on the sideboard. "It's a Liberty and Company English
Arts and Crafts piece."

"Are you interested in antiques?" Sierra asked.

"I'm a fan of *Antiques Roadshow*," Mary said. "And

I do love Arts and Crafts items like this. The bullet glass on the top doors is original. The entire piece is in excellent condition. "

Now that she was looking at it closely, Sierra had to agree. "I like it." Okay, so she hadn't really noticed it much until now but she'd been distracted by a naked vampire and demanding ghosts.

"I understand you inherited this house from your grandfather," Bob said.

"My great-uncle, actually."

"Did you visit him here as a kid?"

"No. I didn't actually see the house until I walked into it a few days ago. Please sit down." She gestured to the couch.

Bob sat on one end and Mary on the other, leaving Sierra to sit in the middle.

"Do you mind if I record our interview?" Bob asked. "It's standard procedure."

Sierra's previous interviews had been via e-mail or Skype.

Bob held up his smartphone.

"Okay," Sierra said.

He nodded his approval. "You write about ghosts. Your first three books feature Nicki Champion, ghost hunter. Your publicist told me your latest book continues Nicki's story, is that right?"

"Yes. She has a new case to solve."

"A new haunting to solve?"

Sierra nodded. "Right."

"I don't know if you've heard that legend has it that this house is haunted."

"I had heard that rumor, yes."

"Have you sensed any ghosts here?"

She sidestepped the question by saying, "I write fiction."

"I realize that. But how much of your fiction is autobiographical?"

"Some of it."

"Care to give me some examples?"

"Nicki doesn't have roots. She moves around a lot. So did I," Sierra said.

"What about now? Are you ready to put down roots here in Chicago?"

"For the time being, yes."

"You didn't answer about sensing ghosts in this house."

"That's right. I didn't."

"Are you refusing to answer on the grounds you might incriminate yourself?" Bob teased her.

"I'm not in court." Her laugh sounded nervous even to her own ears.

"I'm sensing a spirit presence," Mary said. Pointing to the sideboard, she said, "Over there."

Sierra looked but saw nothing. Was that where Ruby went when she disappeared? Into the sideboard? How weird was that? Perhaps not that weird, given the goings-on of the past twenty-four hours.

"I don't want to brag but I do have a sixth sense about these things," Mary was saying. "Do you mind if I take a photo of the sideboard?" She snapped it with her digital camera before Sierra could protest. Looking down at the image, Mary made a face. "Damn. I was hoping for an orb of light indicating a spirit."

"I don't know why she'd see any orbs since there

aren't any spirits over there," Ruby said from the other side of the room. "Relax. She can't see me."

Go away, she mouthed to Ruby.

"There is definitely a spirit in this room." Mary looked around.

"She may feel the connection because she's a descendant of one of the previous owners," Bob said. "Maybe you've heard of him? Hal Bergerstock. He was rumored to be one of Capone's crime bosses."

There was no rumor about it.

"Tell me about him," Sierra said.

"He died before I was born," Mary said. "But my mom told me about him. He came from her side of the family. She remembered him puffing on his cigar as he played cards with his buddies. He'd slip her a hundred-dollar bill sometimes just to make her laugh while he was playing. He was incredibly generous that way. And he was very protective of his family and the business."

"By business, you mean the Chicago outfit," Sierra said. "The Mob, in other words."

"Those were different times. Prohibition was a big mistake." As Mary went on a mini-rant, Sierra wondered if this was the real reason Bob and Mary were sitting on her couch. This wasn't about her books. It was about Hal.

"People still tell me how generous he was. A big tipper. The young son of the mechanic who took care of their fleet of cars needed an operation that they couldn't afford so Hal paid for it."

The sounds of Swedish House Mafia's "Don't You Worry Child" suddenly filled the room.

"I write to this song," Sierra yelled over the high volume of the song.

"A little loud, isn't it?" Mary yelled back.

The music stopped as suddenly as it started.

"How do you explain that?" Mary asked suspiciously.

"I have a defective iPhone docking system. The music goes off and on intermittently. I need to take it in to be fixed."

The overhead light above the dining table flickered off and on.

"I've got an electrician coming to fix that," Sierra said.

"You do know that these are all signs of a haunting, right?" Bob said.

"Just because I write about ghosts doesn't mean I live in a haunted house." Sierra eyed Bob and Mary suspiciously. "Is that why you came here? About the house? Not me?"

"About both," Mary said.

She felt used. But since they were here, she might as well return the favor and use them right back. "What do you know about this place?"

"I gathered a file." Mary opened her smartphone.

"E-mail me what you've got," Sierra said, getting up to grab her own phone and confirming that Mary sent the file. After quickly skimming through the info, Sierra asked, "What about the murder of one of the girls who worked here?"

Mary frowned. "I didn't find any reference to that. But I'm sure we'd get more answers if we held a séance. I've done them before and gotten answers from the other side. Not that I've ever held one here in this house. At least not yet."

Sierra wasn't eager to stir things up any more than they already were. "I'm not sure . . ."

"Come on. I'm sure you've attended séances before, right? For research, I mean."

"Actually, no I haven't." She didn't want to be present when spirits were called forth. She had enough trouble dealing with the ones who just showed up on their own. She didn't want to go looking for trouble.

"Then this would be a great opportunity for you," Mary said. "Do you have any candles?"

"I . . . um . . ."

"Oh look. Here are some on top of the fireplace mantel. It's like fate placed them there for us. To do this right, we need a fourth person," Mary said. "Another man would be great."

"What's going on?" Ronan demanded as he joined them in the living room.

"We're preparing to do a séance," Mary said.

"Who the hell are you?" Ronan said.

Sierra put a hand on Ronan's arm, to prevent him from doing what, she wasn't sure. Flashing his fangs at them or something. "Mary is the photographer who came with Bob the reporter doing a story on me."

"And you are?" Bob asked in his best reporter's voice.

"Ronan is a friend of mine," Sierra said. Turning to face Ronan, she added, "Mary is Bob's wife and photographer. She says she's a descendant of Hal who lived here during the Capone years and that she's done séances before." Staring into his eyes, she tried to add the visual message *Don't do anything you'll regret.* Ronan could read her mind supposedly. So why wasn't her message getting through? Unless he was deliberately ignoring her.

She could tell that he was not responding to her look, no compelling talent on her part obviously, so she whispered, "They may be able to help you reach your sister."

"Or they could be fakes." His voice was so soft she wasn't sure if he actually spoke or if she somehow read his mind. She tried really hard to hear what else he was thinking but nothing came across.

"I've never been to a séance before." Ruby was excited. "Maybe they'll all be able to see me." She fluffed her hair. "How do I look?" She frowned down at her corset. "I wish I was wearing more than this. You know, I did own some of the most divine gowns straight from Paris. There was this one pleated silk Fortuny dress that was the palest peach color. I adored that dress."

"Normally I'd use the dining table but it's too large for us to sit around and hold hands," Mary said. "I think if we move the four chairs into a circle in front of the fireplace, that should be fine."

Sierra didn't know how fine it was going to be. She had a scowling vampire and a fashionista *Great Gatsby* ghost to deal with before things even got started.

"Sierra, you sit here. Ronan, you can sit beside her and I'll sit beside you and then Bob fills the fourth chair. But before we take our seats, let's move this small end table into the center. Okay, now we'll put the candles on it. Light them." She pulled a lighter from her bag. "Turn off the lamp. There." The flickering candlelight provided a mellow yellow old-time illumination. "Great. Now, we take our seats." She reached for her camera.

Ronan reached for her.

Sierra reached for Ronan.

Bob and Ruby were the only ones standing still.

Ronan turned Mary to face him. Looking deep into her eyes, he said, "No photographs,"

Sierra recognized that he was using his compelling voice.

"No photographs," Mary repeated in a monotone before setting her expensive camera back down.

"Continue the séance," Ronan said.

"I will continue the séance," Mary said.

"Right," Bob said. "Let's get this party started."

Sierra sat down and grabbed hold of Ronan's hand. She squeezed it hard as a warning to behave. He responded by rubbing his thumb over the sensitive web of skin between her thumb and index finger.

OMG that felt good! His movement instantly brought back the memory of her sliding her fingers through his hair. Now as then, she licked her lips but she really wanted to lick his—his lips, his skin, his everything.

Damn this vampire-bond shit. She was getting hot and damp again.

Mary took hold of Ronan's other hand, filling Sierra with jealousy. Okay, this was getting out of hand. As in his hands should only be touching hers. Whoa. Stop right there, she silently ordered herself. Behave.

Bob took hold of Sierra's other hand, bringing her back to reality and the task at hand. Damn, there was that word again. *Hand.*

Right. Focus!

"Spirits, are you with us?" Mary said. "Make your presence known."

The fireplace suddenly came to life with a whoosh of flames.

"I sense you here, spirit," Mary said.

Ruby moved closer to Mary.

"You're an old soul," Mary murmured.

"Hey, I'm not that old," Ruby said, clearly offended.

"The spirit is that of a man," Mary said.

Now Ruby was really outraged. "Charlatan!"

"A man with a beard," Mary continued.

"I do have a beard, but I'm not a man," a new voice said.

Sierra took a cautious look over Bob's shoulder. A heavyset woman stood here wearing circus garb. "I have a message for Bruce," she said.

"You're Mother," Sierra said.

Mary looked around. "Whose mother? I'm not sensing any mothers. Just a man with a beard."

"She's not very good at this," Mother said. "Maybe I should come back later. Bring Bruce." She disappeared as suddenly as she'd appeared.

"I sense a new presence entering the room," Mary said.

"Who was that bearded lady?" Ruby demanded. "And what was she doing coming into my house?"

Sierra sensed the dark malevolence of Hal's spirit. An instant later she smelled cigar smoke.

"Great-great-uncle Hal, is that you?" Mary asked.

His darkness faded as he looked at his descendant. *Supposed* descendant. For all Sierra knew, Mary could be lying through her teeth. But she could see Hal and not Ruby, so that had to mean something. Mary probably was related to the gangster ghost.

"How can I help you?" Mary said.

"Get rid of her." Hal pointed to Sierra.

"He's not happy that you're in his house," Mary said.

"No shit," Sierra muttered.

"Why haven't you crossed over?" Mary asked.

"Yeah, why haven't you?" Sierra said.

Mary looked at Sierra. "So you sense him too?"

Sierra just shrugged.

"He says he's protecting the treasure," Mary stated.

"He does?" Sierra said. She hadn't heard Hal say that.

"Maybe we can help you with the treasure," Mary suggested.

That's all it took for Hal's rage to return. He flipped the table over and sent the lit candles flying.

Chapter Fourteen

"Shit!" Sierra quickly stood as one of the lit candles almost landed in her lap.

"Shit!" Bob yelped as one of the candles *did* land on his lap and his wife slapped his crotch to douse the flames.

"That was illuminating," Ronan said.

"This séance is over," Sierra said.

"The séance may be over but not the interview," Bob said.

"You only wanted to interview me to get into this house. It was just an excuse."

"I was just trying to get information about my great-great-uncle Hal's life," Mary said.

"Information about his treasure, you mean. Do you even know what it's supposed to be?"

"Not the specifics, no. But family legend has it that it is worth a great deal of money."

Legends occasionally turned out to be true. Like legends about ghosts and vampires. "Did you really

think that you could just stroll in here and make contact with your ancestor's spirit and get a bunch of loot?"
Sierra said.

"Of course not," Mary said.

"I thought it was worth a try," Bob admitted.

"So what was your plan? To have Hal tell you where
it is and then break into my house later?"

"No," Mary vehemently denied. "We were going to
share it with you."

"Share what?"

"The treasure."

"Which consists of what?"

"Valuables. Lots of valuables."

"I think it's best if you leave now," Sierra said.

"You don't want me writing a bad story about you,
do you?" Bob said.

"I don't think your employer would appreciate you
threatening to trash me in your article."

"It would be your word against mine," he said.

"No it wouldn't," Ronan said in a deadly voice.

Uh-oh. Do not piss off the vampire. She put her
hand on Ronan's arm in an attempt to restrain him.
Right, like she'd have the strength to hold him back if
he went full vamp on them. And then there was the fact
that whenever she touched him, she wanted him—even
more than she craved Godiva dark chocolate truffles
when she was writing the end of a book on deadline and
that was saying a lot.

Instead of flashing those impressive fangs of his,
Ronan looked deeply into Bob's eyes. "Sit down."

He did.

Then Ronan gazed into Mary's eyes. "Sit."

She did.

"Tell me everything you know about this treasure."

Sierra looked around, expecting Hal to throw something at them like furniture or something. But the ghost must have used up his energy for the time being.

"There might be a map," Mary said. "We don't know where. My grandmother remembered stories about a map. Her sister didn't."

"Is there a key?" Ronan asked.

"To the map?"

"To the treasure," Ronan said.

Mary shook her head. "I don't know anything about a key. Maybe the map leads you to a key and the key unlocks the treasure box? I don't know."

"The treasure is in a box? Is it money?" Ronan demanded. "Gems? Gold bars?"

"I don't know," Mary said in a monotone.

Ronan returned his attention to Bob. "You will write a glowing story for your paper about S. J. Brennan and her books. You will not return to her house or bother her again. You will no longer believe Hal's treasure is real."

Bob nodded as if in a trance.

So this was compulsion. Sierra could see how that ability would come in handy.

"Hal's treasure is not real. You will not return to Sierra's house or bother her," Ronan told Mary. "Now you and Bob will leave."

Sierra didn't say a word until they were gone. The way her luck had been going lately she might just somehow knock them out of their vampire trance or something if she spoke up.

But the minute the door closed after them, she said, "Wow, that really works. I mean, I've seen it on TV, but never for real. When will it wear off?"

"It doesn't."

"Not ever?"

"They're human. They don't have forever."

"They . . . um . . . they really were human, right? I mean, you can tell if they weren't? If they were vampires, I mean."

"I can tell, yes. They were human. Compulsion wouldn't have worked on them otherwise."

A knock at the front door made Sierra jump.

"Relax," Ronan said. "They aren't coming back." He opened the door. "It's Bruce."

"I saw the reporters leave," Bruce said. "How did the photo shoot go?" He nodded his approval of her outfit. "I told you that black would look good on you with your coloring. Of course, the fashion pundits are saying that this season is all about color. Red and orange are supposed to be hot, although not necessarily worn together."

"I think your bearded lady came to the séance today," Sierra said.

"Mother was here?" Bruce looked around eagerly. "Is she here now?"

"No."

"I didn't know you were going to hold a séance today," Bruce said in a hurt voice.

"I didn't know either. It was kind of a spur-of-the-moment thing," Sierra explained.

He looked at the chairs and the candles. "It looks

like you still have everything set up. We could reconnect with Mother."

"Not right now. I'm too drained," Sierra said. "Maybe later."

"Sure." He sighed and gave her a sad puppy-dog look. "I understand."

She felt guilty and might have given in had Ronan not hustled Bruce out.

"So now we know why Hal is eager to get rid of me and why he's hung around for so long," Sierra said when Ronan returned to the living room.

"It could just be an urban legend like the treasure in Al Capone's safe."

"Maybe it's tied to your story," Sierra suggested.

He shook his head.

"How can you be sure?"

"I can't," he admitted.

Personally she found it hard to believe that there were two supposed treasures in this house. Although all Ronan had said about his missing item was that it was a key. But it could be a key to a hidden safe holding a treasure. Hal's treasure.

Consisting of what? She doubted the angry ghost would reveal any details about his treasure, like what it consisted of. Cash? Gold bars? Those would be worth a nice sum given the way the price of gold had skyrocketed in the past decade.

But gold bars were heavy. Okay, maybe gold coins. Oh wait, hadn't there been a story about a rare Liberty silver-dollar coin worth three million dollars? Maybe the treasure consisted of rare coins?

Her head was spinning with all the possibilities. How could she find out more? Google, here she came.

Too bad that Mary didn't have more information on what the family legend was about the missing treasure. Maybe Ruby knew something.

"Did you know that Hal had a treasure?" Sierra asked her once the two of them were alone in Sierra's bedroom.

Ruby shook her head. "How was I supposed to know? He doesn't confide in me. That woman could have been lying about being related to him. Maybe she made the whole thing up."

"It would explain why he stays here and why he is so adamant about getting rid of everyone."

"You can't get sidetracked by Hal. Just get rid of him, that's all I asked."

"It's not that easy," Sierra said.

"Hal has kicked your vampire's butt," Ruby said.

"He has not!"

Ruby just smirked.

"How did you know Ronan's sister's name?" Sierra demanded.

"He must have mentioned her at one time."

"Do you know her?"

"Not unless she worked here. Hah!" Ruby pointed her finger in Sierra's face. "I saw that look. A nice girl would never work in a brothel, huh?"

"I never said that." She had thought it a couple of times, though.

"The look on your face said it all."

"Adele died in 1919."

"They had brothels back then."

Sierra ignored that comment. "Did she ever haunt this house?"

"How should I know? I never believed in ghosts until I became one. I still find it hard to understand sometimes," Ruby admitted.

"Are you able to reach other spirits outside of this house?"

"No. Are you?" Ruby countered.

"Apparently so. That's how Mother showed up."

"You invited her in. Without asking my permission, by the way."

"I was trying to help Ronan," Sierra said.

"Help me first. Get rid of Hal first. Then I will help you find Ronan's sister. If you take Hal's treasure from him, then he has no reason to stay."

"Can he hear us talking like this?" Sierra asked.

"I'm not sensing him right now. Are you?"

Sierra shook her head. "I need more information. I don't even know what I'm looking for."

She spent the next few hours on the Internet, researching Hal, his affiliation with the Chicago Mob, and this house. Doing so prevented her from thinking about the vampire bond she shared with Ronan. His wound had healed with supernatural speed. Hers hadn't. Staring down at the cut on her arm, she wondered how such a small thing as a drop of her blood could cause such a change in her circumstances.

Right. Like the fact that Ronan was a vampire hadn't been the biggest change of all.

All those around her acted as if it was no big deal to

be a vampire. Maybe it wasn't if you'd been one for decades and decades.

She tried to focus on getting some pages written on her book.

> *Nicki sensed someone was following her. Shit. She didn't need this. She'd already had a hell of a day going to the hospital to see Bernie's wife, who was still in intensive care and sedated.*
>
> *Nicki had seen someone suspicious loitering around the waiting room. He had a shaved head with swastikas on it. She asked the attendant, who admitted that she didn't know who he was and that he'd only asked about Bernie's wife but was not listed as family. The young man had run out before Nicki could catch him.*
>
> *She was now on a Chicago street in a neighborhood known for trouble. She'd gotten a tip that her runaway young man was from this area. Bending down, she reached for the knife in her boot. Turning, she confronted him.*
>
> *"You brought a knife to a gunfight," he mocked her.*
>
> *"Yeah, I did," she drawled before shooting him in the kneecap.*

Sierra paused. Maybe Nicki shouldn't shoot the guy before she even knew who he was. She hit the delete button and tried again.

> *"Yeah, I did," she drawled. "What's your connection to Bernie and his wife?"*

Sierra paused again. She really should come up with a name for poor Bernie's wife but she had yet to find one that really fit. Okay, she could fill that in later. Keep writing.

> *Skinhead said, "My name is xxx."*

Sierra couldn't think of Skinhead's name either. She used *xxx* as a place holder to fill in later. Forget the name. She hit delete.

> *Skinhead waved his gun at her. "You don't get to ask questions, bitch."*
> *Pissed off, Nicki shot him in the kneecap and both legs and arms.*

Hold on. Sierra just remembered she hadn't even given Nicki a gun in this scene. She had a knife. Besides, Nicki shouldn't go around shooting suspects before interrogating them. Not good even for a first rough draft.

Time for a break, Sierra decided. Clearly this scene wasn't going well and she wasn't thinking straight. So she headed for the kitchen. She needed some chocolate chocolate-chip ice cream. *Now.*

Grabbing the carton from the freezer, she removed the lid and reached for a spoon, dug it into the ice cream and stuck it in her mouth. Yummm.

Dark, sinfully delicious . . . which immediately brought Ronan to mind. Those dark eyes of his reminded her of chocolate. They could go even darker with passion. Were all vampires as hot as he was?

Damon and Nick were good-looking, granted, but they did not have the power that Ronan did.

"You were thinking about vampires," Ronan said, appearing suddenly behind her.

She whirled to face him, holding fast to her spoon and dessert. "How do you know that?"

"A lucky guess."

"You're lying." She thumped her hand still holding the empty spoon against her chest. "Yep, you're lying. I can tell. It wasn't a lucky guess."

He remained silent.

She stared at his mouth, wondering what lie he would fabricate next. Then she wondered how he'd learned to kiss so incredibly well. Was that a talent he'd had as a human or one he'd learned as a vampire? Had he had a lot of women before and after? Where had he learned those tongue moves?

"I don't kiss and tell," he said.

Shit. He really *could* read her mind!

"Stop doing that," she said. "Stop reading my mind. Or I won't help you."

His expression instantly darkened. "Don't threaten me."

"Then don't invade my mind."

He ducked as a plate flew from the cabinet at his head. "Tell your ghost to stop doing that." He grabbed it before it fell onto the floor.

"She's not my ghost."

"Why does she keep trying to decapitate me with dinnerware?"

"She wants me to focus on helping her before she'll help us."

"Maybe we don't need her help. Maybe you can reach my sister another way."

"Hmmm." Sierra thought about it a moment, taking the time to eat a few more huge spoonfuls of ice cream. "There may be a way." She set the frozen dessert back in the freezer and headed to her bedroom. "Follow me."

Ronan did, so closely that she almost ran into him when she grabbed what she was looking for and turned to exit the room.

"Careful." He put his hands out to steady her.

She instantly felt the connection between them heat up. She wondered if she could read his thoughts. Looking into his dark brown eyes, she saw hunger there. Hunger for her or her blood?

For *you*.

Did he really think that or was it just wishful thinking on her part? She hated to think she was the only one consumed with these feelings, this incredibly strong need. Had the vampire bond merely built on what she'd already been experiencing from the moment she'd walked into this house? She had no answers here. Only questions. A lot of questions. And a lot of aching, pulsing desire to have sex with him for days on end.

Maybe she wasn't lacking the slutty gene after all. Ronan certainly brought out her inner slut.

But it wasn't real, right? This was a temporary condition and she would revert to normal . . . when they had sex. Okay, then. She'd freak out and yank him into her bed if she didn't focus her thoughts elsewhere, like on the vintage wooden Ouija board she had in her hand.

Pulling free, she hurried to the living room and set it

on the table. She moved aside a few magazines and put the pointer on the wooden board before sitting on the couch.

"Put your fingertips on it the same way I am," she told Ronan as he sat down beside her.

"My fingers are bigger than yours."

Naturally his comment made her think about his other body parts. "Don't say a word." She was rather pleased with the way that order came out. She sounded like Nicki.

She eyed Ronan, but he wisely remained silent. She just hoped he hadn't been butting into her thoughts about his body parts a second ago or about having sex with him for days on end. The dispassionate expression on his face revealed nothing aside from the fact that he was good at keeping his thoughts to himself.

"Spirits, are you with us?" she said.

"Don't push the pointer," she warned Ronan. "Just let it move where it wants to go."

The pointer headed to the YES section on the top corner of the board.

"We want to speak to Adele McCoy," Sierra said.

The pointer circled aimlessly.

"Are you Adele?" Sierra asked.

The pointer moved to NO.

"Do you know Adele?"

More aimless movements until it eventually went to YES.

"Did you do that?" she asked Ronan.

"I don't think so," he said.

"Maybe you being a vampire is giving the board a weird vibe."

The pointer quickly moved to YES.

Ronan yanked his fingers away. "Do it yourself then."

"I'm not sure I can," Sierra said.

"I can't believe you've never used one of these before."

"Not with a vampire."

"You should know all this stuff," Ronan said impatiently. "You write paranormal novels, whatever the hell that means."

"It means things that aren't normal."

"Like vampires."

"There are no vampires in my books. Only ghosts. Yes, I did some research on vampires in case I wanted to include them at some point in the future, but I certainly didn't go around interviewing them."

"Obviously. We don't do interviews," he said.

"And apparently you don't do Ouija boards either." At her comment the pointer moved on its own, heading toward the *Cosmopolitan* magazine on the table beside it. "Oral Sex. Yes or No?" the heading screamed out in bold letters.

The pointer rushed back to the board and YES.

"Great," Sierra muttered. "We've gotten in touch with a perv on the other side."

"You don't like oral sex?" Ronan said.

"I can't believe you're asking me that."

"I can't believe you don't like it." His voice was like rough velvet.

She was speechless. La-la-la. Do not think about it. Do not envision it. Do not imagine Ronan getting her horizontal on the couch, removing her clothes and spreading her legs. Do not picture him lowering his head and practicing his dark magic on her down there with those bold tongue thrusts and erotic kisses. Do not want it. Stop, stop, stop!

As if on cue, the Ouija board flew across the room straight into the fireplace.

"Good thing there was no fire going." A second later, flames filled the fireplace.

Sierra made a grab for the board before leaning back and letting it burn. She could buy another vintage one on eBay. She needed her fingers to write. She needed a clear mind to write. She needed to stop having hot fantasies about Ronan. She also needed to rein in her wayward ghost buddy.

Looking around the room, she tried to locate Ruby. "That was uncalled-for," she said.

No answer.

Ruby was probably pouting. Which meant this might be a good time to try to reach another spirit. Or not. One séance and one burned Ouija board was enough for one day.

Sierra ended up working late into the night, editing four chapters that were still in draft form. Then she checked her e-mail and found one from her lawyer. *We'll talk when I get back,* was all it said.

He wasn't scheduled to return for over a week. By then, Ronan's deadline would have passed. She didn't want to think about what would happen to him if he didn't find the key he needed.

She clicked on the next e-mail, which was from her energetic publicist Katie. *How did the interview go?*

"It ended with a séance that led to a burning Ouija board," she muttered as she typed the lie: "It went fine."

She looked up to find Ronan standing in the doorway. "Bruce called. He wondered if you could do your thing tomorrow at Zoe's house?"

It took her a moment to translate what *thing* was, but then realized he was referring to a séance. Given the fact that they didn't know what Hal could hear, it was probably best to say as little about such things as possible.

"I guess that would be okay," she said.

"Would ten in the morning work?"

She nodded.

"Vampires don't need much sleep," he said abruptly.

Since she had no idea where this conversation was going she remained silent, waiting for him to elaborate.

"So I'll be watching out for you," he said.

She didn't reply.

"So you can sleep in peace."

Right. How could she not sleep like a baby given the fact that a hot, sexy vampire would be watching out for her? What the hell did that even mean?

"It means you can go to bed safe in the knowledge that you are being looked after," he said.

"Do you plan on tucking me in?" She meant for the words to come out sarcastically, but they sounded more like an invitation.

"If you want me to."

"I want this to be over," she said in frustration.

"You can't want that more than I do."

Slamming her laptop shut, she marched over to her bed, grabbed a pillow, and threw it at him. "Stay in that chair. Do not get any ideas about taking advantage of this situation."

He easily caught the pillow.

An hour later, Sierra tossed and turned in her bed. She'd put on a baggy T-shirt and flannel pj bottoms that she sometimes worked in. She was in the dark but unable to fall asleep. Normally she'd turn on a light and read on her iPad. But she didn't want to do that. Turning the light on would make Ronan's presence in the room more evident. In the dark, she could pretend he wasn't really in the corner.

Yeah, right. She could pretend all she wanted but the fact remained that she *wanted* him. And he knew it. Not being able to have sex with him made her want it even more. Did he feel the same way?

She desperately needed to think of something else. Like what she would post on Facebook the next day. Her author page usually had several daily posts to keep her readers interested. Yeah, she'd think about that . . . and all she came up with were images of Naked Ronan.

An hour later, she was still wide awake. She couldn't take it any more. She flipped on the bedside lamp.

"Something wrong?" Ronan asked in that deep, rough voice of his.

For once, she wished he could compel her . . . compel her to fall asleep.

"I'm too tired to sleep," she muttered. "How can you just sit there in the dark doing nothing?"

"I like the dark. And I wasn't doing nothing. I was reviewing what we know about the situation and the possibilities."

"Hal may have heard us talking about it in the living room earlier," she said.

"Which is why I'm here with you. No one is going to hurt you," he said in a steely voice. "I'll make sure of it."

Sierra looked down at her arm, where her wound was healing nicely. Hal had already drawn first blood. And Ronan was a vampire who consumed blood. Ronan hadn't told her where he was getting his food source. She assumed it came from the bar she'd seen near the cupcake shop. She wasn't sure she wanted to know any details beyond that.

Those images really weren't conducive to pleasant dreams.

"Go to sleep," he said in what she recognized to be his compelling voice. At least he hadn't come closer to look deep into her eyes or she would have been a goner. She would have looped her arms around his neck and tugged him down onto the bed beside her. Then she would have ripped off his clothes and licked her way from his chiseled cheekbones to his chiseled abs. Where was all this licking coming from? She'd never had those thoughts before.

Sighing, she turned off the light and willed herself to sleep. Her last conscious thought was, *Why did life have to be so complicated?* Falling for a vampire went far beyond complicated and entered the realm of . . . She drifted off before she could come up with the right word to complete that sentence.

Chapter Fifteen

"You can't leave this house!" Ruby had plastered herself against the front door again the next morning.

Sierra paused while fastening her coat. "I'm just going next door to Zoe's house."

"How do I know you'll come back?" Ruby demanded.

"Because I've got this stupid bond thing going with Ronan and I can't be far from him." Sierra had a headache. She really didn't need ghostly trouble this morning. She'd barely gotten five hours of sleep last night. The good news was that Hal hadn't thrown any more furniture or objects at her. The bad news was that Sierra had vividly hot dreams about sex with Ronan that always stopped right before she could reach a climax.

"Is Ronan going with you to Zoe's house?" Ruby said.

"Yes."

"Then the two of you could leave me here and never come back."

"All my stuff is here," Sierra said.

"You already tried to take off once."

"Not without my laptop and my laptop is here."

"You could have backed it up to the cloud," Ruby said.

Sierra stared at her in amazement. "What do you know about the cloud?"

"Not much," Ruby muttered. "I've just seen on your laptop that you are able to do that."

Sierra was stumped. She didn't know how to reassure a panicky ghost that she would return. Not because she really wanted to come back to this cosmic chaos, but because she had to, thanks to Ronan.

Okay, maybe it wasn't fair of her to blame him. He hadn't deliberately forged that blood bond with her. Or so everyone kept telling her.

"What are you going to do over at Zoe's house anyway?" Ruby asked suspiciously,

"What are you, my mother?" Sierra said in irritation.

"You sound guilty."

Sierra shoved her hair away from her face. "I do not."

"And you look guilty too."

"That's not guilt, it is exhaustion," Sierra said. "I didn't sleep very well."

"Afraid Hal might throw more furniture at you?"

"No, Ronan stayed with me."

"I know." Ruby smirked.

"Then why did you ask?"

"To see if you'd lie to me."

Ronan showed up behind Sierra. She sensed him there before she saw him. Was that something new? A new ability she'd developed since the blood bond thing? She was already trying to deal with the reading-her-thoughts stuff. Surely dreams didn't count, right? No way was he able to view her dreams of last night. That was her opinion on the matter and she was sticking to it.

"We're going to be late," he said.

"For what?" Ruby yelled in his right ear.

Ronan instantly slashed out with his right arm, so fast his movements were a blur.

Ruby yelped as his arm went clear through her image.

Ronan remained on guard, eyeing his surroundings with lethal intensity, ready for battle.

"Ruby doesn't want me leaving the house," Sierra told him. "That was her screaming in your ear, by the way."

"I thought it might be Hal, ready to toss something else our way," Ronan said.

"That's why we have to leave the house temporarily," Sierra said.

"Because you're afraid of Hal?" Ruby said.

"No, because this is the best way to move forward and achieve our goals." Sierra was deliberately being vague. She didn't want Hal overhearing their plans. Not that she was sure what their plans were specifically, other than to hold another séance to contact Bruce's friend. Oh, and presumably to see if they could reach Adele as well.

"Swear on your mother's grave that you'll come back today," Ruby demanded.

"I can't swear on my mother's grave that I'll come back today," Sierra said. "My mother is still alive."

"Swear on your father's grave—"

"I hated my father." Her voice was cold.

Ronan realized this was the first time Sierra had talked about her family. He'd told her about his but she had not shared her past history with him. Not that he could blame her. He was a vampire, not the first thing that came to mind under the heading of a good confidant.

He tried to access her thoughts and was hit with a wave of two powerful emotions—fear and anger.

He saw the hazy image of a burly man threatening a woman and hitting her with his fists. Then he saw that woman, her eyes blackened and her lips swollen from a beating, holding the hand of a little red-haired girl.

"Where are we going, Mommy?"

"Shhh."

"Wait. I want to bring Boo with me." She pointed to the worn and tattered teddy bear on the bed. The man had his arm over it as he snored.

"No time," her mother whispered. *"I'll get you another one."*

Once they were outside, Sierra had tears running down her cheeks and was about to turn back when her mom grabbed her by the shoulders. "He is going to hurt us! We have to be quiet and fast. We can't go back. Ever!"

Sierra was silent but her tears continued to trickle down her pale cheeks. He'll hurt Boo if we leave him. But she obeyed her mom and left her beloved bear behind.

Ronan could feel her pain. He knew she'd confided in that bear, whispered her fears to it in the night, and hugged it when she'd needed reassurance. Boo had been more than just a stuffed toy. He'd represented comfort and safety.

She'd lost that and had never quite regained it again. Ronan hated the fact that once again a dangerous bully was threatening Sierra. The need to protect her from Hal and any other threats, which had already been great, increased with a fierceness that burned deeply in his gut.

She abruptly turned to face him. "What are you doing?"

"Nothing."

"You're lying. I can tell, remember?" She glared at him. "So now you know why I hated my father."

Ronan nodded.

"Isn't it enough that you've tied me to you with bonds I can't break? Do you have to invade my last bits of privacy as well?"

Ronan didn't know what to say so he kept quiet.

"I want you to swear on your sister's soul that you will stop reading my mind unless I give you permission to do so."

"And have him swear he'll bring you back while he's at it," Ruby said.

Sierra repeated Ruby's words.

"I swear I'll bring Sierra back," Ronan said. He couldn't swear not to read Sierra's mind because doing so might end up saving her life. He was already reeling at how quickly Sierra had messed up his mind. After spending the night watching over her, he was more intrigued than ever.

He hadn't been able to view her dreams while she

slept, but he'd heard her little moans, which had sounded like they were inspired by pleasure not fear. She'd tossed and turned a lot after that, loosening the sheet and blanket to reveal her bare shoulder where the huge T-shirt had slid off.

She had the pale skin of a natural redhead. He already knew how soft she was to the touch, how warm, how responsive. And he knew how smart she was, how creative. He'd read her books last night, all three so far in the series. And he'd been impressed by how much of herself she put in them. The heroine, Nicki, had all the power and always won in the end. He suspected that came from the little five-year-old who had been forced to leave her teddy bear behind and flee into the night. No one was ever going to bully her again.

Yet here he was, forcing her to stay, inadvertently bonding her to him. Yes, he wanted her as much as she wanted him. He'd been hard-pressed not to go to her and caress every inch of her body. He'd been hard, period.

But he was fighting for his afterlife here. For his sister's soul. No way should he even be thinking about sex with Sierra. He needed to stay strong and resist temptation. Maybe they'd be able to reach Adele at the séance today and he could learn more about her situation.

He held the door open for Sierra. "Let's go." His voice was brusque.

She wisely obeyed and didn't bring up his mind-reading abilities again.

"Thank you for offering us the use of your house," Sierra said as they entered the premises next door.

"You're welcome," Zoe said. "Bruce and Pat are already here, waiting for you."

"Let's do this," Bruce said eagerly.

"You're sure Hal can't leave the house?" Pat asked.

"As sure as I can be about any of this," Sierra replied.

"How sure is that?" Bruce asked.

"Ninety-five percent," she said.

"What do we do if he does show up?" Bruce said.

"Duck," Sierra said.

"Vampires don't duck," Ronan said. "We fight."

Sierra ignored his comment. Instead she told Bruce, "I can't guarantee that your friend will show up again."

"I know," Bruce said. "But she showed up before, so that's a good sign."

Ronan tugged Sierra aside as the others set up four chairs in a circle. "What about your father?"

"What about him?" she said curtly.

"Does having this séance put you at risk of his spirit showing up?"

He could tell by the look on her face that this wasn't the first time the possibility had occurred to her. "It's been my experience that once the evil have gone to hell, there is no further contact available to them."

"We don't have to do this," he said gruffly.

"I sense that Bruce's friend has something very important she needs to share."

"We can stop if it gets to be too much," Ronan told her.

Sierra was still angry that Ronan had invaded her thoughts earlier. It was one thing to be bonded to him physically, but it was quite another to be invaded in such a personal way. She felt as if there was nowhere she could go to have some privacy or freedom, which left her feeling jittery and unsafe.

And that was what had brought the memory of her father back to the forefront of her mind. She'd managed to squelch those fears since his death. Yes, occasionally something would happen to trigger a reaction of panic. Overall, she'd refused to let her life be ruled by that. Until she'd had the misfortune to get hooked up to a vampire.

"Would it throw things off if my grandmother and I joined the séance or should we just watch?" Zoe asked.

Sierra said, "Is your grandmother . . . ?"

"A witch?" an older woman asked as she joined them. She had white hair and vivid blue eyes and was wearing a flowing caftan. She looked like Betty White's twin sister. "Yes, I'm a witch. I'm Irma Adams and you must be our new next-door neighbor I've heard so much about."

"Um, nice to meet you," Sierra said. She was still trying to get used to this supernatural world she'd inadvertently moved into.

"Well, can we join the party?" Irma asked.

"I honestly don't know," Sierra said. "I haven't held many séances and never with, um . . ."

"Vampires and witches?" Irma supplied helpfully.

"I participated in the séance yesterday," Ronan reminded Sierra.

"Zoe, maybe you and your grandmother should sit this one out," Bruce suggested. "Let's see what happens with three vampires and a medium."

"I'm not a medium," Sierra said.

"She's an entity empath," Ronan said. "That's why she can't be compelled."

"We can't be compelled because we're witches," Zoe said as she handed Sierra a candle.

Sierra sat between Bruce and Pat. That way she didn't have to hold Ronan's hand and be distracted. The look he shot her let her know that he was aware of her move.

"I brought a photo of her," Bruce said. "In case that might help." He set it on the table near the candle then touched Mother's face with his trembling index finger. "Parting is such sweet sorrow." At Sierra's surprised look, he got defensive. "What? You don't think a clown should know Shakespeare? Mother had me read all his plays." He looked down at the crisp blue shirt he wore. "Too dressy, or not enough?"

Sierra squeezed his hand reassuringly. "You look fine."

"I want her to be proud."

Shit. Those words hit Sierra hard and took her back to a milestone moment in her past. She'd been in third grade and the school was having a Father/Daughter Day. Sierra didn't have a father. They usually told people that he was already dead before his actual death.

But on that particular day, Sierra had seen how the other girls had reacted. So she'd asked her mom that evening, "Why did he hate me?"

"Who?"

"My father. Was I bad? Carla told me that her dad is proud of her because she got an A on a test yesterday. Was my father ever proud of me?"

"I'm proud of you," her mother had said fiercely

before gathering her in a tight hug. "Very proud of you. Always. Never doubt that. And you were never bad. *He* was."

"Sierra?" Bruce said.

"Let's get started," she said gruffly. "We need to hold hands."

Bruce took her right hand and Pat her left. She was surprised to find that both had cooler skin than Ronan.

"Spirits, are you with us?" Sierra said.

Unlike in her house, she didn't sense any strong residential spirits here. Maybe the witches kept them away. Sierra had no idea about the relationship between ghosts and witches. She couldn't think about that now. She had to focus.

"Spirits, are you with us?" she repeated.

Nothing.

"Mother?" Bruce said aloud. "Are you here?"

"I'm here." She showed up as she had the day before, dressed in circus garb in patriotic red, white, and blue. Her beard was dark brown as was her hair.

"She's here," Sierra said.

"Tell him to talk fast, I don't have a lot of time," Mother said.

"She wants you to talk fast," Sierra told Bruce.

"I don't know where to start." He sounded nervous. "I wrote a speech with everything I wanted to tell you, but it's in my shirt pocket and I'm afraid to let go of your hand, Sierra."

"Just tell her what you're feeling," Sierra suggested gently.

"I wanted to thank you for everything you did for

me, Mother," he said in a rush. "I'm a vampire now. Maybe not what you envisioned for me. But I've found happiness with Pat here. I'm . . . I'm . . . I miss you. You were gone so quickly that I never had the chance to say how grateful I am and how much I love you."

"I always knew," Mother said.

Sierra repeated her words.

"I hate that you died alone," Bruce said. His eyes had the glimmer of dampness. "I should have been with you. We were going to watch a movie together. If I'd been there and we'd gone out to the movie theater, I might have been able to save you."

Sierra could feel Bruce's fingers trembling in her clasp and the emotion in his voice was evident.

"My time was up," Mother said bluntly.

"She said her time was up," Sierra relayed.

Bruce shook his head, as if unable to accept that. "Are you okay, Mother?" he said. "Do you need anything?"

"I need you to move on with your life," Mother replied. Her expression softened. "And I loved you, too. You were a good kid." She turned to look over her shoulder. "I have to go now."

Her image was fading. "Wait," Sierra said. "Do you know Adele McCoy?"

Mother shook her head. "But I know of Hal. You'll find what you're looking for in his grave." Then she was gone.

"What? Did she need anything?" Bruce said.

"She wants you to move on with your life," Sierra said, still surprised by Mother's final words about Hal.

"What about Adele?" Ronan said.

"She didn't know her."

"Can't you try to reach Adele the way you did for Bruce?" Ronan said.

Sierra knew how desperately he wanted to reach his sister, so she tried to do so. "Spirits, are you with us? I'm looking for Adele McCoy."

Instead of a luminescent ghost, Sierra saw the dark image of something dangerous. Evil incarnate. She was so startled that she released Bruce's and Pat's hands and leaned back in her chair as far as she could go.

The entity disappeared as quickly as it had appeared. It hadn't been Hal. She had no idea who it was and she really didn't want to know. She hadn't seen features or anything other than the overwhelming aura of malevolence.

"What's wrong?" Ronan demanded. "What did you see?"

Before Sierra could answer, the front door flew open and Daniella rushed in. "Danger and death. It's coming!"

Chapter Sixteen

"Danger and death?" Zoe repeated. "But we're all immortal. Except for . . ."

They all turned to look at Sierra.

"What's going on?" she asked suspiciously. That image of evil she'd seen had spooked her and she didn't spook easily.

"I'm not immortal," Daniella said.

"Just about," Zoe said.

Which left Sierra wondering how you could be "just about" immortal?

"Daniella is a hybrid. She's part druid," Zoe explained. "So she gets premonitions sometimes. She and Nick are a couple. Yes, Nick is a vampire as well, in case you were wondering. But you probably already figured that out."

Would it never end? Was no one normal around here?

"My premonition wasn't about me or about Nick," Daniella said. "It was about someone in this room."

Once again all eyes turned to Sierra.

Enough already. Sierra wanted out. She leaped to her feet and nearly stumbled over the cat Bella.

"Watch it!" Bella growled. A talking cat. Of course. Why not?

"Let's not panic," Zoe said. "Daniella's premonitions aren't always what they seem."

"That's true," Daniella said. "The last one I had warned that Damon and Zoe shouldn't have sex or Vamptown would go up in flames. Clearly that didn't happen. Although there were flames involved and fire hazards. Never mind, that's not relevant now."

Sierra sat down again. She had to. There was no escape. She was tied to Ronan as surely as if he had her bound with a rope or chains. How convenient for him. How dangerous for her.

She wanted Ronan to read her mind so she opened her thoughts and let them pour out in his direction. She let him know how much she hated this, how deeply she resented it.

She could tell by the set of his jaw that he'd received the message loud and clear.

"I saw ghosts and headstones and graves," Daniella said with a shiver.

"Maybe that's because we had a séance here," Zoe said. "Bruce was able to communicate with Mother."

"Not directly," Bruce said. "Sierra communicated with her."

"How do you know that really happened?" Bella the cat said. "I'm just asking."

"Why would I lie?" Sierra said. Then something else came to her. "Mother said you were a good kid, Bruce."

"I never told you that." Bruce's eyes welled up. "She used to say that to me. She really was here. I told you so." His last words were directed at the talking cat.

Sierra was still concerned about that fleeting image of evil. What was that about? Did Daniella's premonition have something to do with that appearance? Sierra had never experienced anything like it before.

No way was Sierra doing any more séances. This was it. Things were getting too messed up.

"Save me," a voice whispered.

Sierra looked around, expecting to find Mother even though this woman's voice sounded very different. She didn't see anything but she detected a sense of desperation along with the smell of lilies of the valley. Zoe was a soap maker. Perhaps the scent came from one of her soaps? Sierra remembered someone telling her that Zoe had a workroom in the apartment upstairs.

But why smell the floral scent now? Then she saw her. Adele. Barely there. Very weak. With eyes that broke Sierra's heart. They were Ronan's eyes. And they were pools of desolation.

Ronan was at Sierra's side in an instant. "Where is she?"

"We're working on it." She directed her words to Adele. "What can you tell me?"

"Nothing."

Sierra saw the look of terror on Adele's face before the spirit glanced over her shoulder. Then she was gone.

Ronan was frantic.

Sierra could tell that he'd seen what she had in this particular case.

"What's going on?" Zoe asked. "Who is Adele?"

"Ronan's sister," Sierra said. "She died in the flu pandemic of 1919."

"I'm sorry to hear that," Zoe said.

"Parting is indeed such sweet sorrow," Bruce said.

"Parting is shit," Ronan growled.

"Maybe Daniella's premonition had something to do with Adele's death," Zoe suggested.

"Or Mother's," Bruce said. "What do you think, Sierra?"

She thought she was going to go mad if she didn't leave.

"You. Me. Outside now," Ronan told Sierra.

She barely had time to grab her coat.

Once in front of their house, he started questioning her. "Why could I see her? Why couldn't I hear her?"

"I don't know. You didn't see Ruby earlier. So it can't be because of our bond or you'd see other ghosts that I see. That means it must be because of your ties to Adele. She's your sister. Your family. Your blood."

"Not my blood any longer." His voice was gritty with emotion.

"What do you mean?"

"My blood is vampire blood," he said curtly. "Just tell me what my sister said."

"I asked what she could tell me. I figured you didn't want me asking what she knew about a key so I just asked her what she could tell me. Her answer was that she could tell me nothing."

"I saw the terror on her face."

"We may have a clue," Sierra said quickly. "Mother told me that she knew of Hal and that we'd find what

we're looking for in his grave. He's buried in a cemetery a few miles from here. You could go there."

"*We* could go there. And we will."

The earlier empathetic Ronan who said they could
end the séance if it got to be too much for her was gone,
replaced by a furious vampire willing to do whatever it
took to free his sister.

"I'm not into cemeteries," she said.

"You prefer mausoleums?"

She didn't appreciate his sarcastic question. "No."

"You deal with the afterlife all the time. Yet you
claim this bothers you?"

"*All the time* is an exaggeration," she said.

"You do write about it."

"That doesn't mean I want to live it."

She recognized the look on his face. He'd had it
when she'd first arrived and he'd bellowed at her to
leave. Back then she'd bellowed right back at him. So
what was different now?

First, there was the fact that he drank blood and had
fangs. And then there was the fact that they shared this
damn vampire bond. But it was the other look on his
face, the tortured remorse when he'd viewed Adele's
terror, that grabbed hold of Sierra like a fist to her heart.

Adele's terror haunted Sierra as well. Ruby had shown
anger and various other emotions, including fear, but
not the abject horror that Adele had displayed. Sierra
couldn't put it out of her mind.

Did it make her feel better to think she was volun-
tarily going to a place filled with thousands of spirits,
many of them unhappy if not downright dangerous?

No. Because this wasn't voluntary. Free will had disappeared the moment a drop of her blood had blended with his.

She wanted to show her anger. She wanted to rant and rave. So she did . . . a little.

"I hate this," she shouted.

"So do I," he shouted back at her before regaining control. "We'll go to the cemetery as soon as it's dark."

"You came back!" Ruby joyously proclaimed the instant Sierra entered the house.

Since Ronan had seen Adele, Sierra needed to confirm her suspicion that that had happened because Adele was his sister. "Do you see Ruby right now?" Sierra asked Ronan.

He shook his head.

"You already know he can't see me. Why would that change? What did you do next door?" Ruby demanded suspiciously.

"We visited with our neighbors," Sierra said.

"You're wasting time. If you don't get rid of Hal soon, I'll be doomed," Ruby said with a dramatic hand to her forehead.

"Yeah, right," Sierra said.

Ruby stood a little straighter. "No shit. Really. It has to happen by Valentine's Day."

"What are you talking about?"

"I was murdered on Valentine's Day. I told you that."

"You never mentioned that you had that as a deadline," Sierra said.

"I thought I did."

"No, I know for a fact that you did not."

"Because I thought you could get rid of Hal quickly," Ruby said. "You're a ghost hunter—"

"I'm an author writing about a ghost hunter," Sierra corrected her.

"You see ghosts."

"Trust me, I wish I didn't."

"Too late. You can still do this, right?" Ruby floated after Sierra, following her into her bedroom. "You need to step on it though. No more dillydallying."

Sierra sat down and wrote out a flow chart like she did for her writing. The problem with that was that she wasn't a plot writer. She was a "pantster." She wrote by the seat of her pants, hence the name. It was as if she was walking in a thick mist. She saw just enough of the story ahead of her to keep going but not clearly enough to anticipate everything that might happen. It's what kept it fresh for her.

So she wrote what she already knew about Ruby and Hal. Just the facts as they'd been told to her. Ruby was murdered by Hal because she wanted to stop being a prostitute. Hal stayed in the house because of his treasure, whatever the hell that was. Ruby was stuck in the house because she wanted vengeance against Hal. She wanted the dark spirits to take him away. So did Sierra.

"What was your life like before you got into this line of work?" Sierra asked Ruby.

"Poor. Very poor."

"So you became a prostitute for the money?"

"What other reason could there be?" Ruby said.

"Did you grow up in Chicago?"

"Yes."

"What about your parents?"

"They died of the flu when I was twelve."

"In 1919?" Sierra asked.

Ruby nodded.

"When did you come to this house?"

"I used to walk by it on my way from the tenement to church. Hal didn't own it then, I don't think."

Could she somehow have passed by when Adele died? Sierra wondered. The odds were completely against that, probably one in a billion. Was there a connection between Ruby and Sierra's family? "When did your parents die? What day and month?"

Ruby gave her the info. Sierra checked the city's death records. Adele had died the day before. While she was at it, Sierra checked the property records for the house to see who owned it after Adele's death. The house was purchased by Gregori Dimitrov and then was sold to Hal in 1923.

Dimitrov was a new name in this puzzle. Did he have something to do with the key Ronan was seeking?

Sierra's great-uncle's father purchased the house in 1930 at bargain-basement prices because of the Depression. Did the key have something to do with her own family?

"You're a redhead. I thought you'd get mad more often," Ruby said out of the blue.

"My hair is auburn." Sierra felt like pulling her hair out in frustration.

"Which means red. What's the big deal?"

"I'm sick of people using me for their own purposes." Sierra got up and started pacing around her bedroom.

"What people?"

"You're right. I didn't mean people. I meant ghosts and vampires using me," Sierra clarified.

Ruby shrugged. "Only the strong survive."

"You survive to drive other people mad."

"That's not what I meant by thinking you'd get mad more often. I meant angry."

"I am angry. Can't you tell?"

Ruby squinted at her. "Not quite."

Sunset was fast approaching, which meant that the time to leave for the cemetery was coming. Sierra switched on the overhead light and wished her emotions weren't so conflicted about this entire mess. She hated the fact that Ronan could order her around. She hated the fact that one kiss from him turned her into a sex maniac. Yet she respected his loyalty to his sister.

She had to stop letting her emotions get the best of her. She needed to view this entire thing as research for future books. Not that she'd tell anyone about Vamptown or reveal its presence in her writing.

"You wouldn't be able to," Ronan said as he stood in the doorway.

"Wouldn't be able to what?" Sierra said.

"Tell anyone about Vamptown."

Damn. He was reading her mind again. "Why not? Because of the vampire bond between us?"

"Because I compelled you while you slept."

"No you didn't. I still know about Vamptown. And I'm an entity empath. I can't be compelled. You said so yourself earlier today," Sierra reminded him.

"Normally that would be true."

"As if there is anything normal about any of this," Sierra muttered.

"Agreed."

Nerves nearly closed her throat, making it hard for her to swallow or speak. "What did you do?"

"Prevented you from speaking or writing about Vamptown. The only exceptions are the nonhuman residents of Vamptown. You are still able to talk to them about it."

"Is this why I have had a headache all day? Because you messed with my mind?" Her nerves were now laced with a huge dose of anger. "What exactly did you do?"

"Don't panic. I didn't touch you."

Okay, she could tell that much was true.

"Not that I didn't want to," he added.

Also true.

"What about my dreams?" Sierra demanded. "Could you read them like my thoughts?"

"No. All I did was focus my mind-reading abilities on a certain frequency . . ."

"What am I? A radio?"

Ronan ignored her snarky comment. "Pat e-mailed me the specific instructions last night while you slept."

Was that why the oldest vampire had been so quiet during the séance today? He had a guilty conscience. Yeah, right. Like vampires had a conscience.

"Otherwise you'd be a security risk," Ronan said. "Trust me, you do not want to be a risk of any kind to a vampire, or in this case an entire clan of vampires."

"How do you know whatever you did even worked?"

Ronan pointed to her laptop. "Go ahead. Try to e-mail someone about Vamptown."

"Okay. I will." She sat down and entered her publicist Katie's name.

You'll never believe this but my house in Chicago is surrounded by an enclave of

Sierra hit the keys for *vampire* but nothing showed up on her screen.

Men with

She typed *fangs* but that didn't show up

They drink

Blood refused to appear on the screen too.

She was so aggravated that she hit the send button by mistake. Shit.

Katie, being the efficient professional that she was, e-mailed her back.

You are surrounded by men with what? Are you in danger?

She tried to type *yes* but that didn't work either.

She turned in her seat to confront Ronan. "I write for a living. You are stealing words from me!"

"Only if you try to use them to reveal our presence. You better e-mail your friend before she calls the police and Alex has to come out. He went easy on you the first time. He won't be that nice this time."

I'm fine, she typed. *Dealing with an ass of a character in the book.*

Glad to hear you are ok. You just got another great review for your summer book. Here's the link. Check it out, Katie wrote.

Ronan closed her laptop. "There's no more time," he said. "We need to leave now."

Sierra was so angry she could hardly see straight.

Which wasn't helping anything. She needed to regain control. Taking several deep breaths helped. "How are we supposed to get there?"

He held up a set of keys. "I borrowed Zoe's car."

Sierra snatched the keys out of his hand. "I'm driving."

If she couldn't control the situation, at least she could control Zoe's Mini Cooper.

Sierra heard the voices before she got out of the car. They weren't human voices.

Pointing to the closed gates blocking the cemetery entrance, she said, "It's after hours. The place is closed. How are we supposed to get in?"

"Simple." Ronan took her in his arms and leaped over the high wrought-iron fence as if it were nothing more than a mere speed bump.

Setting her back on her feet, he looked around. "Which way to Hal's grave?"

Normally Ronan's supernatural vault would have thrown her but she was distracted by the surge of voices filling her head, getting louder with every word. She was infused with cold. Not normal February-in-Chicago cold but ridiculous, the-surface-of-Neptune cold. Rubbing her hands together didn't help.

"I told them I wanted a musical note on my headstone," one ghost complained.

"At least you got a headstone. Mine is falling over," another said.

She could hear them but didn't see them as clearly as she did Ruby or Hal. Instead these were more vague shapes and images that would come and go. A head here, a body there. Totally *Sleepy Hollow*.

"What's wrong now?" Ronan demanded.

"There are a lot of spirits here." And they were making themselves known. "It's hard to focus."

"Try harder. Pretend you're doing research for your book. As long as it doesn't involve vampires or Vamptown, your characters could have sex in a cemetery."

"Nicki would never have sex in a cemetery," Sierra said. "She's much too classy for that."

"I read your books. She's not that classy."

"Yes she is!" Sierra's teeth were starting to chatter. There was no point arguing with Ronan. She brought out her trusty flashlight. A strange mist was rising from the ground all around them. Angels wept atop headstones at an angle befitting the Leaning Tower of Pisa. Sierra had always wanted to go to Italy someday. Now she just wanted to get out of this cemetery.

Sierra shrieked and her heart almost jumped out of her chest as her flashlight beam picked up a face staring at her. It wasn't a ghost. It was Tanya.

"What are you two doing in a cemetery?" Tanya asked. "Is this research for your next book?"

"What are you doing here?" Sierra asked shakily.

"Following you, but I got lost along the way. So fill me in," Tanya said. "Why are we here?"

"Research," Sierra said.

Tanya nodded and clutched her faux-fur coat closer. "I knew it. Tell me what we're looking for."

"Hal Bergerstock's grave." Sierra had found a photo of Hal's headstone in the material Mary Nolan had shared under pressure.

"Want me to dig it up for you?" Tanya offered eagerly.

"No!" Sierra emphatically shook her head. "The grave should be this way." She squinted in the increasing misty fog, trying to read the names on the headstones they passed. So intently was she focused that she almost ran right into Damon, who suddenly stood in front of her, appearing out of nowhere.

"What the hell is going on here?" Damon demanded.

"We're digging up Hal's grave," Tanya said cheerfully. "We could use some help."

Damon shot a dark look at Sierra. "Was this your idea?"

"Uh." She wasn't sure how to answer that one. "How did you know we were here?"

"We monitor unusual activity in all the area cemeteries," Damon said.

"In case of a zombie uprising or something?" Sierra asked.

"Or something." Damon turned to Ronan. "Would you care to make a comment here?"

"No." Ronan's eyes gleamed with an unnatural light.

"I suppose you're going to tell me there's no need for concern, right?"

"Right," Ronan said.

"And I should trust an indentured vampire because?" Damon said.

Since Ronan stubbornly remained silent, Sierra spoke up. "Because he's telling the truth."

"He hasn't said anything," Damon pointed out. "If you make trouble, I swear—"

"Don't swear in a cemetery." Tanya looked around nervously. "It's bad luck."

Tanya wasn't the only nervous one. Sierra was sensing several dark presences growing in power. The fog was rapidly increasing, billowing up and separating her from the sparring vampires.

Sierra felt as if she were being pulled far away. She was suddenly alone. She swayed and had to reach for a nearby heart-shaped headstone for support. Because standing right before her was her worst nightmare—her father.

Chapter Seventeen

"I told you I'd come after you," her father said, his voice reptilian.

Stunned, Sierra dropped her flashlight. Her heart skittered in fear as she watched it roll over a grave before coming to a halt against a headstone.

ROY BARNES.

She could see the letters clearly even without artificial illumination. Leaning down, she quickly scooped up the flashlight and cradled it against her body the way she had cradled Boo as a kid. Once she realized what she was doing, she aimed the flashlight at Roy.

From the top of his buzz-cut shorn head to his size twelve construction boots, he looked the way she remembered him—big and mean. They said he'd had his heart attack during a bar fight and died on the spot. He sure as hell looked ready to do battle right now.

"You don't scare me," she said.

"Liar."

His accusation, while true, hit her the wrong way,

firing up her anger. "Bully," she shot back. "Shit-faced bastard!"

"That's no way to talk to your father," he roared.

"You're not my father. You never were. You provided sperm, that's all. Nothing else. Not support, not kindness. Certainly not love."

"I supported you and your bitch of a mother for five years."

"You beat and intimidated us."

"What do you know?" he scoffed. "You were just a kid."

"I know enough." She eyed him with extreme suspicion. "I thought spirits in hell couldn't return to this world."

"Apparently they can if you stand in their cemetery dealing with other spirits and prying open caskets," he mocked her.

She'd had enough. "You aren't welcome here. So go back to that hellhole you crawled out of."

He laughed. He had the gall to actually laugh.

"Go!" she bellowed at him. "Begone!"

He drifted closer.

Sierra felt frozen in place. She refused to back down. Evil spirits like him fed on fear. Even as a human, he'd fed on fear. So she displayed none.

Her showdown with him continued for a moment or two before he started to waver in front of her, then slowly dematerialized. Like the Cheshire cat, only his face remained visible, his eyes glaring at her with vicious intent. Finally that too was gone.

She almost sank to the ground in relief.

"Sierra! Where are you? Come back," Ronan cried out.

The mist cleared, allowing her to find her way back to Ronan and his vampire friends. They stood beside the casket they'd just dug up.

Seeing the disapproval on Sierra's face, Ronan said, "It's the only way to get rid of Hal."

Sierra was still trying to recover from her confrontation with her father. She certainly didn't need to be staring inside a casket at a putrid pile of bones covered in maggots. She'd seen enough horror movies to know the risks here.

Dizziness threatened to overcome her. The sheer number of spirits nearby was nearly overwhelming. She took several steps back from the open gaping hole in the ground, suddenly terrified that she was going to either fall in or be yanked into it.

"Open it!" Tanya said eagerly.

Sierra shut her eyes. She couldn't bear to look.

"What the hell?" Ronan's voice was rough with disbelief.

"It's empty," Tanya said.

Sierra cracked her eyes open a smidge. "No body?"

"No body," Ronan confirmed grimly.

"So this was a dead end, no pun intended," Damon drawled.

"Then where is Hal's body?" Sierra asked.

"Why do we care?" Tanya asked. "Is this for your next book? It must be, right? If you're going to mention my assistance in the acknowledgments, please make sure you spell my name correctly."

"Nobody is going to be listed in any book," Damon said emphatically.

"You've had a thing against books since that incident with Zoe," Tanya said.

"What do we do now?" Sierra asked.

"We keep checking." Ronan felt along the satin padding.

"Hal's body won't fit in the padding," Tanya said.

Sierra knew he was looking for a key or something to indicate the location of the treasure that Hal was so fiercely protecting.

"Sierra and I can wrap things up from here," Ronan assured Damon. "We won't be long."

Damon looked down at his cell phone. "Good. Because I'm needed elsewhere."

"I'm not," Tanya said.

"Yes you are." Damon took Tanya by the arm and the two of them departed with vamp speed.

As Ronan quickly checked the lining of the coffin, Sierra was distracted by another spirit nearby. He was a young man wearing dark pants and a white shirt. She could see him clearly. His dark hair was slicked back in the style of the twenties.

"Have you seen Ruby?" he asked.

Sierra nodded. Going on a hunch, she asked, "Are you Johnny?"

The ghost nodded. "I've been waiting for her. Why is she still at the house? I can't go there."

Sierra didn't know how long she'd have with Johnny. His energy was fading quickly. Unlike Ruby, he wasn't accustomed to materializing.

"Did you kill Hal? Do you know where his body is?

What do you know about the treasure?" Sierra asked in a rush.

But Johnny was gone.

"Another ghost?" Ronan asked.

Sierra nodded.

"I found something." Ronan held up a piece of paper and quickly studied it before putting it in his pocket.

"What is it?"

"I'll tell you later. First I've got to return the casket to its grave." He did so with amazing ease and speed.

"It still looks like a fresh grave," Sierra said.

An instant later, it was covered with grass as it had been before. Ronan looked down at his smartphone where a beep indicated a new text. "Damon asked Zoe to return the grave site to the way it was."

"So not only does Zoe lend us her car, she cleans up our mess again," Sierra said. "Talk about a nice neighbor." She paused at the sudden strong smell of cigar smoke. "Hal?" she whispered, looking around.

The surrounding ghosts had faded away, replaced by a man wearing a stylish and expensive-looking suit. He had dark hair and a narrow weasel-like face with sunken eyes of an indeterminate color. He gave her the creeps and that was saying a lot considering what she'd already been through that night.

"I'm Baron Voz," he said.

Right. Of course he was. All the nightmare demons seemed to be coming out of the darkness in this cemetery. First she'd had a confrontation with her father and now here was this man who had turned Ronan.

"I see you know who I am," Voz said.

"And *what* you are," she said.

Voz shook his head. "Tsk-tsk, Ronan. You really should learn to keep your mouth shut."

Ronan instantly stepped in front of Sierra as he had when the clock and mirror had come flying at her. "Leave her alone."

"You bonded with her."

Ronan neither confirmed nor denied Voz's statement.

"You only have two days remaining to find the key," Voz said.

"It's not a fair agreement," Sierra said. "You didn't provide enough information. You've set Ronan up to fail."

The moment she said those last words, she knew it was a mistake. Ronan stiffened and anger radiated from him. He may actually have growled.

Voz laughed. "Even this weak human thinks you will fail."

"That's not an option," Ronan said.

"No, it's a foregone conclusion," Voz said. "You will fail and be indentured to me forever."

Sierra wanted to say that she would help Ronan, that he wasn't alone, but knew that wouldn't go over well so she kept silent.

"If you are still bonded with him when the deadline comes, then I get you too," Voz told Sierra. "Two for the price of one. Well done." Reading the fear on her face, he added, "Not feeling so smart now, are you? You should have run away the minute you saw Ronan in the house. But hey, it's your funeral. One of the lines from your book, I believe?" Voz mocked. He tugged on his cuff. "Not that I read that kind of pulp fiction."

If Sierra wasn't so scared, she'd be really pissed right now. How dare he insult her work. As soon as she could breathe, she was going to tell him a thing or two. He disappeared before she could do so.

Ronan instantly turned to face her. "I had no idea."

"He insulted my book!"

"Forget that. You are at risk because of me."

"I was already at risk from Hal."

"Hal is a flea compared to Voz."

"Okay, that might be a bit of an exaggeration." Looking at the spirits regathering all around, watching them, she said, "Let's get out of here."

The spirits moved forward.

"Don't even think of following us," she warned them. "This guy is a vampire and he doesn't like ghosts."

Ronan bared his fangs and the place cleared out. Except for Johnny. His image was weak but his voice was strong. "Tell Ruby I love her."

Sierra remained quiet for most of the drive home. Ronan was so tall he barely fit in Zoe's red Mini. She doubted he even had a license. No way was she letting him drive. At least that had been her intention until they'd gotten to the car and her hands shook so badly she couldn't open the damn door.

So here she was being driven by a surly vampire back to a home haunted by violent ghosts. What joy. Not.

Sierra was a mess. Confronting her father that way had taken more courage than she thought she possessed. And then she'd had to face Ronan's nemesis.

She'd let her defenses down once Ronan had assured her that he wasn't going to turn her into a vampire. The other vampires in Vamptown had backed up his claim and made a similar one themselves.

But they didn't know about Voz.

Finally she spoke up. "You need more help than I can give you," she said bluntly.

"I've got the map," Ronan told her. "I found it in the lining of the casket."

"Goody for you," she said sarcastically, angered by the way he'd ignored her comment.

"Don't you get it? This will lead me to the treasure and the key for Voz."

"How do you even know that the key is connected with Hal's treasure?" she said.

"It has to be. What are the odds of the house having two treasures?"

"About the same as the entire neighborhood being populated with vampires," she shot back.

Ronan was quiet for a few minutes. "Our vampire bond was an accident," he reminded her.

"Don't bother. I've heard it before." She drew a deep breath, fighting the urge to curl up into a fetal position. "Listen, the bottom line here is that you have to have your vampire friends help you with this because I am not joining your vampire gang."

"We aren't a gang. It's more like a clan—"

"I don't need to hear the details," she said as he parked in front of their house. "I am not going to become a vampire. I refuse to allow that to happen. End of discussion. Show me the map out here where Hal can't see us." She dug in her purse for her flashlight and aimed it at the piece of paper Ronan handed her.

She looked it over. It was drawn in dark ink with no

identifying information, such as "X marks the spot" or even north/south. "Something isn't right with this."

"What are you talking about?"

"It looks like it's been cut in half," she said.

Ronan swore as he took it from her and studied it himself.

"Are you sure the rest of it isn't still in that casket?" she said.

"Yes."

"Hal was probably too smart to put all his eggs in one basket or all his map pieces in one place. Although we still have no idea where his body actually is."

"Maybe that's where the rest of the map is. With his body."

"Well, you've got forty-eight hours to find it and the treasure. I don't have superhuman powers."

"You speak to the dead."

"And I yell at the undead!" she shouted at him. "It doesn't seem to be doing me any good." She'd been roped into this mess against her will. Her stomach rumbled with hunger pains. Maybe that was why she was so dizzy. "If I don't eat, I'm going to pass out," she said, getting out of the car.

Pulling out her smartphone, she ordered a deep-dish Chicago-style pizza with extra mushrooms. She had to change her order when she learned it would take an hour to make it and deliver. So she ordered a thin crust pizza instead.

As soon as she walked inside, she headed for the bathroom to take a shower and wash the cemetery dust off. "Do not talk to me for at least an hour," she warned Ruby before she slammed the door in the ghost's face.

She'd smudged the bathroom earlier with sage to prevent spirits from entering the room. The technique worked best in small spaces, so it wouldn't do for her bedroom. But she had to have one small iota of privacy. If she couldn't even pee without an audience then she was going to loose it completely.

Not that she wasn't already on the verge, teetering there. Tears ran down her cheeks as she stood under the shower, using some of the soap that Zoe had given her as a housewarming present before wondering if it was spelled. Hell, even the soap around here wasn't safe.

Muttering under her breath, she reached for her makeup kit, which had a small bar of soap from the last hotel she'd stayed in. That should be safe enough.

Okay, she had to calm down. She had to be logical.

But that was hard to do when wild thoughts kept zinging in her head. How could she be sure that her father wouldn't come after her? What if he'd followed her home from the cemetery? What if he joined forces with Hal to punish her?

This was playing out more like a horror movie by the minute.

And then there was the entire Voz thing, where he would turn her into a vampire if they didn't find the key in time. Unless Sierra was no longer bonded to Ronan. Which meant she had to have sex with him in the next forty-eight hours. Better make it sooner than that to be on the safe side.

Not that there was anything safe about having sex with a vampire. She was going to have to talk to Zoe and Daniella about that. She needed to get them alone, without Ronan being present. Or Hal.

She washed her hair and let the water sluice over her, rinsing away the bubbles but not her anxiety. Was that evil incarnate she'd sensed this morning after the séance at Zoe's house a manifestation of her father? Or did it represent Voz somehow? But Voz was a vampire, not a spirit.

Maybe evil was evil. It didn't matter what paranormal world it originated from. This was all new territory for her. Wondering what her heroine would do didn't help because Nicki had never had to deal with anything like this. Plus there was the fact that Nicki was a fictional character.

The lack of hot water made Sierra finally turn off the shower. She couldn't stay in there forever. After drying off, she tugged at the pile of clothes she'd grabbed on her way in—underwear and a soft microfleece top and pants in black.

She was finally starting to feel warm again after that incredible otherworldly cold in the cemetery. She quickly blow-dried her hair and then emerged, ready to welcome the pizza delivery guy.

He arrived a few moments later. She paid him and gave him a nice tip before closing the door and carrying her dinner to the dining room table.

The aroma made her mouth water. The sight of Ronan standing nearby wearing black pants and a soft black V-neck sweater also made her mouth water. There was something about a guy going SOS—sweater on skin. He'd apparently decided to clean up too after his time in the cemetery. His dark hair was still slightly damp and fell over his forehead.

Oh yeah. He definitely looked good enough to eat. And to lick. And to kiss and nibble.

He gave her a fiery yet cursory look and then headed for the wall where the built-in bookcase had been before Hal pulled it down. He started feeling the wall.

"What are you doing?" She stood next to him. Big mistake. Because the wall suddenly shifted and shoved them into a pitch-dark space.

Chapter Eighteen

"What did you do? Get us out of here!" Sierra demanded.

"This must be a hidden passage," Ronan said.

"Ya think?"

"You don't have to be sarcastic about it," he reprimanded her.

"My pizza is out there and I want it now."

Her eyes adjusted enough to the darkness that she could just barely make out Ruby, playing her tiny finger violin. "So you want your pizza. Tough tinsel. I want to head into the light. We all have problems."

"Do you know how to get out of here?" Sierra asked.

"No," Ronan said.

"Yes," Ruby said.

"Then get us out," Sierra told Ruby. "Or I won't tell you the message I got from Johnny."

"When did you see Johnny?" Ruby instantly demanded

"At the cemetery."

"Tell me what he said or I won't let you out," Ruby said.

Sierra had had enough of being bossed around by supernaturals for one night. Her mother had raised her not to use a certain four-letter word. So instead, Sierra gave Ruby the finger. "F you!"

"I'm guessing you are speaking to Ruby the ghost," Ronan said.

"Yes."

"How's that working out?" he asked.

"Not very well at the moment," Sierra admitted

"The two of you can fight it out later," Ronan said. "I don't have time to waste."

"Like I do?" Sierra retorted. "There's a pizza out there with my name on it." She sensed his movement. "Wait. Where are you going?"

"I'm going to see where this tunnel goes," Ronan said.

"You can come back another time to do that. Another time when you have a flashlight." Like the one she'd brought to the cemetery and dropped on her father's grave.

"I can see just fine in the dark," he said.

"He's a vampire, remember?" Ruby told Sierra. "But he shouldn't go exploring."

"Ruby doesn't want you exploring," Sierra told Ronan.

"You and the ghost can stay here then," he said.

"No way!" Sierra latched onto his arm.

"Afraid of the dark?" he drawled.

She had been temporarily when it had gradually occurred to her after her father's death that he might come to her. Seeing him at the cemetery tonight had shaken her to her core. So had seeing Voz. So while normally Sierra wasn't afraid of things that go bump in the night, this night was a little different.

When she didn't answer his question, Ronan put his arm around her and tucked her close against him. "You're safe with me," he said.

Was she safe? Really? He was a vampire. How safe was that? She had a vampire bond with him so every time he kissed her she wanted to have sex with him. Not just *want* as in *I want to lose a few pounds* but as in *I want to, need to, have to.* No way by any stretch of the imagination could that be safe.

No, it was more like spontaneous combustion. That's what it was.

Sierra should run in the opposite direction but she was locked in a secret tunnel with him in the dark. And she had that bond thing going on, meaning she was stuck on him like white on rice. She slid her arms around his waist and rested her head on his chest for a moment. She could hear his heartbeat. Slow and deliberate.

"I thought vampires didn't have a heart," she said.

"Who says I do?" Ronan countered.

She loved the way his voice rumbled through her. "I can hear your heart beating."

"We have organs. If you mean a heart that pumps blood, then yes, I have a heart."

"But you don't think you have a heart as in feelings?"

"No." His voice was curt.

She shifted so she could see his face. It was pitch-dark but her eyes had adjusted a bit. Ruby was illuminated so Sierra had been able to see her. But Ronan was a mystery.

"If you have no feelings then why did you agree to save your sister?" she said.

"I owe her that much."

"Loyalty is a feeling."

"I knew her before I was turned."

"So you're saying that since you were turned, you haven't had any feelings?"

"No." Now his voice was curt and cold.

Ronan was determined to ignore the way she cuddled against him. Why did she have to ask so many damn questions? Why couldn't she keep her mouth shut? Hell, why did she have to show up in the first place?

Because she was his key to communicating with the ghosts.

Shit! What if *she* was the key that Voz was talking about? What if the key was a person not a thing? His reaction was profound, twisting his gut and sending all his protective instincts into overdrive. Yes, Sierra asked questions and she got under his skin. But as much as he tried to deny it, she was *his* and he would die for her. The realization hit him like the proverbial ton of bricks. He would never allow her to die for him or to suffer because of him. She was already too much at risk as it was.

If Sierra was the key, no way was he turning her over to Voz. Never. No matter what the consequences might be.

He struggled to get his thoughts in order. His sire's proclamation at the cemetery tonight had thrown Ronan.

He knew some things about vampire bonds, but did not know that because of the bond Sierra would have to go with him if he was returned to being an indentured vampire.

She'd told Voz that the Master Vampire had set Ronan up to fail. Which made it sound like she didn't have much faith in him solving this mystery.

He tried to be logical. If Sierra was the key, then why hadn't Voz just taken her at the cemetery? Yes, Ronan would have fought viciously to the death to protect her, but Voz was the one entity in the world that was stronger than Ronan. Voz knew that as surely as Ronan did.

So it couldn't be Sierra. He heaved a sigh of relief. The mere thought of his redhead being touched by Voz had almost driven him over the edge.

But what if that "key" person was Ruby or even Hal? None of this made sense. They weren't people any longer. They were ghosts.

Just as he wasn't a person anymore. His days of dating in high school and college, of falling in and out of love, of wanting to follow in his father's footsteps and become a doctor were long gone. He'd lost his humanity in the war to end all wars. When he'd left this house, people were growing victory gardens and angry mobs were hanging effigies of the German kaiser. After completing boot camp, he'd gone on a transport ship with thousands of other guys. German subs prowled the Atlantic, sinking ships and threatening theirs.

They'd landed in France and were ordered to the front lines within days. He'd heard the horror stories about the conditions in the trenches, but nothing had prepared him for the reality. The deadly hail of shrapnel and high-explosive shells. Death also threatened from the German planes above, diving down so you could hear the wail of the propeller before dropping their bombs. Land mines littered the ground, ready to rip a soldier apart the instant it was detonated with a footstep.

He should have died then. Instead Voz had found him and dragged him away, draining Ronan's blood and replacing it with his own. The battles had continued long after any mortal wars ended. Ronan had killed countless vampires and some humans along the way. Going to that cemetery tonight had made that memory hit home. Vampires didn't get graves. They got even.

He was a vampire now.

Sierra had no intention of becoming a vampire. She'd been very blunt about her feelings on that issue.

She was allowed to have feelings. He wasn't.

Ronan switched his attention back to his surroundings. The darkness reminded him of the dungeon in Voz's castle. But he had no more time for those visceral memories. He needed to focus. The wall was brick and covered in cobwebs. He brushed them away. He'd need both hands for this.

"Stay here," he told Sierra, setting her a few feet behind him.

He should have known she wouldn't obey orders.

She hooked her hand in the waistband of his jeans. "Just making sure you don't take off and leave me here."

"I would never do that."

"Damn right you won't," she said. "Because I've got hold of you."

He didn't point out that if he moved at vamp speed, he could still take off and she wouldn't be able to do anything about it.

Instead he concentrated on the surface of the bricks, looking for one that might jut out or differ from the others. He quickly realized he could do this faster if he didn't have Sierra tethered to him. Maybe the best thing to do was to see where this passageway went. So he reached around for Sierra and once again tucked her against his side.

Looking ahead, he discovered that the floor seemed smooth up to the right-angle turn. When they turned the corner, they moved toward what he assumed was the back of the house where they reached a metal spiral staircase going down.

"Can you see anything?" he asked Sierra.

He watched her squint. "Not much."

"We're standing in front of a staircase." He put her hand on the metal railing.

She touched it briefly before yanking her hand away. "Someone died here!"

"What? Who?" he demanded.

"I don't know. I can't tell."

He listened for fear in her voice but instead heard frustration. "Are you going to be able to . . . never mind." He whisked her over his shoulder and moved down the steps at vamp speed before setting her back on her feet.

"What the hell was that?" she demanded.

"An expedient move," he replied.

"I could have managed those stairs on my own, thank you very much."

"You're welcome."

"I was being sarcastic."

"I know. Look at this." He pointed to something scratched onto the cement wall of the tunnel they were in before remembering she couldn't see in the dark the way he could. "It looks like part of the map. But not all of it."

"I can't see anything."

"That's okay."

"No it's not."

"Why? Are you sensing something?" he said.

"Yes, I'm sensing that I am losing patience with you."

"That's it? That's all?"

"My pizza is getting cold," she reminded him. "How long do you plan on keeping us locked up in here?"

A few feet ahead was a dead end. Ronan pushed on the wall and ended up knocking the bricks out. They tumbled onto the concrete floor.

"You could have done that upstairs," she said. "Are we in the basement?"

"Yes."

"Our basement?"

He was surprised at how her use of the word *our* got to him. As if they were a team, meant to be together.

"You're going to pay to have that fixed," she said.

Ronan didn't know how to fix this situation. He had to get that key.

He stepped over the pile of fallen bricks and helped her into the basement. He steadied her a moment before reaching for the light switch.

She blinked and shielded her eyes at the sudden influx of illumination. "So that was the tunnel system that runs under the house."

Ronan was no expert on the tunnels, but he knew that this particular branch hadn't been used in decades. He'd have to consult with Damon to see what he knew.

"I'm going upstairs to eat my pizza," she announced with a regal tilt of her head that made him want to kiss her.

He let her go. Because he knew that he wouldn't stop with just one kiss.

She'd no sooner left than Damon appeared. He eyed the demolished bricks. "First you're digging up coffins, now you're destroying walls."

"Did you know about that passageway?" Ronan asked. "It leads upstairs from the dining room down here."

"I was not aware of a passageway within the house. Only the bootlegging tunnels connecting Vamptown. Did you find anything interesting in the passageway?"

"Sierra said someone died on the staircase in there."

"You found a dead body?"

"No."

"A skeleton?"

"No. Sierra just had a feeling, that's all."

"And you care because?"

"It's my house."

"And you're awfully attached to it, aren't you?" Damon eyed him suspiciously. "Remember I told you that we keep surveillance on area cemeteries? I saw what went on."

Ronan remained silent. A hell of a lot had gone on in that cemetery.

"I saw Sierra talking to someone who wasn't there."

"There were a lot of spirits at that location," Ronan said.

"So you think that finding this missing treasure of Hal's will be enough to get rid of him?"

"If he doesn't kill us first."

"He's a ghost. What can he do?"

"He's already done plenty."

"Are you referring to the vampire bond between you and Sierra?"

Ronan nodded.

"And where does Voz fit into all this?"

Ronan remained silent.

"I saw him there in the cemetery with you for a moment before the feed mysteriously went dead."

"Thanks for enlisting Zoe's help with returning the grave site to its previous state," Ronan said.

"You're avoiding my question. What did Voz want?"

"He was just checking up on me."

"Why?"

"He wanted to make sure I was settling in here."

"Because he's a warm and fuzzy kind of Master Vampire, right?" Damon mocked.

"No." Ronan suspected that Damon was well aware of Voz's ruthless reputation.

"What then?"

"He has a hard time letting go."

"Obviously."

"What is Voz's connection to Hal?"

"None that I am aware of," Ronan answered honestly.

"That tat at the back of your neck did more than

make you able to tolerate sunlight, you know. It made you part of our clan," Damon said.

Ronan had been part of Voz's vampire gang—always a lesser being, never an equal. He'd never been part of a clan before. That didn't change the fact that he had to do this alone. He'd already involved Sierra in ways he'd never expected and now regretted.

"One way or another, this will all be over soon," Ronan said. "You have my word on that."

Ruby met Sierra at the top of the stairs. "I told you not to investigate that passageway."

Sierra walked past her, opened the pizza box, and stuffed a slice in her mouth. She gobbled it down in a few bites and reached for another piece.

"Are you listening to me?" Ruby demanded.

Sierra shook her head and kept eating.

When Ruby floated closer, she warned the ghost, "Do not mess with me. I am eating this damn pizza without anyone bothering me. I've had it. Do *you* hear me? I've had it with spirits and ghosts and vampires and everything! Now go away and let me eat in peace!"

Ruby didn't go away but she did allow Sierra to finish her dinner.

Sierra put the leftovers in the fridge.

Ruby sat on the kitchen counter, swinging her feet. For the first time, Sierra noticed the shoes she was wearing. They were black and had a shiny shoe clip on the vamp, which was fashionable in the twenties. But for the first time she noticed the heels, which were covered in colored rhinestones and glittered in the kitchen light.

"Have you been wearing those shoes all along?" Sierra asked.

Ruby looked at her footwear. "Yes."

"Are you sure?"

"Forget about my shoes. Tell me about Johnny. I've been patient."

"He said to tell you he still loves you."

Ruby burst into tears. At least that's what Sierra thought happened. She'd never actually seen a ghost cry before. It wasn't a pretty sight.

Not that Sierra should be judgmental about it. She was an ugly crier herself.

"He said he's waiting for you," Sierra added, hoping that might make Ruby feel better.

It did. "He is?" She just about beamed. "He's waiting for me?"

"That's what he said. He can't leave the cemetery to tell you himself."

Ruby jumped down from the counter and floated closer. "How did he look?"

Hmmm. How had he looked? He looked like a ghost. A pale and translucent ghost. "He had dark hair."

"And his eyes? He has the dreamiest eyes."

"Right."

"You didn't see his eyes?" Ruby demanded.

Sierra paused. She had no idea what color his eyes were.

"Did you really see him or are you just making this all up to shut me up?"

"Why would I do that?"

"To make me shut up. People are always trying to shut me up."

"Not Johnny though, right?"

"No." Ruby's voice softened. "Not Johnny. He'd listen to me and make me feel like I was the smartest girl in the world. No one had ever made me feel that way before."

Sierra could relate to that. No one had ever made her feel the way Ronan did. But most of that was because of the vampire bond connecting them.

Or was it? She'd been attracted to him before she even knew he was a vampire. Seeing him naked had certainly gotten her attention. He wasn't the first man she'd ever seen naked. Okay, he *was* the first vampire she'd ever seen naked. The first she'd ever seen clothed, for that matter.

Who was she kidding? She was falling for Ronan. Right. Falling? Wrong. She'd already fallen. Done and done. He was the one for her. She could be conflicted about it all she wanted, but it didn't change that basic fact.

That's why she was doing all this for him. Screw the vampire bond. She could only blame that for so long. But she'd keep blaming it for now because it made her feel less terrified that way.

"Why didn't you want us exploring the passageway?" Sierra asked. "Was it because of the spiral staircase?"

Ruby's pale face reflected her anxiety. "I don't want to talk about it."

"Someone died on that staircase," Sierra said. "Do you know who?"

Ruby shook her head vehemently.

"Had you ever been in the passageway before?"

"Maybe."

"Before or after you died?"

"Why does it matter?"

"I'm assuming Hal knew about the passageway?"

"Hal knows everything," Ruby muttered. "That's why he's so hard to get rid of."

"And don't you forget it, girlie," Hal said from the doorway to the dining room. He paused to take a puff of his cigar. "Where's your vampire watchdog?"

"Ronan is nearby so don't try anything," Sierra warned Hal.

"I'm right here," Ronan said. "What's going on?"

"Hal is here."

"I can tell. I can smell his cigar," Ronan said.

"Tell your sissy vampire dog to stay out of my tunnels," Hal said.

"He doesn't like us going into his tunnels and he wants us to stay out of them," Sierra said.

"You'll never get your hands on my treasure," Hal said. "I'll see you dead first!"

At his words, the lightbulbs in the kitchen ceiling fixture over their heads exploded.

Once again, Ronan shielded Sierra with his body even as he moved her with freaky fast speed. Slivers of glass rained down on the place where they'd stood a split second earlier. The sound of Hal's laughter filled the air before he was gone.

Chapter Nineteen

"Something happened," Ruby said.

"No shit," Sierra said. "Hal just went all Angry Birds on us." Seeing the confused look on both Ruby's and Ronan's faces, she muttered, "Never mind."

"We can't go in the basement anymore," Ruby said. "Hal and I. We can't go in the basement."

"Why not?"

"We don't know."

Sierra sure hoped it didn't have anything to do with the evil she'd sensed at the séance earlier. That's all she needed. Some mysterious terrible thing rising from the basement. What next? Zombies? Mummies? She sure as hell hoped not.

Her heroine Nicki would say, "Bring it on." Easy for her to say. She was a fictional character living in the world Sierra created. Sierra hadn't created this world of vampires and witches and ghosts. She just lived in it.

"I've had enough for one day," Sierra said. "I'm going to bed."

Ronan remained by her side as she marched into the bedroom and plopped on her bed. "I have a headache." An instant later she felt something cold clamp around her ankles. She tried to scoot back or sit up but whatever was holding her wouldn't let go. She was on the verge of screaming when the Bearded Lady appeared at the foot of her bed. "Let Bruce help you," she said.

"How?"

But she was already gone.

Damn. Why didn't any of these spirits hang around long enough to give specific instructions or directions instead of these vague one-liners?

"What's going on?" Ronan demanded.

"Mother showed up again. She said I should allow Bruce to help me."

"In what way?"

"She didn't say. She just grabbed my ankles to get my attention and then said that one line and disappeared."

"What is her connection to all this?" Ronan said.

"I have no idea. Aside from her connection to Bruce, I mean. She did give us that clue about Hal though. She'd heard of him."

"How?"

"She didn't say. Maybe he has a reputation among spirits? A bad reputation. What are you doing?" Sierra asked.

"Calling Bruce," Ronan said.

"Let me talk to him," Sierra said.

Ronan frowned. "Why?"

"Because I'm better at interviewing people than you are."

"Perhaps. But Bruce is a vampire not a person."

"I'm still better." She grabbed the phone from Ronan's hand. "Bruce, it's Sierra here. I was wondering if you could give me some more information about Mother. You were both in the circus, right? Where was it located?"

"It was a traveling circus," Bruce said. "We went all over. Mostly the Southern and Midwest states."

"What was the name of the circus?"

"Cirque Dimitrov," Bruce said.

"Wait a second. Gregori Dimitrov owned my house at one time. Before Hal and after Ronan's family."

"I knew he had a place up North, but I had no idea it was here."

"Was he a vampire?"

"No. His business partner, his brother Ivan, was a vampire. He's the one who turned me."

"He turned you but not his brother?"

"Ivan and Gregori had an argument shortly before Mother died. Gregori took off after that. We never saw him again."

"Is it possible Ivan turned Gregori and didn't tell anyone?"

"I doubt it. Ivan once told me that his brother wasn't worthy of being immortal. I was worthy because my act made Ivan laugh more than anyone else ever had. I didn't want to die the way Mother had so when he asked if I wanted to live forever, I said sure, why not. I may have been drunk at the time," Bruce admitted.

"I think it is more than just a coincidence that there is a connection between Gregori and this house and the circus and you and—"

"And the Romanovs," Bruce added helpfully. "That's

where they got the money to start the circus. They smuggled some of the Romanovs' treasure out of Russia after the revolution."

"What do you know about this treasure?"

"Not much. Only what I told you basically. Why? Do you think Gregori hid it in your house? Surely someone would have found it by now."

"Probably," Sierra said. "Thanks for your help."

"Pat might be able to provide you with more information but he's out of town and unavailable. He'll be back tomorrow. Shall I have him give you a call?" Bruce said.

"Yes, thanks."

"What was all that about?" Ronan demanded when she disconnected the call and handed him back his phone.

"One of the previous owners may have smuggled some of the Romanovs' treasure out of Russia."

"I was still human when they were overthrown and arrested," Ronan said. "I'd already been turned when they were murdered. Not that I played any role in that bloodshed."

"Did Voz?" Sierra asked.

"I don't know. He may have used others."

"So that could be it. That could be the connection between Voz and . . ." She paused as she once again felt a cold grip on both her ankles. "Mother, is that you?"

Then she sensed it with every cell of her being. That terrible evil. Terror froze her vocal cords, preventing her from screaming as she was rapidly yanked off the bed and onto the floor.

Ronan grabbed her arm and held her in place. "What the hell?"

Sierra tried to kick out and managed to get one foot free but it went through something she couldn't see but could feel. It was some sort of putrid plasma that wanted to suck her in.

"Don't let me go!" she frantically told Ronan.

"Never." He pulled her closer but it was as if she was mired in quicksand. Ronan went full vamp. She could feel his strength increasing along with his fury. "Release her!" he roared.

For a moment she was afraid she'd be pulled apart, like a wishbone at Thanksgiving or a prisoner locked in a medieval torture dungeon. Suddenly, without warning, she was released. The sucking noise as she pulled her foot free confirmed her fearful realization that she'd nearly been taken in. Her foot was covered in black slime.

That did it. She turned on her side and threw up. "Get it—" Barf. "Off." A dry heave. "Me!"

Ronan slid his hands under her thighs and lifted her in his arms. In the blink of an eye, she was downstairs in the basement.

"You're safe here," he said.

He set her on top of the washing machine and turned on the water from the laundry tub. Gently reaching for her feet, he shifted them so the water rinsed away the slime. She watched it slide down the drain. What if it came back up again? She shimmied back, almost falling off the washer.

"Close the drain," she shouted. "Use the plug!"

Ronan did.

"It could return."

"Not here," he said. "We're in a secure area."

"Since when?"

"Since Damon secured it. He's a vampire Demon Hunter."

"Was that a demon?" she asked unsteadily.

"It may have been."

Sierra wrapped her arms around Ronan's neck and rested her forehead on his shoulder. Tremors continued to grip her body.

He ran his fingers through her hair, trying to soothe her. "I've got you now."

"Are we interrupting something?" Damon asked from the stairway. Zoe was right next to him

"Something tried to grab Sierra," Ronan said. "It may have been a demon."

"What did it look like?" Damon demanded.

"It was invisible to me," Ronan said.

"Me too," Sierra said, releasing her manic hold on Ronan and sliding to the floor to stand on her own two feet.

"Did it speak?"

"No," Ronan said.

Sierra shook her head.

"What happened to your foot?" Zoe asked.

The slime was gone but the moldy dark color was back.

"Shit!" Sierra was so light-headed she thought she'd crumple onto the cement floor.

Ronan scooped her up and set her back on the washer. Unfortunately there was no comfy chair or couch for her to recline on. In fact, there was no furniture down here at all.

"We washed the slime away," Ronan told Zoe. "It went down the drain. Sierra is afraid it might come back."

Zoe moved close and studied Sierra's foot for a moment before saying, "I'm going to do a protection spell for you. Is that okay?"

Hell yes. Sierra's lips trembled too much for her to speak the words out loud so she nodded instead.

Zoe began reciting the spell.

> *By forces of day and spirits of night*
> *By solemn vow and powers strong*
> *When evil lurks or harm be in sight*
> *Be you safe from all evil forever long*

A puff of sulfur-smelling smoke popped the plug off the drain.

"That's a good sign," Zoe said. "It means the spell disarmed the demon power in the sink."

"What about my foot?" Sierra said, holding it out.

"Give it a minute," Zoe said.

Sure enough, the moldy darkness disappeared.

"So let me get this straight," Damon said. "Not only is Hal the ghost after you, but now some demon is as well?"

"Have you heard of invisible demons?" Sierra asked. "It was yanking me into some sort of plasma shit. I couldn't see anything. Just feel it." Another thought hit her. "Ronan said you secured this site yet there was some kind of bad stuff in that slime in the sink."

"You brought the slime in," Damon explained.

"And I got rid of it," Zoe said. She slid her arm around Damon's waist. "We make a good team."

"Yes, we do." Damon kissed Zoe briefly but intensely. "And to answer your earlier question, Sierra, there are rare instances of demon plasma consumption, where a demon force tries to suck its victim into a deadly invisible vortex." He got out his smartphone and texted. "I'm contacting my sire Simon to see if he has more information on this phenomenon. He's been doing this longer than I have."

While he did that, Sierra asked Zoe, "Will that protection spell you did work on keeping me safe from Hal?"

Zoe shook her head. "It's mainly designed for demons."

"Do you have another one for ghosts?"

"Not really. Especially since you are an entity empath. You are more sensitive to spirits than others," Zoe said.

"What if I don't want to be that sensitive anymore?" Sierra said.

Zoe gave her a sympathetic look. "I'm sorry. That's beyond my powers."

"Simon texted that he'll check into it and get back to me," Damon said.

"I'll check with Pru," Zoe began when Damon interrupted her.

"Simon said he'd relay the message to her as well."

"They are a couple," Zoe explained. "Pru is a witch like me and Simon is a vampire Demon Hunter like Damon."

"Not quite like us," Damon said.

"Right," Zoe agreed, giving Damon another quick but intense kiss. "No one is quite like us." Looking around, she said, "You're going to need some furniture down here."

"Why do we have to stay down here if I've got a demon protection spell?" Sierra asked.

"Because this is a secure site. No ghosts," Ronan said. "I think you've had enough excitement for one night."

"True," she said. "I'm not sure how I'll ever sleep on that bed again."

"I can get you a new bed. What style would you like?" Zoe asked.

"This isn't a design makeover from HGTV," Damon said irritably. "Just give her a bed. Big enough for two."

Zoe wrinkled her nose at Damon before beginning her incantation.

> *Air and fire*
> *There is a desire*
> *Air and earth*
> *For what it's worth*
> *Whatever is said*
> *Please, we need a bed.*

While she did that, Ronan rushed upstairs and brought down Sierra's laptop and phone. He did all that in a millisecond.

"Get some sleep," Zoe suggested. "Call us if you need anything."

When Sierra was alone with Ronan she said, "I have

to tell you something. I saw my father at the cemetery tonight. When I wandered off, I didn't go looking for him at all. It's as if I was drawn there. I called him a shit-faced bastard. Maybe that made him mad enough to turn into a demon. Or maybe he always was one. I don't know. I don't know anything anymore."

"How do you know it was your father in the cemetery?"

"Aside from the fact that I was standing next to his headstone with his name on it, I could see him," she said.

"Could you see him tonight?"

"No, I saw nothing. But that doesn't mean it wasn't him." She looked at the bed. "I can't believe Zoe did that." She cautiously sat on it. "Not bad." The sheets were plain white and the comforter was as well. Nothing fancy. Just a plain bed. Created by a witch who had recited a demon protection spell on Sierra.

She reached for her laptop and then started doing research. She'd investigated everyone else so she might as well investigate Baron Voz and then the Russian circus guys. She didn't get far with Voz.

"All I can find is a reference to him during the Crusades. That's not possible, right?"

"Wrong," Ronan said. "He became a vampire around that time."

She kept looking on the Internet, trying to ignore the fact that she had to pee. Yes, she'd smudged the bathroom off her bedroom with sage but she wasn't ready to go back upstairs yet.

As if reading her mind—wait, Ronan *could* read her

mind. "There's a small WC behind the stairs," he said. "Just a toilet and sink."

"Thanks." She rushed over to it and shut the door. Small was right. When she sat on the john, her knees bumped against the sink, which she faced. From side to side there were maybe a few inches bracketing the toilet. She couldn't even stretch out her hands. She had to keep her elbows bent. Had Zoe spelled this room as well as the bed? Sierra hadn't noticed it before but then she hadn't spent much time down here. The first time she'd tried to explore, her flashlight went out. Then earlier tonight, she'd been in the passageway and couldn't wait to get out and go upstairs to eat her pizza, which she'd thrown up all over her bedroom floor.

"It's all cleaned up," Ronan told her through the door. "The mess upstairs, I mean."

Okay, then. Definitely time to slam her mental barrier back in place. No more thought sharing as she sat on the john. Because the bottom line here was that by midnight the day after tomorrow they had to find the key or she'd be turned into a vampire. Unless she and Ronan had sex. So that was a given. They were *definitely* having sex.

She just needed to work out a few details first. And she needed to do that without Ronan listening in on her thoughts and her plans.

Chapter Twenty

Sierra greeted her friends the next afternoon. "Thanks for coming."

"Is there a reason we're sitting outside on this chilly February day when there are two perfectly warm and toasty houses in front of us?" Zoe asked as she tried to make herself more comfortable in the plastic resin chair Sierra had set outside. She'd ordered them express from Amazon the other day, before the cemetery stuff.

"We're out here because this conversation needs to be private." It was only after Sierra said the words that she realized they were almost the same as those that Ronan had used when he'd told her about his sister. She handed a mug of hot cocoa to Zoe and one to Daniella, who sat beside her.

Sierra hadn't gotten much sleep last night. No surprise there, given what she'd gone through yesterday. She didn't feel safe in her own house so she'd taken this meeting outside. She couldn't hold it in the basement. Ronan was using that space to piece together what he had of the map from Hal's coffin and the passageway wall. Tomorrow was Valentine's Day. Time was not just running out, it was freaking racing.

She'd still been unsettled this morning and avoided her bedroom and the rest of the house, including the kitchen. Ronan had actually handed her the hot chocolates in mugs as he escorted her outside before returning to the house. Somehow he'd also dug up an extra mug. A vampire good with a Keurig. Who knew?

"How are you doing today?" Zoe asked. "Was there any more trouble after we left last night? I already filled Daniella in."

"I'm hanging in there," Sierra said. "We still aren't sure what came after me."

They were interrupted by the arrival of Nick. Sierra hadn't seen him since her first night in the house. He wore a black leather coat, as did most of the vamps around here, and had a cashmere scarf in his hand. "Ladies." He nodded to Sierra and Zoe but went right to Daniella, tugging her to her feet before tenderly wrapping the scarf around her neck. "To keep you warm," he murmured before kissing her with undisguised hot passion. When they finally broke off the embrace, he kissed her cheek and fondled her fanny. "That was to keep you warm."

Sierra was hot just from watching them. When Nick walked away, she saw the adoration on Daniella's face. Saying they were a couple was putting it mildly. They were clearly something very special. The same could be said for Damon and Zoe. Which is why they were the perfect ones to share this discussion.

"What did you want to talk about?" Zoe said.

"Sex," Sierra said. "Or more specifically, sex with a vampire." After what she'd just witnessed, she suspected she already knew the answer but still she had to ask. "I'm assuming it can be done?"

"Oh yeah," Zoe said. "It can be done."

"It can be done *incredibly* well," Daniella agreed.

"Um . . . is it different than other sex?" Sierra asked.

"Absolutely. It's better than anything I've ever experienced," Zoe said.

"Ditto," Daniella said with a huge smile on her face.

"Is there pain involved?" Sierra asked.

"You know, I voiced that same question myself," Daniella admitted. "Nick's reply was that vampires don't have fangs on their privates."

Zoe tried to squelch a snort to no avail. "I can't believe you asked that!"

"Didn't you?" Daniella said.

Zoe shook her head.

"Well, you're a witch," Daniella said. "You know more about these things than I do."

"Not where vampires are concerned," Zoe said, before turning to Sierra. "You are thinking of having sex with Ronan?"

"Yes."

"Just thinking or planning?"

"Planning."

"Because of the vampire bond you two share?" Zoe asked. "You want to break it?"

"Yes," Sierra said. "Wouldn't you?"

"I can't answer that," Zoe said.

"Why not?"

"Because I don't know the answer."

"It's a matter of free will, right?" Daniella said. When Sierra nodded, she continued, "I can understand that part. The vampires in our lives find it very aggravating that they can't compel us to obey them."

"That's putting it mildly," Zoe said.

"What about your mind?" Sierra asked.

"As in, are we out of our minds?" Daniella said.

"No, as in, can your vampires read your mind?" Sierra said.

"Sometimes it seems like Nick can," Daniella said with a secret smile.

"Ronan really can read my mind," Sierra said. "That's a side effect of the vampire bond thing. I asked him to swear on something he holds dear that he'd stop doing it unless I give him permission but he refused. I am able to block him sometimes if I really focus on doing that. And I have to be fairly close for him to read it. He said he couldn't read my mind out here and I believe him. Besides, I can tell if he lies. Another effect of the bond thing."

"I bet they wouldn't like it if we could read their minds," Zoe said. "Wait, sometimes I can read Damon's mind."

"Because you're a witch?" Sierra said.

"No, because he wants me to know what he's thinking. It's written all over his face," Zoe said with a grin.

"I have a hard time reading Ronan," Sierra admitted.

"So the only reason you want to have sex with Ronan is to break the vampire bond?" Zoe asked bluntly.

Sierra squirmed in her seat. The chairs looked a lot comfier online than they were in reality. Perhaps that was because Zoe's question made her uncomfortable. "Maybe not the only reason but the main reason."

"Were you attracted to him before you knew he was a vampire?" Zoe said.

"He was nude when I first met him, remember?" Sierra said.

"And that attracted you to him?" Zoe said.

"You make it sound like I'm attracted to any guy I see naked, which is certainly not the case," Sierra said.

"Are you having any premonitions about them having sex?" Zoe turned to ask Daniella.

"Not yet. I'll let you know if that changes. But just because I don't have a premonition, that doesn't mean that there might not be danger ahead," Daniella said. "Remember, I did have a premonition yesterday about danger and death."

Sierra was pretty sure there was plenty of danger ahead. She just needed to do everything she could to make sure that one of those dangers wasn't her being turned into a vampire against her will. Oh yeah, and that the death wasn't hers. There was that too. No big deal.

Ronan was in the basement, studying the map on the passageway wall and trying to calibrate it with something in the house. So far no luck. There were no recognizable sites on the map.

Maybe that information was on the missing segment. He'd used his smartphone to take a photo of the passageway wall and put it together with the piece from Hal's empty casket. He'd even taken the casket portion of the map to the passageway to see if putting the two together that way made a difference. It didn't.

Ronan rubbed his hand over his face. He was trying to concentrate here but the memory of Sierra being yanked off her bed stayed with him. The force that had tried to take her was incredibly powerful. It had taken all his strength to hang on to her.

He could hear Sierra's voice outside. He could hear all the women outside. She'd asked if he would be able to read her mind if she was outside and he'd said no. She hadn't asked if he'd be able to hear her with his vamp-heightened senses. Sierra was talking about breaking the vampire bond and having sex with him tonight.

He immediately got hard at the thought. It wasn't just a thought on her part. Sierra had said the words out loud.

Had he met her without all this shit hanging over his head, he'd have conquered her immediately that very first night. Not against her will, but with her blessing. Yeah, he was that good. Vamp senses were heightened in all things, including sex.

But now things were complicated. However, the bottom line was that he couldn't risk failing in his mission to find the freaking key for Voz and thereby putting Sierra at risk. He had to protect her. That need had grown within him as intensely as his desire for her.

Sierra had only seen a brief flash of him going full vamp. She hadn't seen the entire transformation. Not that he planned on doing that in front of her. But none of this was going as he'd planned.

His thoughts were interrupted by the arrival of Pat through the Vamptown tunnels.

"Damon gave me an update on the occurrence last

night," Pat said. "I also got a message from Bruce that Sierra wanted to talk to me."

"She's outside right now."

"I saw. Far be it from me to interrupt their girl talk."

It occurred to Ronan that if he could hear Sierra's conversation, then so could Pat. "I'll have her come down."

"You're a braver vampire than I," Pat said with old-world syntax. "How are you adapting to the sunlight? No side effects?"

"None. Were you expecting some?"

"I've never used our tat ink on an indentured vampire before."

"Formerly indentured," Ronan corrected him.

"Right. So you're transitioning to functioning in the daylight just fine?"

Ronan was getting suspicious. "What aren't you telling me?"

"That unknown attacker last night may have been a mutant vampire hybrid."

"I've never heard of such a thing."

"Bruce said Sierra was asking about a previous owner of the house. Gregori Dimitrov owned this house for four years. He sold it to Hal in 1923."

"Were you here then?"

Pat nodded. "I've been in this area since Abe Lincoln's time."

"You were a vampire when my family lived here?"

"I had nothing to do with the deaths in your family," Pat said curtly.

The possibility hadn't occurred to Ronan until that moment. He hadn't discovered that the area was known as Vamptown until his return several days ago. Since then he'd been consumed with the search for Voz's key and his growing attraction to Sierra.

Voz had held back Adele's soul from moving on. Had he lied? He'd sworn on his family's coat of arms but did that make it real or true?

"What is the connection between vampires and spirits or ghosts?" Ronan demanded.

"Normally there is none," Pat said. "But Master Vampires are different. You know that already."

Ronan nodded.

"They are more powerful than other vampires and have more abilities."

"Is this mutant vampire hybrid a Master Vampire?" Ronan asked.

"No. I think it could be Gregori. I ran my suspicions by Simon, Damon's sire and a longtime Demon Hunter. He agrees with my analysis. Rumor had it that Gregori wasn't turned properly. When his vampire brother Ivan refused to turn him, Gregori may have ended up with a defective transition."

"Damon thought it could be a demon plasma consumption attempt last night. He didn't say anything about mutant vamps."

"He didn't know. We only heard back from Simon a short time ago."

"Was Gregori a vamp when he bought this house?"

"Not when he bought it, no. But by the time he sold it, we knew something was off but didn't know what. He was never included in our clan the way you were."

"What happened to him?"

"I've been trying to track him down. He was in the South around New Orleans for some time. Then he disappeared. He could be continuing to deteriorate."

"So he's what . . . part vampire, part demon?"

"That's a simplified way of putting it."

"How can he be annihilated?"

"Beheading. I fear his demon portion makes fire useless in destroying him."

"Zoe did a protection spell for Sierra last night. Will it work against him?"

"We don't know for sure," Pat said. "One would hope so."

"I don't deal in hope," Ronan said flatly.

"I heard that Hal's casket was empty," Zoe said. "Do you think that's why he's haunting this house?"

"You dug up a casket?" Daniella's voice reflected her surprise.

Sierra shook her head. "Not personally, no. I didn't do that."

"My family owns the local funeral home. We tend to frown on digging up graves without proper legal authorization," Daniella said.

"We're dealing with a dangerous poltergeist ghost here," Sierra said. "That calls for unusual measures." Then Daniella's words sank in further. "How long has your family owned the business?"

"Several generations."

"So it's possible that they may have handled Hal's funeral arrangements?" Sierra asked.

"Probably. We keep the records going way back."

"Can you get me in to see them?" Sierra asked. "Maybe if I can locate Hal's final resting place, it will help solve the problem."

"What problem?" Ronan said as he joined them.

Sierra, Daniella, and Zoe were all wearing winter coats but Ronan was just wearing his customary black sweater and black pants. The weather didn't seem to affect him the way it did others. So camping in the backyard shouldn't have been a problem for him when Sierra had suggested it at their first meeting. But of course his ability to manage that would have raised the red flag that Ronan wasn't just another guy.

"Did you know that Daniella's family owns the local funeral home?" Sierra said. "They may have records about the real location of Hal's body."

"I did hear something about her connection but it didn't occur to me before," Ronan said.

"Because we had no reason to think that Hal wasn't where he was supposed to be—in his coffin at his grave site." Turning back to Daniella, Sierra said, "Do you have time now to take me over there—"

"Take *us* over there," Ronan interrupted her.

Pat joined them. Ronan asked him, "Do you have a problem with that?"

"Not as long as you limit your investigation to Hal's remains," Pat said.

Sierra immediately suspected something was going on between the vampire community and the funeral home. She just as quickly decided she really didn't want to know any details about that subject at the moment.

"We can walk there. It's only a couple of blocks," Daniella said.

Ronan took hold of Sierra's hand during the walk, as if hanging on to her protected her from being taken. At least that's how it felt to her. There was little conversation during the short trip.

Once inside the Evergreen Funeral Home, Daniella paused to gently rearrange the flower arrangement on the marble table in the front foyer. Looking around, Sierra noted the muted wallpaper and dark wood that combined to create a feeling of class and comfort.

"I have to introduce you to my dad and brother," Daniella said. "They run the place. If I don't say something, they'll get suspicious. My brother is here now." She knocked on the funeral director's door and led them inside. "Hey, Gordon, I'd like you to meet some friends of mine."

As the introductions were made, Sierra was aware that Daniella's brother was flirting with her. She could also tell that Ronan was aware of that fact and not happy about it. Ronan tugged her closer and put his arm around her shoulder, no doubt declaring her his property.

"And this is my dad and his wife, Franny," Daniella added as the newcomers joined them.

Sierra could definitely see the family resemblance between the two men, who shared the same lanky build, dark hair, and blue eyes.

"This is Sierra Brennan. She's an author," Daniella was saying. "She writes as S. J. Brennan and she's doing some research for her new book so I said I'd give her a tour."

"I should be the one to give her the tour," Gordon immediately said. "You don't really know much about the business."

"I'm most interested in the history of the place," Sierra said. "You may have heard the story that my house was once owned by Hal Bergerstock, a member of Al Capone's gang."

Gordon nodded. "I have heard that, yes."

"It's true. I was wondering if you handled the details when he died? The funeral, burial, that sort of thing."

"When was this?"

"Back in 1929."

"Hold on," Daniella's dad said. "My grandfather told me about this case. The wife decided at the last minute to have the body cremated and bury the empty coffin."

"Why?" Sierra asked.

"She wanted him to burn because he had a mistress who came to his funeral service and made a scene."

"What would have happened to any personal belongings like a wedding ring?" Sierra asked.

"In most cases, jewelry is removed and kept by the family. Otherwise it's kept with the body and burned."

"That's very helpful information. Thanks." She and Ronan made a hasty exit. As Sierra and Ronan walked back to the house, she said, "At least we now know what happened to Hal's body."

"Maybe that's what pissed him off," Ronan said. "Being cremated instead of buried."

"I don't think so. He referred to his treasure."

"He's dead. Whatever this damn treasure is, he can't do anything with it."

"He doesn't want anyone else having it," she said.

"If that key was burned to a crisp with him, then we are in deep shit." Ronan's voice was grim.

A package from Amazon stood on the front porch.

She'd ordered a new nightgown the day before and clicked on overnight shipping. That was all before she'd almost been yanked into hell or wherever.

"Why was Pat here?" she asked.

Ronan filled her in. Mutant vampire-demon hybrids? It was getting to be all too much for her to decipher. Maybe she'd be able to think more clearly once she had sex with Ronan.

Taking the Amazon package, she headed for the tiny basement bathroom, washed up, and changed into the nightgown. It was pure silk and felt like a dream against her bare skin.

The bias cut reminded her of the gowns from the twenties while the apricot color reminded her of the Fortuny dress that Ruby had talked about. Staring at herself in the mirror, she said, "You can do this."

Ronan was waiting for her. "I realize a visit to a funeral home isn't exactly a normal version of a romantic afternoon out," he said.

"Hardly."

"But we both know what's going on here." At her confused look, he said, "Sex."

"Uh, I think I'd know if we were having sex right now. I would know that, wouldn't I?" she asked with a nervous chew on her bottom lip.

"Yes, you'd definitely know. I meant we know where this is leading. So we may as well get started."

"Just like that?"

"Given the power of the vampire curse, it may be difficult if not impossible to go slow the first time."

"The first time? Do you mean—"

"That we'll be doing this more than once. Yes."

"Okay, then. I . . . uh . . . let's get started. Where do you want me?"

"Just relax."

Sure, because there's nothing to be nervous about after all. It's not like I'm about to have sex with a vampire to prevent my being turned into one.

Only then did Sierra notice that the utilitarian bed she'd slept on last night had been transformed into something out of a fairy tale—a four-poster bed with a filmy white canopy. It was the most romantic thing she'd ever seen.

She looked over her shoulder at Ronan. "Too dainty for you?"

"When I first got here I slept in a coffin," he said.

"Ew."

"I realize you're only having sex with me so you won't become a vampire." His voice was curt.

"That's not the only reason."

"It's not?"

"No. There are other factors, like the strong attraction between us."

"Caused by the vampire bond."

"It existed before that," she admitted before saying, "Why do you want to have sex with me? Or is that a dumb question?"

"It kind of is."

"Gee, thanks. So I could be just any female?"

"No." He brushed his thumb over her lips. "You could never be 'just' anything. You're you. Special."

"Because I see ghosts?"

"For a hundred thousand reasons."

"That many, huh?"

"I won't have another death on my hands," Ronan said gruffly. "I won't have your blood on my hands. I want my hands on your breasts and on the rest of your body."

"I want that too."

"I won't have Voz take you." Ronan's voice was fierce with the emotion he claimed he didn't have. "He can't take you if our bond is broken."

She sat on the bed, because it was that or fall down. Even the sound of Ronan's voice was making her go all jelly-kneed. She ran her hand along the bed linens. She'd always wondered what the softest sheets imaginable would feel like. Now she knew. She'd never actually wondered what having sex with a vampire would feel like but she was about to find out.

Wait, he was probably reading her thoughts right this second.

Don't rip my nightgown.

"Then take it off," he said.

"I just put it on." She took his hand and placed it on her breast. "It feels so good."

He ran his hand down her body, over her stomach, to her thigh and then to the juncture between her legs. She'd already removed her underwear. He rubbed the heel of his palm against her feminine mound while inching up the hem of her gown with his free hand.

The first brush of his thumb against her clitoris sent a spiral of sinful sensation into her womb. She moaned her pleasure. He whisked her nightgown off before lowering her onto the bed and continuing his darkly talented seduction. First he slid one finger into the wel-coming slippery dampness of her vagina. Then he re-placed his hands with his mouth and his tongue.

A swirl here, a lick there. His actions shot her to another level of bliss. The clench of her orgasm rolled over her like a tidal wave . . . after wave . . . after wave. She screamed his name and gripped his shoulders. Otherwise she thought she might fly off the bed—not from an enemy but from her response to Ronan.

She didn't have to speak. He knew what gave her the most satisfaction and he repeated that move with a twist here and a nibble there. She'd never felt anything like this.

The physical bond was incredible but there was more. There was a sense of recognition. Of something missing suddenly found.

Then Ronan abruptly stood. It took him the blink of an eye to remove all his clothing and stand before her as magnificent and nude as he had been the first time she'd seen him. Only there was one difference. Now his sex was rampant with desire. He was clearly fully aroused and ready to go.

She was spread-eagled and naked on the bed when he finally kissed her on the mouth. Instantly she wrapped her legs around his hips and lifted up to urge him in.

She felt a primal need to mate. Did he feel it too? Was the vampire bond creating this need so intense it bordered on pain?

"Now!" She could barely form the words. "Take me now."

He thrust his tongue between her parted lips as he thrust his penis between her parted legs. She took all of him. The friction of his body against hers and within hers was sizzling and fiercely divine. She was enthralled by his power, entranced by his touch. Threading her fingers through his thick hair, she matched his passion. She loved the way he kissed her, the way his body filled hers.

He slid deeper until she sheathed him from tip to root. The walls of her vagina clenched around him as he possessed her. Tremors continued to ripple deep within her as she teetered on the edge of her orgasm.

There was a carnal rawness in each of his delicious thrusts. She broke off their kiss with a breathless cry of impending ecstasy.

Primitive needs took over.

"Mine," Ronan growled. "You're mine. Say it."

"Yours," Sierra gasped.

He held her chin and had her look at him as she came, the powerful spasms radiating through her. She watched his eyes darken and glow as he came. His animalistic snarls of pleasure didn't frighten her. They empowered her.

Because this was what she'd been waiting for her entire life. Their bond hadn't been broken, it was strengthened.

Chapter Twenty-one

Sierra woke up in bed alone. She panicked for a moment, thinking Voz had taken Ronan. Today was Valentine's Day. But the deadline was supposed to be midnight tonight.

Then she saw the note on the pillow beside hers. *I'm in the passageway. Call out when you wake up. Ronan.*

She touched the paper with her fingertip, tracing his words. This was the first time she'd seen his writing aside from his scrawled signature on their temporary lease agreement. Maybe she was just being sappy but his handwriting seemed deliciously old-fashioned to her now.

There was nothing old-fashioned about the way Ronan made love. Because that's what it had been to her. There was no hiding her feelings by labeling it as sex. The vampire bond might be broken but the ties between them were more powerful than ever.

She loved Ronan. And not just because he was good

in bed. Okay, off-the-charts totally EPIC AWESOME in bed. But there was more to it than that.

She loved the way he could catch a dish flying through the air. His sense of humor. His fierce loyalty. His old-fashioned sense of chivalry. His dark chocolate-brown eyes. The way his smile was slightly lopsided.

She was accustomed to being haunted by ghosts but not by being haunted by the power of her love for Ronan. She refused to allow Voz to have him. She'd do everything in her power to save Ronan, just as he'd saved her.

She might not have superpowers or magical abilities but she had other skills. The bottom line here was that yes, she'd fallen in love with a vampire. And yes, that created some unique challenges like the fang-and-blood thing not to mention the immortality stuff. But in order to work those out, she first had to make sure that Ronan wasn't taken from her by Voz.

Which meant she had to get up and get moving. She found clean clothes laid out at the foot of the bed. After washing up in the tiny bathroom under the stairs and pulling on the black pants and red top, she called out Ronan's name. He was beside her in an instant.

"Everything okay?" he asked.

"I was just following orders. You said to call your name when I woke up."

"Like you called it so many times in the night as you came," he said.

"And I came so many times. I had no idea it was even possible to have that many orgasms."

"Was it too much?" He cupped her cheek with his hand. "Are you okay today?"

She wanted to tug him back into bed and show him exactly how okay she was today. But first things first. "I will be fine when we find that key Voz wants. Any progress on that front?"

"I searched every inch of the passageway."

"That map is confusing. And why would Hal need a map to begin with? He knew where he put the treasure in this house. It's not like he buried it in a desert or wilderness somewhere. The treasure is in this house."

"Or the backyard. I dug it all up, by the way."

"Why? Did you think Hal was buried there? People bury their goldfish in their backyards. Not humans. Besides, Daniella's dad already told us that he was cremated."

"There have been plenty of serial killers who buried bodies in their yards or under the cement floor of their garage."

"So you thought the key could be on a body Hal buried in the backyard? Did you find anything out there?" she said.

"Some bones. Not human, though."

"And no treasure?"

"No. I even ran a metal detector across the property. Nothing," he said.

"Okay then. So we can knock those two locations— the passageway and the backyard—off the list of possible hiding places. What about the front yard?"

"I dug that up too."

"At vamp speed?"

"Of course."

"And no one saw you?"

"It was still dark. Before the sun came up."

She could only imagine what the neighbors would think. Wait, the neighbors were witches and vampires. "I still think we're missing something."

"We're missing the third piece of that damn map," Ronan said.

A warbling scream came from upstairs.

The door at the top of the stairs flew open and Ruby stood there, frantic. "It's Valentine's Day! Hello? Why aren't you doing something?"

"Can she see us?" Sierra asked Ronan.

He shook his head. "It doesn't appear so. Remember, this is a secure site."

"Maybe she could hear me if I stand on the stairs. I'm still here," Sierra told Ruby. "Ruby, can you hear me?"

"Yes, I can hear you but I can't see you. Something new invaded the house the other night and now everything is out of whack."

"Do you know what it was? Had you ever seen it before?" Sierra asked.

"I didn't see it at all," Ruby said.

"Yeah, me either," Sierra said.

"But it was evil. Even worse than Hal. That doesn't mean that Hal can stay though. He has to go. Today!" Ruby shouted. "He has to go today!"

"Today is the anniversary of her death," Sierra told Ronan.

"Not my death, my *murder*," Ruby said. "And no, I wasn't part of the Valentine's Day massacre. I had no idea that was going to happen. Why are you hiding down there? What's going on?" She paused a moment. "There's someone knocking at your front door."

"Ignore it. They'll go away," Sierra said.

"It's Tanya."

"I'll get rid of her," Ronan said.

The knocking stopped and instead Tanya showed up in the basement with them. "I used the tunnels. I figured you couldn't hear me. Maybe you were writing with your headphones on." She looked around at the messed-up sheets on the romantic bed. "I like what you've done with the place."

Tanya was dressed conservatively for her in a black skirt and a fuzzy red angora sweater. She had a large tote bag over her shoulder.

"This really isn't a good time," Sierra said, going back down the steps to face Tanya.

"I've been doing some research and self-publishing is the latest thing. Also fan fiction. I already wrote a chapter about Nicki and posted it. But here's the bottom line. You need a street team."

"Is that a vampire thing?" Ruby asked from the top of the stairs. "Can that help you get rid of Hal?"

"It's a marketing promotional sort of thing," Sierra said.

"I'm the perfect person to head your street team," Tanya said.

"Let's talk about this some other time," Sierra said.

Tanya shook her head. "You snooze, you loose. Not that you two have been doing much snoozing down here. I really do wish you'd talked to me before you did the deed, Sierra. I was going to give you some helpful hints. You may not know this but I'm a graduate of the Mansfield School. I was their star pupil."

"How about I meet you tomorrow at Heavenly

Cupcakes," Sierra said, "and we can talk about your childhood schooldays—"

Tanya interrupted her. "The Mansfield School was not for kids. The full title of their establishment was the Mansfield School of Undressing."

Sierra blinked. "You're kidding, right?"

"Not at all. Back in the fifties, they had a third-floor office downtown on State Street. The teachers gave us invaluable lessons. For example . . ." Tanya took hold of the hem of her sweater and started shimmying.

"Don't you have someplace else you have to be?"

"No," Tanya said.

"I was talking to Ronan."

"I'll be nearby," he said.

Once he was gone, Sierra drew a deep breath. "Look, I know you're only trying to be helpful here."

"Because clearly you need help."

"But this isn't a good time."

"Okay, then I'll give you the one-minute lesson. We can't have you practicing faulty disrobing techniques. You do not want the word to get out that you are a sloppy undresser."

"Who's going to put a word out like that?"

"No one once I'm done with you," Tanya said. "Now pay attention. Do you see how I crook my knee? Do that while you are stepping out of your dress or skirt, sliding your clothing over your hips before gracefully stepping out of it. As for your top, never clumsily yank it over your head, getting your arms all trapped." Tanya demonstrated. Luckily she was wearing a bra because Sierra did not want to be flashed by the tanned vampire.

Tanya smoothed down her angora sweater and started

over. "Instead you peel it off with elegance. Do you see the difference?"

"Yes."

"Good. Now how is the book coming?"

"Slowly."

"I don't want to hear that."

"Then don't ask."

"What's the problem? Is it Ronan? Is he distracting you? I can take care of that."

"No, it's not Ronan. I'm in the research phase right now."

"Is that what you call bedding an indentured vampire?" Tanya said.

No, Sierra called that incredibly satisfying.

"Fine. Don't tell me. I like the way your books surprise me," Tanya said. "But I am going to need to see an advance copy of your next one. When does it come out?"

"In three months. The one I'm writing now comes out next year. But all that information is on my website," Sierra said.

"Which could also use updating. My rates are very cheap. Just feed me."

"Blood?" Sierra took a hasty step away. "No way."

"I meant feed me scenes after you write them."

"I don't share my work with anyone until my editor Lily Janeway reads it."

"Okay, then I can be the next in line after her." Tanya pulled an iPad out of her bag. "Here, look at this. I think the blue and black colors tie in well with your book cover and the theme of ghosts. This would be your logo for your street team."

Sierra had to admit that what Tanya was showing her looked good. Shrouds of smoke swirled around her name, S. J. Brennan, and the title of the book. "That's really impressive."

"So you like it?"

Sierra nodded.

"Then I have the job?"

"I could get you a galley of the next book for your iPad."

Tanya squealed in delight, almost dropping her tablet as she yanked Sierra close for a hug. "I haven't been this happy in a long time. I have a hard time bonding with other females. I'm not talking about sire bonds or vampire bonds. I mean BFF stuff." She finally set Sierra free. "Okay, I'll get right on this. First I'll set up a Facebook page exclusively for your street team. Then we'll get some book graphic cards going. Sharlene does those. I love her work. And we need to recruit people to come like your author page. Not recruit in a vampire way, but in a social media way. Draculina can help me with that. I've never met her but we message each other online. She gets me. Anyway, sorry I can't stay to chat but I've got to get working. You need to be working too. Your fans are eagerly waiting for your next story."

Tanya rushed past Ronan on her way out through the tunnels.

"What was all that about?" he said.

"It's about my books not the treasure. And before you ask, no, I didn't tell Tanya anything about the treasure."

"She's probably already heard the buzz around Vamptown about Hal."

"Will any of the other vampires try to interfere with the search?"

"Aside from Gregori, you mean?" Ronan said.

"Right. The evil mutant hybrid vampire. Hal's treasure must be really good if Gregori wants it."

"We have to get to it first."

'And we will." She thought for a moment before speaking her thoughts out loud. "Why is that framed large photograph still on the wall upstairs?" Sierra asked before going on to answer to her own question. "Because Hal is a gangster ghost with a narcissistic streak, right? But what if there's more to it than that?"

"I took it off the wall and looked behind it when I first got here," Ronan said.

"Did you look inside the mat or the frame?"

"No," Ronan admitted. "I'll go get it off the wall and bring it down here so we can examine it more closely."

Yes, he could move at super vamp speed but she feared losing him. It wasn't logical, perhaps. But she trusted her gut. "I'm coming with you," Sierra said.

"No way."

"I can distract Hal while you grab the photograph."

"He might not even show up," Ronan said.

"Oh, he'll show up." She marched up the basement stairs.

An instant later, Ronan stood in front of her.

"You can't stop me," she said. "You can't compel me. You can't kiss me. Well, you can kiss me but it won't be go-off-the-deep-end like before." No, it wasn't like before when they shared the vampire bond. But it was even more powerful in a way because of free will. Returning his kiss was her choice now. Not that he kissed her. He was too aggravated with her. "Come on. We're wasting time."

"Yes, you're wasting time," Ruby said from the top of the stairs.

Ronan glared at Sierra but allowed her to pass. He stayed right by her side.

Sierra hated to admit it, but she was still a bit jumpy about being in the unsecured house. She just hoped that Zoe's protection spell would keep her safe from Gregori.

Then she saw the graffiti on the living room wall, written in red.

L E A V E N O W!

"Who did that?" she demanded.

"It wasn't me," Ruby said.

"Is that blood?" Sierra asked.

"I think it might be your lipstick from your bedroom," Ruby said.

"My Chanel lipstick? That set me back nearly forty dollars! No one messes with my makeup," Sierra growled.

She was about to march upstairs when Ronan snared her by his side. "You should let me take care of this."

"I am not letting this go."

"It's just lipstick."

"No it's not. It's not about the lipstick. It's about my life and I want it back," she said fiercely.

"Don't do anything reckless. Do I have your word?" Ronan said.

"I am not a reckless person."

Ronan just gave her a look.

"Hey, I thought I was moving into a new house and that's it," she said. "Okay, maybe there was a slight chance it might be haunted. I did take that possibility into consideration. But I never imagined any of the rest of this shit, and trust me, I have a great imagination."

"Your word," Ronan reminded her.

"Fine. You have my word."

"I still would prefer that you wait in the basement."

"I know. Let's get this over with." As she headed up the steps she remembered her first day in the house, when Ronan had followed her on this staircase and she'd been worried about her butt being too big. Now she was remembering the feel of his hands gripping her there as he teased her clit with his tongue, making her come again and again.

She almost stumbled at the erotic memory.

"Everything okay?" Ronan asked from right behind her. His breath brushed her ear. What if he pushed her against the wall and took her from behind right here on the stairs?

Sierra couldn't blame her wayward thoughts on the vampire bond any longer. "Can you read my thoughts right now?" she said.

"No." He lifted a strand of hair from her nape and placed a kiss there. "Why?"

"No reason." Her voice sounded alien, part breathy Marilyn Monroe, part raspy Janis Joplin.

"Did you change your mind?"

"No." She hurried up the stairs and into the bedroom on the left.

No hint of cigar smoke. That was a good sign. The dark coldness was still present so Hal hadn't left the premises. Not yet. But he would soon. This had gone on long enough.

"I'm not sensing him in the immediate vicinity. Go for it," Sierra said.

Moving with vamp speed, Ronan grabbed the photograph. The moment he touched the frame Hal appeared. "Get your filthy hands off that!"

"Hal . . ." Sierra barely got that one word out before Hal turned to face her.

"Back off!" A second later, the French doors leading to the small balcony flew open and Hal sent Sierra flying through the air out those doors.

She grabbed hold of the balcony railing as she whizzed by. Roaring his anger, Ronan threw the photograph outside even as he saved Sierra.

"I've got you," he said, wrapping her in his arms.

She heard the frame crash on the cold ground below. Ronan cradled her as he leaped to the ground in a single smooth movement.

"If I'd lost you . . ." His voice was thick with emotion.

"You didn't. And I'm not losing you," she told him. "Voz can't have you. We are finding this damn key, no matter what."

"It's not worth risking your life."

"It's not worth indenturing yours."

"Most people would consider me a monster," he said.

"Most people don't see dead people," she retorted.

"Haven't you figured out yet that I'm not most people?"

"Yeah, I get that now."

"It took you long enough." She kissed him. "Now let's go kick some ghost butt!"

Chapter Twenty-two

"I hate this invisible shit," Ronan bit out with obvious fury. "How am I supposed to fight something I can't see?"

"By letting me help you because I can see them," Sierra said.

"Right. And that just worked out so well, nearly getting you killed just now."

"I'm more likely to twist an ankle on one of these holes in the backyard here," she said as she looked around. "You weren't kidding when you said you dug it up. It looks like giant mutant gophers attacked. Not that I am comparing you to a giant mutant gopher."

He frowned at her. "Did you hit your head on that balcony?"

"No. I always sound a little flustered when I fly through the air, first propelled by a poltergeist ghost and then saved by you."

"You should have stayed in the basement."

"Okay, enough of the I-told-you-sos. You can let me go now."

He did so reluctantly.

"How badly is the photograph damaged?" Sierra asked as Ronan plucked it off the ground.

"It's seen better days."

"Haven't we all," she said, brushing off the rust from her hands that came from her grab on the balcony railing.

Pulling her close, Ronan paused a moment to hug her before zapping them down to the secure site in the basement.

He set the frame parts on the large table he'd been using. The wood had broken into pieces. There was also a large tear in the wide mat and the backing on the photograph.

Sierra turned the picture of Hal facedown. She couldn't stand to look at him at the moment.

"He used up a lot of energy sending me out those French doors, but he will rebound in time and he's going to start smashing my furniture. Normally I might not be that upset but I really like that Liberty Arts and Crafts sideboard in the dining room."

"I'll get it."

"It weighs a ton," Sierra said, but Ronan was already gone.

He reappeared and set the sideboard near the bed. He wasn't even out of breath.

"Feel better now?" he said.

She nodded, still amazed by his abilities.

"Careful with the wood," he said as she moved one of the pieces of Hal's photo frame.

Only then did she realize it looked an awful lot like a wooden stake. She'd never use it on Ronan but it might come in handy should that evil vampire-demon hybrid show up. "I could use this on Gregori in an emergency."

"It wouldn't work."

"Why not?"

"Because the only way to annihilate him is to sever his head from his body."

"That's probably above my skill set," she said.

"It's not above mine," he said grimly before returning his attention to the stuff in front of them.

Obviously Ronan was faster than she was at going through the pieces of matting and backing. "I found something." He peeled away the matting and revealed something in between. "This is it!"

He set the small piece of paper on the table along with the other two.

"That's great!" She leaned over his shoulder to look at it. The piece definitely completed the map. That was the good news. The bad news was that it still made no sense.

Ronan swore under his breath.

"Maybe if we turned it another way," she suggested.

They tried turning it every possible way.

She really was concentrating on deciphering the symbols on the map but the bottom line was that she had to pee real bad.

"I just need to use the bathroom," she said apologetically. "You keep trying to figure it out. I'm sure we can do this. The map thing, I mean. Okay, I'm leaving now. I'll be right back."

Sierra rushed to the bathroom and emptied her bladder. After she flushed, the water kept running longer than it should have. She knew enough about home maintenance to remove the lid to the tank and check inside. As she did so, she couldn't help wondering if maybe Hal had hidden his treasure or the key to it inside the plumbing fixture. Probably not, since odds were that someone would have checked it in the intervening decades. Still, she did look but found nothing.

Meanwhile the water kept running. At this rate it was going to overflow and flood the bathroom.

Bending down, she turned the water shutoff valve while jiggling the toilet handle. To her surprise, the handle went way up and as it did she heard a click.

Great. She'd just broken the only safe toilet in the house.

But no. The click didn't come from the toilet. It came from the wall behind it. Peering in the tight space, she saw a lever. She pulled it. She thought nothing happened until she noticed one of the large tiles on the floor was elevated.

Afraid to let go of the lever, she nudged the tile with her foot and it came loose. Beneath it was a metal strongbox with the initials HB on the top.

"Ronan, I found it!"

He burst into the bathroom.

"It's there, beneath the floor."

He snatched it up. She was just about to release the lever when she noticed something attached to it inside the niche where it had resided. A small chain with . . . a key at the end of it!

"And I bet this is the key," she said, removing it and

showing it to him. "Are we supposed to open it or are we supposed to hand it over to Voz first?"

"Our agreement didn't say anything about revealing a treasure," Ronan said. "Just the key."

"Maybe we should ask him first. I don't want to screw anything up for you."

And just like that Voz stood on the threshold to the tiny bathroom. "A wise woman," he said.

"I thought this was a secure site," she said.

"Secure against ghosts." Voz studied her for a second. "Ah, I sense the vampire bond between you and Ronan has been broken. A pity. I would have enjoyed adding you to my collection."

"You're not adding anyone," Ronan said, standing before Sierra protectively. "Take the damn key!"

"No," Voz said.

"No?" Sierra repeated in confusion.

"No, I won't take that key because it's not the right one. It's not in that strongbox either," Voz said. "Tough tinsel."

His mocking reference to Sierra's book infuriated and scared her. Both emotions kept her from speaking up.

"How will we know if we find the right key?" Ronan demanded.

"She'll know." Voz pointed to Sierra. "When she sees it, she'll know. You've got two hours left." With those words, he disappeared as fast he'd appeared.

"Right," she muttered. "I'll know it when I see it? Like that's a lot of help. No pressure there."

"We might as well see what's in this box," Ronan said. "Maybe opening it will make Hal disappear."

Sierra handed him the key.

A horrible howl from upstairs made her blood chill.

"Quick, before he breaks more furniture," she said.

"This better not be empty like his damn coffin," Ronan said.

It wasn't.

"Are those . . . ?" she whispered.

"Diamonds?" Ronan said. "They sure look like they are."

"Maybe they're fake."

"Sierra!" Ruby screamed.

"I have to make sure she's okay," Sierra said.

"Stay close to me," he said.

They reached the top of the stairs in time for Sierra to see Hal, his face contorted with fury. "What's going on?" he yelled.

Dark spirits came spilling out of the wall, grabbed him, and hauled him away. It was over very fast.

"That was freaky," Sierra said. "I am definitely getting new wallpaper." Had those dark spirits been living in her wall all the time? She sure hoped not. She decided they must have merely used the wall as a portal. Still, who wanted a portal to hell in their front foyer?

"What about me?" Ruby peered around the doorway from the living room. "Are those dark things going to come for me too?" Ruby's voice trembled.

"No," Sierra reassured her. "You didn't murder anyone. Did you?"

"I wanted to."

"That's not the same."

"Then where is the white light for me?" Ruby looked

around. "I'm not seeing it anywhere. That can't be a good sign. What does it mean?"

"I don't know," Sierra admitted. "This is all new territory for me. I'll get back to you."

"Where are you going?" Ruby demanded.

"To find a solution."

Sierra had to admit that despite the freaky occurrence she'd just witnessed with those dark spirits hauling Hal's ass to hell, her mind felt clearer without his presence in the house.

Twenty minutes ticked by. She felt every second of every one of them to the depths of her soul. They had to figure this out. The fates couldn't be so cruel as to take Ronan from her now that she'd fallen in love with him.

The thing was that Sierra already knew Fate could be a bitch.

Some people believed bad things happened for a reason. Sierra had a hard time buying into that philosophy. She'd always leaned more toward the Shit Happens school of thought.

But that was before she met Ronan. Before she knew about witches and vampires.

She'd always known there was an afterlife, which was more than many did. But that knowledge wasn't helping her figure out this freaking map.

She didn't even realize that Ronan had disappeared for a second until he handed her the carton of chocolate chocolate-chip ice cream from her freezer upstairs. He even brought a spoon. How could you not love a guy like that?

She wished she had time to savor her emotions for

Ronan but she didn't. So she instead ate what was left of the carton of ice cream while studying the map. With her last bite, it suddenly hit her. "This looks like a maze and it isn't all in this house. This is just a small part of the picture. I think I know where we are supposed to go. There," Sierra said. She pointed to the spot where Tanya had appeared.

"That leads to the Vamptown tunnels," Ronan said. "I checked them out very carefully my first week here."

"Maybe, but keep in mind that I can see things you don't," she said. "Like ghosts."

Ronan shoved one of the cement blocks and the pocket door slid open.

The tunnel had a lightbulb every ten feet or so. The instant she stepped inside, she felt something. Focusing on the wall to her right, she saw images appear and then fade.

They reminded her of the Russian lacquer box she'd incorporated into her first book, only larger. She saw what looked like a prince and princess. From her earlier research she knew that these types of images were often based on a variety of folk and fairy tales. The one she had used was based on a village courtship story. This one was different though.

Sierra placed her hand on the princess and the mural became clearer.

"Can you see this?" she asked Ronan.

"No. What are you looking at?"

"An incredible mural painted on the wall in the tradition of Russian lacquer boxes, only much larger. The background is black and the colors of the illustration are really vibrant. Judging from the fine lines of gold leaf used throughout, I'd say this was done by someone from the village of Palekh. They specialized in icon paintings there for centuries. Right up until the Russian Revolution, in fact. I researched this stuff when I was writing my first book."

"Is it a map?"

"No, it's got a prince and princess. In front of a castle." There was so much to look at that it was hard to choose where to focus. Then she saw them. "The shoes!"

"What? Is it Cinderella or something?"

"No. The shoes are the same ones that Ruby is wearing. That can't just be a coincidence. They are pretty unique shoes."

"Like Dorothy's in *The Wizard of Oz*? Voz had a large collection of classic movies in his castle."

"They're not red but they are kind of sparkly," she said.

"Could the castle belong to Voz?"

"I don't know what his castle looks like."

"It's got turrets."

"Not a lot of help," she said.

"It might be another of his properties. He has them all over Eastern Europe."

"And Russia?"

"Probably," Ronan said.

"The shoes are the link. We have to go talk to Ruby."

The ghost was waiting for them at the top of the stairs.

"Less than two hours until midnight, people," she said frantically.

"I know," Sierra said. "And I think I know why you're still here. It's your shoes."

Ruby looked down. "What's wrong with them?"

Instead of answering, Sierra posed a question of her own. "Where did you get them?"

"From another girl who worked here. Her name was Natasha. She called them her happy shoes because the sparkle cheered her up."

"Was she Russian?" Sierra asked.

Ruby nodded. "Yeah, so what?"

"Where are your shoes now?"

"On my feet. Are you losing it?" Ruby said. "You can't go off on me now."

"I'm not," Sierra assured her. "I mean the actual shoes, not your ghost shoes. Were you buried in them?"

"No. I was buried in an ugly dress and shoes that did not match. This is what I was wearing when Hal murdered me."

"Where did he murder you?"

"In this house."

"I mean specifically. Which part of the house? The passageway? The tunnels? Is that why you didn't want to go there?"

"The attic," Ruby whispered.

"The attic?" Sierra repeated. "What attic?"

"There is an attic," Ronan said. "I looked carefully up there when I first arrived, but again I can't see what you can, obviously."

"Why didn't I know about an attic?" Sierra said.

"It's this way." He led her upstairs and into the room he'd claimed as his. There were two doors, which she'd assumed led to closets. Only one did. When he opened the other door she saw a staircase leading up.

"Are you sure Hal is gone for good?" Ruby asked.

"Yes."

Ronan went up first and checked it out before indicating it was safe for Sierra to come up. A single bulb in the rafters lit the place. Unlike the basement, which hadn't had much stuff in it when she'd moved in, this space was crammed with things from the past. Or so it seemed to her.

Ronan pointed to a chipped and battered rocking horse in the far corner. "That used to be mine when I was a kid. Adele played on it after me."

"Ruby, does anything look familiar from your time?"

"I haven't been up here since I was murdered," Ruby whispered.

"I'm sorry," Sierra said. "This must be hard for you. But the faster you help us, the faster you'll be able to go into the light."

"Hal paid off the cops," Ruby said unsteadily. "He said I was holding the knife trying to kill myself when I fell down the steps. It was a lie. I never fell down the stairs. It all took place here in the attic."

"Where exactly?" Sierra asked.

Ruby pointed to the right.

"Let's look here," Sierra told Ronan, who had already gone through several piles with vamp speed.

He removed several chairs and boxes to free a large hinged wicker trunk. When Sierra first opened it, all she saw were rags and yellowed linens. She moved those aside and was about to give up when she saw them. The shoes.

She carefully lifted them out.

"Do ghosts have shadows?" Ronan asked.

"Not usually," Sierra said.

"Then what is that?"

The darkness took shape. The first things to materialize were the eyes and face. The eyes were totally black and totally creepy, like Voz's. But these eyes had blood oozing out of them and fanatic hatred in them. The face was scaly and abhorrent.

Sierra felt terror and repugnance. She also felt the overwhelming evil she'd only felt once before, when Gregori had tried to take her. He flashed his fangs and then flicked his long lizardlike tongue at them.

Ronan instantly grabbed Sierra, who still had the shoes in her hand, and transported her down to the safe site in the basement.

"Whatever happens, do not leave here," he ordered her. Then he was gone . . .

Chapter Twenty-three

Gregori was waiting for Ronan in the attic.

This was something Ronan knew how to do. He knew how to fight other vampires. He was damn good at it.

Kill or be killed.

Ronan had already started going full vamp when he'd left Sierra seconds ago. His fangs emerged and his eyes darkened and glowed. Adrenaline scored throughout his body as he tensed, prepared for battle.

His opponent was ready for him, lashing out with claws courtesy of his demonic side. Ronan had once asked Damon, who was a vampire Demon Hunter, the secret to fighting demons. His answer? Move fast and exterminate faster.

Not all that different from fighting fellow vampires.

But Gregori was no normal vampire. He was a mutant. That lizard tongue of his snaked out and nearly blinded Ronan.

Shit! Ronan grabbed for the sword he'd spotted in the attic earlier. He'd barely got it in his hands when Gregori grabbed him by the ankles and yanked him to the floor.

Ronan kicked him in the face.

Gregori laughed at him and nearly sank his fangs into Ronan's leg before Ronan leaped away.

The level of evil in this creature was beyond anything Ronan had ever experienced. Still Ronan battled on, calling on his anger to propel him to a new level of violence. This mutant had tried to take Sierra.

Bellowing his rage, Ronan matched Gregori blow for blow until Ronan's arms and legs streamed blood. No matter. He'd heal. If he lived.

And the only way he'd live was to sever Gregori's head. The sword was old and rusty but it would be sufficient to do the job if the blow was delivered properly with full vamp force.

Ronan knew he'd only get one chance. It came when he least expected it. Gregori's attention strayed for a millisecond. Ronan gripped the sword hilt with both hands and swung with all his might.

The sword sliced through. Hacked through. Whatever. It did the job. Gregori disintegrated into a putrid pile of dust.

A golden key fell and bounced on the wooden planks. It must have come from Gregori's body.

Ronan lunged, catching it before it slid between the cracks.

Blood pooled in the palm of his hand. At first he thought it was Gregori's before realizing it was his own. The mutant vampire had slashed Ronan's sweater and pants. His wounds were already starting to heal but he was still a bloody mess.

He hated Sierra seeing him like this, but there was no time to waste. He returned to the basement with the key clutched in his hand.

She remained calm despite his appearance. "Are you okay?"

He nodded. "Is this it?" he asked, holding out the key.

"Yes." Sierra grabbed it.

"So it's the key for Voz?"

"No, it's the key for the mural. While you were upstairs I looked at the shoes more carefully," she explained. "These are removable shoe buckles that were in fashion in those days. They come apart and could be used as brooches or earrings. But this one is different than the others. It's in the shape of a key."

"So that's the key Voz wants?"

"No. This key also plays a role in the mural thing."

"We've got less than thirty minutes left."

She took the golden key from him along with the sparkly key from the shoe. She inserted the sparkly key into the box on which the princess was standing.

Sierra had to work hard at keeping her hands steady and focusing on unlocking the box in the mural. She couldn't show Ronan how upset she was to see him so torn up. She felt his wounds as if they were her own. Not literally, but to her soul.

"I'll heal," he whispered in her ear. "Don't worry about me."

The moment the key touched the wall, the box transformed from a flat illustration to a three-dimensional object.

"I can see it now!" Ronan said.

The sparkly key didn't fit in the box itself but the golden key did. The box opened to reveal a pile of gems—not just diamonds but rubies and emeralds as well. There were also several pieces of gold and gemstone jewelry.

Sierra gave the box to Ronan and removed one necklace in particular. It featured an amethyst-and-ruby-encrusted golden key the size of Sierra's hand.

"This is what Voz wants," she said.

"A necklace?" Ronan said.

"A necklace I gave Catherine the Great during a moment of weakness," Voz said, appearing out of nowhere.

"Did you know it was here hidden in the mural?" Sierra said.

"I knew it was hidden somewhere in this house. Gregori had a witch charm it so no one would find it but him. Then he became increasingly demented and couldn't remember how to retrieve the treasure. He had a key around his neck but that wasn't the answer. He needed more. I needed more."

"Did you turn Gregori?" Sierra said.

"No. I would have done a much better job of his transformation."

"I don't understand. If you wanted this necklace why couldn't you just go get it from Catherine yourself? She may have been great but I'm sure she would be no match for a vampire," Sierra said.

"Master Vampire," Voz corrected her. "And I couldn't take it. The necklace had to be given to me. It's been in my family since the time of the Crusades. I needed it back."

"Why? What does it do?" she asked.

"My, you are a nosy little thing, aren't you." It was a statement of fact, not a question.

"Yes, I am," Sierra, said, keeping an eye on her watch. She wasn't about to let Voz talk his way into getting both the necklace and Ronan by going over the midnight deadline. But she also had to be sure, after dealing with Gregori, that she wouldn't be aiding and abetting in the release of mutant vampire demons or something else equally bad if not worse.

She had no idea what she'd do if that were indeed the case. How could she bear to have Ronan returned to the horrible life he'd had? He hadn't told her much about it, but she'd seen the marks on his body, as if he'd been branded.

"The necklace has mystical properties," Voz said.

"Which are?" Ronan demanded.

"It enables me to see into the future."

"Swear on your family's coat of arms that you are telling the truth." Ronan pointed to the signet ring that Voz wore.

The Master Vampire put his left hand over the ring on his right hand. "I swear on my family's honor. Now hand it over."

Ronan reached for the necklace when Voz stopped him. "No, it has to come from her."

"Why?" Ronan asked suspiciously.

"Because it has to be given to me by a woman who is pure of heart."

Shit. Sierra felt like crying. She wasn't a virgin. She hadn't been one when she and Ronan had made love last night.

Voz laughed at her expression. "I don't mean a virgin. You are pure of heart. That is why you are such a strong entity empath. Now hand it over before I rip Ronan's heart from his chest out of sheer frustration."

Sierra shoved it at Voz. "You're cold, hard, and mean."

"Indeed I am," Voz readily admitted. "But I keep my promises." He tilted his head toward the stairway behind him. "Your sister."

"Adele?" Ronan's voice was ragged.

"My job here is done," Voz said before disappearing.

Ronan moved toward the translucent image that was his sister's spirit. "I'm so sorry, Addie," Ronan said.

"It's okay, Ronan," she said. "You saved me."

"I had no idea—"

"I know," she interrupted him. "I don't have much time. But I wanted you to know that I love you."

"Right back at you," he said.

She smiled. "You always did find the words hard to say."

"I do love you, Addie."

"I know you do." She floated down the steps until she was close to Ronan. Leaning forward, she kissed him on the cheek. As she did so, a portal appeared with a glow of white light. "I have to go now. Mom and Dad are waiting for me. I can see them!"

Sierra took hold of Ronan's hand as Adele went into the light and then disappeared.

"She's safe now," Sierra told him.

"How can you be sure?"

"I've seen that light before," she said. "It was the real thing." Just as what Sierra felt for Ronan was the real thing.

"Hey, I'm still up here," Ruby yelled down at them. "We've got three minutes to midnight." She sat on the top step and started crying. "I'm going to be stuck here forever. I mean . . . come on! What's a girl ghost like me got to do to get a little white light around here?"

Sierra saw the male ghost's hand on Ruby's shoulder and for a second feared Hal had somehow returned or that her father had left the cemetery. But no, it was Johnny.

"Hey, now, what's all this? You need to get up . . ." Johnny gulped a bit when he saw what she was wearing but then his face lit up with a smile as she stood beside him.

"Johnny?" Ruby whispered.

"I'm here for you." He took her hand in his. "We're together now. Together for always."

Sierra wanted to correct his grammar but didn't. She also wanted to cry and did. She couldn't help the few tears that escaped her eyes as Ruby kissed Johnny. Then Ruby turned to Sierra and said, "Thank you."

"You're . . ." Sniff, sob, sob. "Welcome."

"I'm leaving you in good hands," Ruby said, pointing to Ronan.

The white light appeared behind Ruby and Johnny. They walked into it together and then disappeared.

"They're gone." Sierra turned and started crying on Ronan's shoulder. Then she took a quick step back. "I'm sorry. You're hurt." She looked but his wounds had already healed.

"I'm a fast healer," Ronan said.

"It's a vampire thing, right?"

He nodded.

"Your clothes are still in shreds though. And we've got the treasure here."

"While you were talking to Ruby I texted Damon to ask Zoe to put a protection spell over both treasures until we figure out what to do next."

"I know what I want to do next. I want to take a nice long shower. Or better yet, a bath."

"My room upstairs has a very large tub."

"Sounds good."

It also felt good ten minutes later to be in lovely lavender water up to her neck. She'd used some essential oils with the Bella Luna label that had magically appeared in the bathroom.

Ronan used her old bathroom off her bedroom to take a quick shower before joining her in the tub.

"You're going to smell like lavender," she warned him with a laugh.

"I've smelled of worse things." He nuzzled her neck. "Mmm." He turned her around so that her back rested against his chest. She sat between his splayed legs. He ran his soapy hands over her breasts, pausing to brush his thumbs over her nipples.

"We need to talk," he said gruffly.

"This isn't a good time," she said, running her hands along his thighs.

"There's no good time to have this conversation," Ronan said.

"What conversation?" she said.

"The one where I tell you that it's not over."

She looked around nervously. "Gregori and Hal are back?"

"No. I meant the vampire bond."

"But we had sex. Several times."

"I know. And that broke the part of the bond tying you to me against your will. You may leave any time you want. Free will and all that."

"Can you still read my mind?"

"Sometimes. It's because I've come to know you so well."

"It's only been a few days," she said.

"Time means something different to a vampire. And from the first moment I met you, I could get images of some of your thoughts."

"What am I thinking right now?" She rubbed against his erection.

"That we should be having sex. And we will. As soon as I tell you something."

"This better be important," she said.

"It is." His voice turned husky as she kept moving against him. "Each time we have sex, it lengthens your life."

"Mmm," she purred

"I'm serious here," he said.

"So am I. Can't you tell?" She caressed him, squeezing and massaging with sensual intent.

"I mean it will literally lengthen your life. Is any of this sinking in?"

She shifted so she faced him. Reaching down, she guided his erection inside her body. "Oh yeah, it's sinking in now." She lifted up and sank down again. "Definitely sinking all the way in."

He moaned then growled. "You'll basically stay as you are."

"Naked in a tub impaled by a hot vampire?"

"With some variation on that theme." He stood with her and carried her to the bathroom counter. "Naked here." He turned as she wrapped her legs around his waist and backed her up against the wall. "Naked here."

"Reaching an orgasm here," she murmured.

The connection between them went beyond the physical. She clutched his bare shoulders as he gave her the ride of her life.

It was only later, *much* later, when she finally regained her breath that she asked, "Were you kidding about that longevity stuff?"

"No." He ran his hand over her damp hair. "I'd never kid about something like that."

"So every time we have sex . . ."

"Your life is lengthened."

"By how much? A year? Two?"

"Fifty."

Sierra was stunned. With all that had been going on, she hadn't had time to dwell on the fact that Ronan was immortal and she wasn't.

It would take time for her to fully process what he'd

just told her. But apparently time was something she'd have a lot of.

"Fifty years, huh?"

He nodded.

"Then we better keep doing it," she whispered against his mouth. "Happy belated Valentine's Day."

Chapter Twenty-four

One month later . . .

"I'm sorry the paperwork took so long," Sierra's lawyer told her.

"No problem. I'm not in a hurry." Near immortality did that to you. Made you stop rushing—unless you were being attacked by a mutant vampire hybrid or a vicious poltergeist gangster ghost. Then time was of the essence . . . but not now.

Wait. Unless she was on a book deadline. Then time mattered too.

"Thanks for giving an advance copy of your new book to my wife," he said. "I believe she's joined your street team, whatever that means."

"It means I appreciate her hard work on my behalf."

"Well, I hope you enjoy your new house." He handed her a manila envelope with the official documents.

"It's actually an old house. Not that it's Southern plantation old or New England Revolutionary War old. But it is all mine."

"Old houses tend to have a lot of things go wrong with them," he said. "Let me know if you need a plumber, electrician, or handyman. I can recommend several."

"Thanks, but I've already got all the help I need."

As Sierra drove home in her brand-new blue Mini, she couldn't wait to arrive and see what Ronan was up to. So much had happened since that fateful day when all the ghosts and the evil mutant vampire had departed.

For one thing, Sierra had bought this car. Ronan wanted her to get something bigger. Nick had recommended a Jaguar. Damon was apparently partial to top-of-the-line Porsches. Bruce had a sentimental fondness for the VW Beetle while Tanya loved the 1956 red Thunderbird convertible.

But Sierra loved Zoe's red Mini, so she'd gone with that. She'd paid cash, having gotten part of the money from selling some of the diamonds. They were indeed real. A majority of the funds from Hal's treasure had gone into very large anonymous donations to various charities that helped families who were victims of domestic violence. She would do the same with the Russian treasure when the time came to disperse it.

Sierra had spoken to her mom on the phone the other night, reassuring her that all was well and admitting that she'd fallen in love. Her mom had demanded details so Sierra had given her a few. Of course she kept the vampire part out of their discussion. Sierra was glad her mom had been incommunicado during the month of February as that had prevented Sierra from having to deal with maternal worrying.

Tanya was waiting at the curb the instant Sierra stepped out of the car. "Ronan is a good influence on you," she said. "That latest sex scene you sent me. Wow." She fanned herself. "Plus we just added another four hundred likes on your author Facebook this morning. How stinking cool is that?"

"Very stinking cool."

"And how stinking smart are you to have put me in charge of your reader street team?" Tanya demanded.

"Um, very stinking smart?" Sierra said.

"Damn right."

"It's too bad that treasure story didn't work out. That would have made great PR," Tanya said.

Sierra and Ronan had agreed to keep the truth limited to Damon and Zoe, who had also vowed not to reveal any information about the gems. They'd gradually pieced together how Gregori returned only recently to the house when he was losing his memory and his mind. The séance at Zoe's house was the catalyst to his arrival. It got his attention because of his link to Mother and the circus along with the house. They suspected that Hal's diamonds had been left by Gregori in the attic by mistake and found by the gangster, who'd temporarily hidden them in the bathroom figuring he'd come back to retrieve them later. But then Johnny had shot him on the spiral staircase in the passageway. Hal had yanked Johnny down with him. The young man died of a broken neck.

Sierra had learned that last part of the story in a dream the night after Ruby crossed over to the afterlife. She knew in her heart that it had been a message from Ruby, wanting to fill in the blanks for Sierra.

"Listen, I've got to run," Tanya said. "I've got a live chat coming up."

Sierra turned to walk toward her house when she almost bumped into Daniella, who said, "Today was the big day, right? You got the papers for the house?"

"Yes." Sierra waved the manila envelope in the air. "They're all in here. I plan on living here a very long time."

"We all plan on staying in Vamptown a long time," Daniella said, before giving Sierra a big hug and a box of cupcakes. "I gave you a selection of our regulars plus the specials of the day—salted caramel, banana walnut, and raspberry coconut."

"Did you send that order to my publicist and my editor in New York City?" Sierra asked. "Red velvet, mocha, devil's food, cookies and cream."

"They went out last night overnight express special delivery."

"Which means what?" Sierra asked. "That Zoe used her magic to put them on Katie's and Lily's desks in the middle of the night?"

Daniella grinned. "Bingo. The same for your agent Annelise. All three got their box of cupcakes. Sorry I can't stay. I've got to get back to the shop. We're working on a big special order."

Sierra had made it to the front porch when Zoe called out her name and waved. Zoe had turned out to be a fantastic friend. Not only had she returned the yard to its original state shortly after Ronan dug it all up, she'd also helped Sierra adapt to living among vampires as well as her newfound version of immortality. And now she had cupcake delivery to add to the list.

There were still a lot of things for Sierra to process.

Living with magic and demons and vampires and witches and talking cats took some getting used to.

She was sad that the impressive Russian mural in the Vamptown tunnel entering her house had faded and disappeared within minutes of its discovery. Sierra had taken a photo with her smartphone before it disappeared but nothing showed up.

"Mystical things aren't meant to be photographed," Ronan had told her.

"Does that mean I can't photograph you?"

"I'm real, not mystical," he'd said.

Sierra was still coming to terms with her new reality and surroundings. The house was shaping up nicely. All the walls had been repainted. The sideboard was back in its original place but the photograph of Ronan's sister on it was new. The kitchen had been redone and now housed new appliances, cherrywood cabinets, and a black countertop to go with her Keurig. She even had a new set of twelve mugs with a SWEET HOME CHICAGO logo courtesy of Bruce as a housewarming gift. They were unbreakable courtesy of Zoe's grandmother.

"I'm home," Sierra called out as she entered through the front door and found a naked Ronan standing there.

No matter how long she lived, she'd never grow tired of seeing him this way. He was crazy gorgeous to her. When she'd once told him so, he'd told her that he had a bump in his nose from breaking it as a teenager. She'd waved his words away. He was perfect to her. Unless he pissed her off. But even then she was still hot for him. She hadn't told him she loved him. He hadn't said he loved her. At least not in words spoken aloud.

But they'd shared their feelings in other ways. Not just by making love but through their mingled thoughts. The mind-reading thing still worked when they wanted it to. It was working right now. *I love you, Ronan.*

His brown eyes darkened, letting her know he received her telepathic message. Then he sent her one of his own. *I love you, Sierra, and always will. You astonish me. You challenge me. You complete me.*

Her heart and her body just about melted. She wanted to jump his bones right there and then. She could tell by his lopsided smile that he knew it.

Looking over his shoulder, she noted, "I see you finished wallpapering the foyer. Good job."

"Should I have left my tool belt on?" he drawled.

"I would just have to take it off. Just like I'm taking this off." The day was warm enough even though it was March that she hadn't worn a coat. Remembering Tanya's instructions from weeks ago, Sierra crooked her knee and shimmied out of her slim skirt. Then she gracefully took hold of her ivory silk top and lifted it over her head. At least that was her intention. She did get her arm briefly stuck but hopefully Ronan didn't notice.

Apparently he didn't because his attention immediately focused on her breasts. Pulling her close, he cupped them in his hand and murmured in her ear. "I want you. Are you ready for some hot vampire sex?"

"Always."

Scooping her in his arms, he hustled her into their bedroom. The romantic canopy bed that Zoe had conjured for them filled most of the space.

The room was done in pale peach that Ronan said reminded him of her bare skin. He made fast work of removing her lingerie but then slowed down to kiss every inch of skin he'd just revealed.

He traced the shell of her ear with his tongue before nibbling on her earlobe. She'd had no idea that area was such an erogenous zone. He'd taught her so much about her body and the pleasure he could give her.

He found nerve endings she didn't even know existed, in the arch of her foot or the small of her back, then licked and nibbled his way over her body, creating a pathway of excitement that reached a crescendo when he reached the pulsing flesh between her parted legs. Once there he teased her with the tip of his tongue. Her clit emitted sharp quivers of delight shooting through to her very core.

She dug her heels into the bed and lifted her pelvis. He gripped her hips with both hands and held her in place as he continued to fiercely seduce her until spasms of bliss consumed her. Then he worked his way up her body, lapping at her navel, sucking on the rosy tip of each breast.

Sierra took his erection in her hands, encircling him and sliding her hand up and down his hard length. He plunged into her with a feral growl, joining them together with ferocious power. She put her hands on his sexy ass and pulled him even deeper. He communicated his approval of her actions by increasing the primal intensity of his possession of her.

The wildly erotic friction of his thrusts soon propelled her over the edge. Blissful spasms took hold of her. Her orgasm continued on and on as Ronan continued on and on until every iota of satisfaction was wrung from her and she vibrated inside and out.

Only then did he come, tilting back his head and shouting her name.

Afterward, she whispered, "That one should have been worth at least a hundred years."

His grin was downright wolfish. "A hundred? More like a thousand."

Sierra knew Ronan was no knight in shining armor. He was a vampire with a dark past. But the future was looking very bright because Sierra would be spending it with him—the love of her very long life.

Don't miss the first two novels in this "sinfully delicious" (*RT Book Reviews*) series by

Cat Devon

The Entity Within
Sleeping with the Entity

Available from St. Martin's Paperbacks